HOTTER THAN EVER!"
Mystery News

SWEET DREAMS, IRENE

"Fresh and appealing . . .
Will linger in any reader's mind"
Murder Ad Lib

"Jan Burke has created a sharp, witty,
and utterly endearing detective."
Susan Dunlop, author of *Death and Taxes*

"A compelling mystery . . .
It's hard to see how Burke can top this one"
Drood Review of Mystery

"Jan Burke is good news for mystery fans"
Linda Grant, author of *Love Nor Money*

"Highly recommended . . .
You shouldn't miss it"
The Purloined Letter

Other Irene Kelly Mysteries by
Jan Burke
from Avon Books

GOODNIGHT, IRENE

Coming Soon

DEAR IRENE

Sweet Dreams, Irene

JAN BURKE

AVON BOOKS ◆ NEW YORK

**To John F. Fischer,
who can do *anything*,
but is especially good at being Dad.**

This book is a work of fiction. Names, characters, places and incidents
are either products of the author's imagination or are used fictitiously.
Any resemblance to actual events or locales or persons, living or dead, is
entirely coincidental.

AVON BOOKS
A division of
The Hearst Corporation
1350 Avenue of the Americas
New York, New York 10019

Copyright © 1994 by Jan Burke
Author photograph by Debbi DeMont Photography
Published by arrangement with Simon & Schuster, Inc.
Library of Congress Catalog Card Number: 93-31179
ISBN: 0-380-72350-6

First Avon Books Printing: February 1995

AVON TRADEMARK REG. U.S. PAT. OFF. AND IN OTHER COUNTRIES, MARCA
REGISTRADA, HECHO EN U.S.A.

Printed in the U.S.A.

RA   10   9   8   7   6   5   4   3   2   1

One

Frank scared the hell out of me on Halloween, and we hadn't even finished breakfast. He accomplished this by looking up over the top of the morning paper and saying some of the most frightening words in the English language: "I'd like for you to meet my mother."

For minute I hoped he was reading a "Dear Abby" letter out loud, but no such luck.

"What?" I said, not so much because I hadn't heard him, but as a stalling tactic.

"I said I'd like for you to meet my mother. Do you have plans for Thanksgiving? Maybe you could ride up to Bakersfield with me and join our family gathering."

"I don't know. I'll have to check with Barbara. She may be counting on me showing up at her place."

He put down the paper and made a who-are-you-trying-to-kid face at me, and said, "You'd rather spend Thanksgiving with Kenny?"

He had me there. "Well, no, I wouldn't." Barbara is my older sister, recently reunited with her ex-husband, Kenny O'Connor. Kenny's dad and I had been the best of friends, even after my sister and Kenny had their messy divorce. His dad, affectionately known simply by his last name, O'Connor, had been my mentor and confidante at the *Las Piernas News Express,* the newspaper I work for. But O'Connor had been murdered that last summer, and in the aftermath of that event, Kenny and Barbara got back together.

O'Connor's death also led to my being reunited with an old acquaintance, the man who sat across the breakfast table from me. Frank Harriman is a homicide detective with the Las Piernas Police Department. Neither of our employers were too nutty over the idea of a cop and a reporter getting together, but we decided we could survive a little criticism, given some of the other things we had survived that summer.

Initially, I had been afraid that our relationship was just a reaction to all of the violence of that time. But those fears had proved unfounded over the last few months.

Fear of thy lover's mother is another thing altogether.

For some women, this would probably have been a moment of victory. They would read it as kind of promotion, a step up the prenuptial ladder. I remembered when Alicia Penderson, an old rival of mine, ran around bragging that her premed boyfriend was taking her home to meet the family over Christmas. She had started picking rings the next day. She wanted, as they say, "a rock." Gibraltar wasn't available or she would have had a setting made for it.

But I have never been much like the Alicia Pendersons of this world, and so I anticipated meeting Frank's mother with much the same enthusiasm as a mallard awaits the opening day of duck-hunting season.

Out of the bag of assorted misgivings I had about being introduced to her, I pulled my question to Frank that morning.

"Why do you want me to meet your mother?"

"Don't you want to meet her?"

"Of course I do," I said. Some might say I lied when I said that, but what I meant was, someday I wanted to know his mother, and have the meeting part all over and done with.

He had put the paper aside now and was studying me. Frank is unfortunately very good at this, and I can seldom hide my feelings from him. Those gray-green eyes were alive with amusement now.

"She'll like you," he said, once again proving his knack for getting to the core of things. I suppose it's a good skill to have in his line of work.

"How do you know she'll like me?"

"I know."

"Frank, I am so comforted by that."

"Too early to be snide, Irene."

"Too early to think about meeting your mother. You're right, I'm afraid she won't like me."

"I like you. She'll like you when she sees how much I like you."

"For a cop, you have a very optimistic outlook on life."

He shook his head. "I thought you'd be happy about it."

"It's nice for you to invite me. I'm flattered. But for starters, why don't you see if your mom wants another mouth to feed on Thanksgiving? She may just want to be with her family."

"She won't mind," he said. More optimism.

He stood up, taking the breakfast dishes with him. Concerned that I had insulted him with my lack of enthusiasm, I got up from the table and went over to him as he reached the sink. I stood behind him and wrapped my arms around him. He's so tall, this put my head somewhere between his shoulder blades. He set the breakfast dishes in the sink and turned around to face me.

"You worry about the damnedest things, Irene. But I'll call and ask her today. Want to get together for dinner?"

"Sure, but it's Halloween. Do you get many kids trick-or-treating over here?" Frank lives near the beach, and I hadn't seen many young families in his neighborhood.

"No, not really—just two or three families with kids on this block. I'm not often home from work in time to give them anything, so Mrs. Fremont usually hands out treats for me." Mrs. Fremont, his next-door neighbor, was about eighty years old. She had lived in that house for most of those years. Mr. Fremont had gone to his reward long ago, and while she still talked with fondness about their marriage, she seemed quite content with her life alone. She lived simply, but was actually very well-to-do. The ocean air must have been good for her, because you would never have guessed her to be over sixty. She was a real live wire.

"How about coming over to my place after you get off work?" I asked. "I don't have a Mrs. Fremont, so I'll be on candy-duty."

"Okay. I'll take you out for a late dinner."

"You've got a deal." I looked at my watch. "You're going to be late, Frank. Want me to take the stuff over to Mrs. Fremont for you?"

"That would be great." He walked over to the freezer and pulled out a bag of miniature Snickers.

"Frozen?" I asked.

"It's the only way I can keep myself from powering down a bag of them myself. It's been driving me nuts just knowing they're in the house. They'll thaw by tonight."

"Why, Frank Harriman, I never would have thought of you as a man with a sweet tooth."

He leaned over and kissed me good-bye, saying, "I don't know why not," and scrambled out the door.

Thinking about my own need to get to work, I made sure his house was locked up and then gathered my purse and overnight bag. Nabbing the cold bag of Snickers as well, I fumbled my way out of the house, then set the deadbolt. Frank had let me park my old '71 ragtop Karmann Ghia in the driveway the night before, and as I was stuffing my overnight bag into the trunk, I saw Mrs. Fremont returning from her morning jog.

"Good morning, Irene!" she called. "When are you going to come running with me again?"

I smiled at her, remembering my surprise the first time I heard this proposal. We had gone running together several times since, and I found I didn't have to make concessions to her pace. "Soon, I hope. I haven't been able to do much running this week."

"All that election coverage," she said knowingly. She spied the bag of Snickers clenched in my right hand. Her bright blue eyes sparkled. "Did Frank leave those for me to hand out tonight?"

"Yes, I was going to come over with them as soon as I got my overnight bag put away." For some reason, I felt myself blush.

She laughed. "My dear, I hope you don't worry about my judging your relationship with Frank. You've been very good for him. Couldn't stand the last one—that was years ago. It's about time that man had a woman in his life again. And as for your spending the night with him—don't forget, I was a teenager at the height of the Roaring Twenties. We could teach you kids a thing or two."

When you're pushing forty, it's always nice to be called a kid.

"Well, Mrs. Fremont, I'm sure you could," I said, handing the bag of candy over to her. "And I know you don't judge me. I guess I'm fretting over an idea Frank has—he wants me to meet his mother at the family Thanksgiving dinner."

"Oh, and you're afraid if his mother doesn't like you, that will be that?"

I thought about her question. "I guess so. That, and the fact that I'm not sure what Frank means by bringing me home to his mother."

She gave me a kind look. "Well, Irene, you know I'm not into this role of being some old lady who imparts her wisdom to the younger generations at the drop of a hat. But let me ask you this—do you and Frank love each other?"

I turned crimson, but answered, "Yes."

"Well then, don't worry about what Frank means by this invitation. Enjoy Thanksgiving—you've got everything you need in life, with or without his mother's approval. Frank is no fool, Irene."

"Thanks, Mrs. Fremont."

"Go on to work. I've got to get going myself—I've got to carve a jack-o-lantern. Happy Halloween!"

"Same to you," I said, getting into the car and waving as I drove off. As I made my way down the streets of Las Piernas, I was already turning my thoughts to being with Frank again. I was looking forward to sharing a pleasant evening together.

I was being optimistic.

As it turned out, that Halloween, someone was up to some very cruel tricks indeed.

| Two

The Wrigley Building, which houses the *Express*, is in downtown Las Piernas. It's been there since the 1920s, when the father of the current editor had already turned his own father's small rag into a good-sized paper. We are always in the shadow of the *L.A. Times*, but the local beach communities have appreciated our special attention to their concerns over the years, so we're firmly entrenched along the coastline south of Los Angeles.

As I entered the building, I was greeted by Geoff, the security man, who was rumored to have been working in the building since opening day.

"Good morning, Miss Kelly," he said. "There's someone here who says he has an appointment with you." I didn't bother to return Geoff's questioning look; he knew it was not my custom to meet people off their own turf, nor at 7:30 in the morning. I turned around and saw additional reason for Geoff's skepticism: the person waiting for me looked to be all of sixteen. He was decked out in black from head to toe, and I doubted his hair was originally that coal black color. But the face was familiar, so I hesitated for a moment. It was a face full of that intense seriousness of purpose that seems built into adolescence.

He nervously stood up, wiping his palm on the leg of his pants before extending his hand to me. "Miss Kelly? I'm Jacob Henderson."

Henderson. So that was why he looked familiar. Son of Brian Henderson, candidate for District Attorney. I faltered only a moment before I took the offered hand in mine and said, "Hello, Jacob. I'm so glad you're on time."

I turned back to Geoff, feeling bad about making him

6

doubt his instincts, but saying, "Jacob and I are going to have a chat downstairs. I think we'll have more privacy there."

Geoff smiled. "Yes, Miss Kelly, I understand. Anybody asks, I'll tell them you were in but had to leave for an interview."

"Thanks." I turned to Jacob. "Would you like to see the presses?"

The seriousness gave way to curiosity, and he nodded. He followed me through the maze which is the downstairs basement of the *Express*. "They aren't running right now," I said, "but you'll get to see them, anyway. They may run a special section while we're down here."

"How do you know they aren't running?"

"There's a low rumble that runs through the whole building when they do. It's quiet now."

We entered the area of the basement which houses the presses. As Jacob looked around in wonder, I took a deep breath and smiled. Ink and newsprint is my favorite fragrance in all the world. I loved being down there.

Coburn, one of the operators, saw us and walked over. "How are you, Danny?" I greeted him.

"I'm great, Irene. Suzanne and I have got a new grandbaby." He pulled out an ink-stained wallet and showed me a photo. I made appreciative noises and he beamed with pride. He put the wallet back and smiled over at Jacob. "Who you got with you?"

"This is Jacob," I said, and they shook hands, Jacob not even flinching at the dark smudges he received. Why not, I thought. Matches the rest of his outfit. "Jacob and I need a place to talk. Can you help us out?"

"Sure, sure. I think I can manage something." We followed him around and through the warren of machinery. We went past a cubicle with vending machines in it, and I stopped and fished some change out of my purse.

"Want a cup of coffee or a soda?" I asked Jacob.

"A Coke would be nice, thank you."

"This early in the morning?" Coburn said.

"Why not?" I said. "In fact, I think I'll have one too. You want anything, Danny?"

Still disbelieving, he shook his head. While I took a chance on the vending machine, Danny talked to Jacob about the presses. I watched them for a while. Jacob was clearly fascinated, and Danny enjoyed the audience. I wondered what was on the kid's mind.

I had been covering the election since the summer, when both the mayor's and D.A.'s races had become fairly wide open. Brian Henderson, Jacob's father, was one of the two leading candidates for D.A. As politicians go, he was an okay sort. I knew he had made some compromises along the way in order to hold a fragile coalition of supporters together, but he still seemed able to take a stand on an issue.

I was not as impressed with his chief opponent, Brad "Monty" Montgomery. Monty struck me as the type who would do just about anything to win an election. I stopped looking for sincerity in politicians long ago, but something in my gut made me especially leery of him.

Unfortunately, the readers of the *Express* needed more than Irene Kelly's gut feelings. They were being fed all sorts of contradictory information through the mail and in ads. The campaign had started out on the up and up, but with only one week to go, the mud was really flying.

Danny saw me standing there with the Cokes, and brought Jacob back over to me. "We're going to be running a special a little later on, Irene. Will you and the lad still be here?"

"Not sure, Danny, but you know I love to watch them run."

Coburn laughed. "That you do, that you do." He led us to a small storage room, pulling a couple of folding chairs out of a small office. "It's not as grand as the conference room of Wrigley's office, but it's a damned sight more private."

"You're great, Danny—thanks."

He smiled and left. Jacob and I settled on to the metal chairs and opened our Cokes. The nervousness was back, and he fidgeted with the pop-top on the soda can.

"Okay, Jacob, I've interrupted my day and gone AWOL first thing this morning so you could talk to me. I have a feeling you're supposed to be in school somewhere right now. Want to tell me why you've come to see me?"

"I called in sick. They won't miss me."

I waited.

"You're the reporter that writes all that stuff about my dad, right?"

"Guilty."

"Well, I need your help."

"In what way? I have to try to write objectively, Jacob, no matter who the candidate is."

"It's not that." He looked up at me, deadly earnest. "I need for you to prevent a witch hunt."

| Three

"A witch hunt? Jacob, if this is some kind of Halloween prank, I swear I'll—"

"It's not! It's not a prank!" he protested hotly. "And it has to do with real witches."

Great, I thought. I'm sitting in a walk-in closet with the maniac son of one of the people I'm supposed to be covering. I took a deep breath and said, "Real witches?"

He calmed down. "Well, no. Just people who *think* they are witches."

"Why don't you try this from the beginning?"

"Monty Montgomery is about to put out a piece of campaign literature that says I'm involved in a satanic cult. He's going to talk about it like there's a bunch of murdering Satanists running around loose in Las Piernas, and that he's going to put a stop to it. He's going to say my dad can't be expected to stop them because I'm one of them."

"Are you a murdering Satanist?"

"No."

"Then it's libel."

"You know how this works. It will take months or maybe years if my dad sues for libel. The damage will already be done. My dad will spend the next five days trying to deny I'm a member of the cult instead of campaigning on the issues, and Montgomery will win."

"You seem to know a lot about campaigns."

He looked at me like I was from Mars. "Well, why wouldn't I? I've grown up with them."

Since Henderson had only run once before, unsuccessfully against a then-popular incumbent, I didn't see how twice in four years meant Jacob grew up with campaigning. But I supposed from the perspective of someone his age, it must have seemed constant, given the time his father would have devoted to it.

"If you've grown up with campaigns, you know your dad will know how to combat mudslinging. What is it that really bothers you about this?"

He was silent, seeming to be debating about what he should and shouldn't tell me.

"Off the record?" he said.

A sixteen-year-old demanding to be off the record. He did know something about politics. "That depends. You came to see a reporter, after all."

"But it's about something that isn't true. It's not news, then, is it?"

And he had grown up with a lawyer. "Okay," I said. "But if I find out otherwise, expect to see it in print."

He mulled this over. "Okay. Montgomery has this photo. It's supposed to show me participating in a witches' coven."

"A witches' coven?"

"Yeah, you know, a group of witches."

"I know what a coven is—but how did he get a photograph of you and a coven?"

"I don't know. I mean, I do know, but I don't know how." He drew a breath. "What I mean is, I was there, but I wasn't there as a witch or anything. And I didn't see anyone with a camera, so I don't know how."

"Why were you there?"

"You're not going to believe me."

I waited.

He sighed. "I was trying to get a friend of mine to leave. She's mixed up with the wrong crowd. I was trying to get her to come home."

"Girlfriend?"

"She's just a friend. Not my girlfriend." He looked down at his hands. "We grew up together. I've known her since we were little kids. Sammy's been our neighbor for years."

"Sammy?"

"Gethsemane—yeah, I know. It's worse than Sammy. Her parents are real religious types. I think that's part of why she's doing this crap with the witches. I don't think she really believes in it. I think she's just trying to rebel against her parents or something. Anyway, we've always talked, and been ... I don't know, we could always just talk to one another. She's my friend. Understand?"

"I understand. Do her folks know about the witchcraft stuff?"

"Yeah. They kicked her out. They're so busy going to church all the time, I don't think they care about anything else."

"So where is she living?"

"She was just spending the night with her witch friends, but I talked her into going down to Casa de Esperanza, the runaway shelter. You know about that?"

"Yes." Casa de Esperanza was, in fact, one of the many gifts Frank's neighbor, Mrs. Fremont, had given to Las Piernas. She had started it back in the 1970s, when I was in college. One semester I did volunteer work there for credit in a psychology class. She had founded the shelter, but she had since handed most of the administration of the facility to other people. She had kept some of it in the family; I remembered that she once told me her own grandson worked there. All the same, Mrs. Fremont still spent a lot of her time at the shelter, lending an ear to troubled teens. She seemed to be the town grandmother.

"Well, anyway," Jacob went on, "I talked Sammy into going to the shelter. She didn't put up much of an argument. I guess even the witch friends were tired of having her over all the time."

"Who are these witches?"

"They're not even really witches. It's just a bunch of high school kids playing dress-up. They read all these weird books and try to do the rituals and all of that, but as far as I know the worst thing they've done is gone into the cemetery after closing."

"Some people think there are occult groups murdering their pets, having strange sexual rituals, worshipping the devil," I said. "Maybe getting into drugs, things like that. Trying to be evil, you might say."

"I know what people think. But it isn't true. Not with this group. I mean, I think Sammy would let me know if they did anything like that. She loves animals—she wouldn't hang out with anyone that killed a pet. Maybe there's some other group of witches out there. I don't know. These people she hangs out with talk like they're really evil, but I think they just like the showy stuff. I think they're all talk."

"All of them? Maybe Sammy's fairly innocent, but when people get into this kind of thing, they sometimes attract people who are more serious about it all."

He brooded over that for a moment. "That's what I'm afraid of, I guess. That's why I keep trying to get her to quit hanging around with them."

He was holding something back, so I decided to wait it out. It was getting stuffy in the little room, but I figured there was more to the story than he had told me thus far.

"There is one guy . . ." he said, then paused, seeming reluctant to say more. "He's older. Sammy told me about him. He's sort of the leader. They never see his face. He wears some sort of goat mask or something. He wasn't there the night I tried to get Sammy to leave. But she was really freaked out, you know, like if the guy found me there he would kill me."

"*Kill* you?"

"I don't know, maybe she was just being dramatic. She is sometimes. Lots of times, really. She just needs attention. But I think she really was scared of something."

Something was bothering me about his story, and I finally figured out what it was. "If you didn't see a photographer, how do you know there's a photo? And how do you know about this hit piece of Montgomery's?"

He turned beet red. If he was nervous before, he was frantic now. "I can't tell you that."

"You're really testing my patience, you know that? There's going to be a witch hunt, only there aren't really any witches. You say you've been photographed at a gathering of these wanna-be witches, but you don't know who took the photograph. You say there's about to be a smear campaign that might cause your father to lose an election, but you can't tell me how you know. And for toppers, you've asked me to keep all of this stuff that *maybe* happened and *maybe* will happen off the record. What the hell am I supposed to do with all this?"

"Please," he said, bursting into tears, "I need your help."

I felt like a bully. I hadn't meant to make the kid cry. I leaned over and put a hand on his shoulder. "Sorry, Jacob, I didn't mean to be so hard on you." I reached into my purse and pulled out a packet of tissues.

He was embarrassed, but he took one.

"Have you talked to your father about this?"

He laughed. There was no mirth in it. "What father?" he said.

"The one you care so much about that you'd come down here and talk to the meanest reporter in town."

He smiled a little at that. "You're not mean. He's not around much. He's—I understand, really—it's important to him to win. But he doesn't have time to sleep, let alone talk to me. He's really worn out."

"He should be proud of you. You care about your friends and your family. You strike me as being a good-hearted person."

"He doesn't think so. He doesn't want people to know about me. I don't know. It's because of the way I dress—at least, that's what my mom says. I guess I'm no different from Sammy. I sort of rebel against him. But I really do like to wear black."

"Can't help you with that, Jacob. You're in one of the world's oldest struggles there. What do you think I *can* help you with?"

"Could you tell people I'm not a witch?"

"It will seem pretty odd if I do that before anyone has said you are one."

"It's going to happen. I—can you keep a secret?"

"Most secrets. If they won't hurt anyone, or compromise the paper. But just because I'm a reporter doesn't mean you can't trust me with a confidence."

"I have a friend who—who works for the Montgomery campaign. We don't usually talk about politics. But when my friend saw this flyer about me being a witch—well, that's how I found out. I don't want to get my friend in trouble."

"Girlfriend?"

He turned red again. "Please don't ask me any more about it, okay? I've told you too much already."

He acted as if he was going to leave. "Hold on, hold on," I said. "I won't tell anyone about your friend." He looked at me as if he were trying to decide if he could trust me. Apparently I passed the test, because he sat back down again.

"Look, Jacob, all I can do is try to find out if this piece is really going to be mailed out, and if it is, I'll do what I can to balance the coverage so that your side of the story gets told. It would help if I could get some kind of quote from your friend Sammy. Do you think she would talk to me?"

"If I went with you, she might."

"Is she playing hooky today, too?"

"Naw, she's in school. They try to make sure kids go to school if they stay at the shelter. It's a rule."

"What time will she be out of school?"

"Two-thirty."

"Okay, so, would she back at the shelter by three?"

"I could go back to school—you know, tell them I'm feeling better. I'll find her and ask her to meet us there if you want."

"Okay. I'll meet you there at three." I pulled out a card

and gave it to him. "Call me here at the paper if you need to cancel."

He took it and read it over. "Okay," he said.

"Do you have any idea of how Montgomery's people knew you'd be out at this witch shindig?"

"No."

"Any chance your friend at the Montgomery campaign might have told them?"

"No!"

"Okay, okay, take it easy. Did you tell anyone else? Or could anyone have overheard you talking about it?"

"I didn't tell anyone. But I did have a big argument at the shelter with Sammy. Maybe someone heard us. I don't know. The walls are kind of thin, and there are always a lot of kids hanging out there."

"One other thing. How are you at taking advice from old fogeys?"

"Depends on the advice, I guess, and the old fogey."

"Well, let's say this old fogey."

"Try me. You're not *real* old."

"Thanks, I guess. I really don't have any business sticking my nose in, so it's just between the two of us, okay?"

"Okay."

"It's just something to think about. The way I figure it, if you're concerned enough about your dad's campaign to come here and talk to me, maybe you're concerned enough to fight a little of the fire Montgomery plans on setting."

"What do you mean?"

"He'll be using your appearance—the black clothes and black hair—to promote his ideas in people's minds. Trust me on this—I used to work in public relations. In fact, a pal of mine named Kevin Malloy could make you an expert in this kind of stuff. People will try to place you in a box—the box you seem most likely to fit in. Those that get to know you, even for as short a time as I have, will doubt you could ever fit in a box labeled 'witch.' But those that don't know you are only going to have what Montgomery says and any pictures of you they see in the paper. And believe me, there will be a picture in the paper if this comes out."

He groaned.

"Anyway, you have every right to wear whatever clothes you want to wear, or to dye your hair pink, if you want to. But there's a price for everything. Ask yourself if it's worth it to change your image for a few days."

"That sounds a lot like selling out."

"Maybe. But again, ask yourself what set of principles you're selling out to. The set that doesn't want to bring harm to others, or the one that says you're free to make any fashion statement you choose. It's up to you. No skin off my nose."

"I'll think about it."

"What do you say we get some fresh air?"

"Yes, I'm suffocating in here."

As we stood up, we heard the throbbing sound of the presses as they started up. Danny met us outside the door with ear protectors. "Better wear these," he shouted, as the roaring grew. He led us back through the aisles. Jacob was enthralled with it all. I had seen it a thousand times or more, and I was still enthralled.

He shook Danny's hand as we left, and we handed over the earmuffs. Jacob was smiling, and I was glad to see him lighten up a little. "Feel better?" I asked.

"Yeah," he said. "I'm still scared about it, but I guess I feel like maybe there's something I can do about it."

"I'll see you at three."

"Okay." He turned to leave. I had started up the stairs when I heard him call out to me.

"Miss Kelly?"

I turned around.

"What kind of classes should I take if I want to work here?"

"Journalism and English are good starting points. You have a school paper at Las Piernas High. Try to get on it."

"I think I will. Bye."

He moved out of the building with a little more energy than he had shown in the halls, and I found myself bounding up the stairs. I don't often encounter young people—my

God, I was old enough to call them young people—in my work, and there was something refreshing about spending time with Jacob. As I entered the newsroom, my mood was shot down by a booming voice filled to the brim with sarcasm.

"Well, good morning, Miss Kelly! Nice of you to join us!"

"Good morning, John. I can't tell you how happy I am to be here with you."

| Four

John Walters, my news editor, sauntered over to me. "That cop boyfriend of yours keeping you up too late at night?"

"I came in at seven-thirty this morning. You can check that with Geoff."

"So where the hell have you been since then? The ladies' room?"

"No, John, I was interviewing someone. And not in the ladies' room."

"Really? At seven-thirty in the morning? Who is this early bird?"

"Sorry. For the moment I'm not free to say. I'll probably be able to tell you more this afternoon."

He stared at me. His face was red, and I could see the veins in his neck and forehead. "Come into my office," he said gruffly.

I followed him across the newsroom, which had fallen silent in the wake of our exchange. As I watched his huge behind waddle in front of me, I wondered what bug could have possibly crawled up it so early in the day.

He opened the office door, ushered me in with a mocking bow, turned to the newsroom, and shouted "Work, damn it!" at the top of his lungs. Then he slammed the door shut so hard everything on his desk jumped.

He turned to me and scowled, but didn't say anything. I decided the best defense was a good offense, mainly because I was pissed. But I kept my voice calm and low.

"You know, John, I really don't mind being paraded through the newsroom like an errant child—you've got a nasty reputation to protect, and as staff curmudgeon it's almost your duty to throw a fit now and then. I'm happy to be of help. But usually, underneath it all, you've got some reason for getting angry. I can't figure out what it is this time. Have I let you down somehow? Is there a problem with the way I've covered the election?"

He sat down. The flush of anger left his face and he started fooling around with a ballpoint pen, stabbing it into the blotter on his desk. He was actually silent. Something *was* wrong.

"What's going on, John?"

"I don't have any problems with your coverage of the election. As usual, you've done an ace job. You haven't let me down in any way."

"So what is it?"

"Wrigley is on my case all the time. He wants me to hand over some of your work to Stacee."

I felt my fists clench. Winston Wrigley III was an ass-pinching SOB who had inherited a job as editor. The publications board could still outvote him, or the staff would have walked out a long time ago. In fact, two years before, I had quit the *Express* after a loud argument with him. He had wanted me to come back but I turned him down until O'Connor was killed. I came back to finish the stories O'Connor was working on when he died, and in the process ended up hooked on reporting again.

"My work to Stacee? Stacee who couldn't find her way around City Hall with a map? Stacee who's so adorable she spells her name in a cutesy kind of way? Stacee who has spent all of six months out of J school?"

"You've forgotten five months of grad school under Professor Wrigley's private tutelage."

"Goddamn that bastard! He questions my ethics—bans me from crime stories because of Frank—"

"Wait a minute, you know he's entitled to do that under the circumstances."

"Oh hell, John. I've heard it all before—if I'm going to bed with a cop, you're not going to put me on a crime story. I might not be able to stay objective if the cops are due for some criticism. Never mind that you and half the reporters on this paper are drinking buddies with these same cops—sex somehow will ruin my brain for being a crime reporter. But you know what, John? It's worse for Frank. Who do you suppose they're going to go looking for the first time somebody in the department leaks some story to the paper?"

"Look, Irene, if you think I don't trust you—"

"I hope it hasn't come to that."

"It hasn't."

I settled down a little. "I've never made a stink out of being forbidden to do stories that involve the cops. I can live with it. I knew that something like that might happen if Frank and I got involved—"

"Yeah, yeah, but you can't help yourselves. Look, don't make me sick, okay? I don't like what Wrigley's trying to pull with Stacee any more than you do. She's not a bad kid, she just seems to be so used to getting her way by using that saucy little body that it hasn't occurred to her yet to use her brains."

"Yeah, well, anyone who lets Wrigley into her underpants can't be the next Einstein."

"Oh, so you've been wise all your life? Shall I talk about a couple of the losers I've seen you hook up with over the years?"

I flinched. "No thanks. Point taken. So what are you getting at, John?"

"Starting tomorrow, why don't you try to let her help you out?"

"You have got to be kidding."

"I'm not. You know it's too much to cover on your own. You've been running yourself ragged."

There was some truth in this, I thought. In the past,

O'Connor and I had covered things together. When I quit, other reporters had worked with him off and on, but no one had really made the contacts and connections I had. When I first came back to work at the paper, I had been glad to have the distraction the long hours gave me. But now, if I was honest with myself, I had to admit I was wearing down. Still—*Stacee?* John was looking at me, waiting for an answer.

"So you think Stacee has talent—outside of the type Wrigley appreciates so much?"

John grinned. "I knew you'd be fair about this, Irene. The kid needs a mentor—someone to show her the ropes. Her writing is okay. Needs a little polishing, but that takes time."

"Hold on, John. This is not an unconditional surrender. I'm not signing up to be a mentor. I've worked hard to build up the trust and confidence of my sources in Las Piernas, and I'm not just going to hand it all to her on a silver platter. If she works with me, I choose what I'm going to let her cover. The paper has as much or more to lose than I do if she starts pissing people off."

"You are getting very uppity in your old age."

"I have a great role model."

"Hmmph."

He didn't say anything for a while, but finally he agreed.

As I left his office, my eyes came to rest on a woman who looked like she was made to order should central casting call up and say, "We need a bimbo." It was Stacee Martin. She looked up at me and smiled a 400-watt, totally phony smile.

What the hell had I gotten myself into now?

Meaning to return the smile, I believe I ended up grimacing, since she looked puzzled in response. I turned and made my way over to my desk, which had once been O'Connor's own. I admit it—I was pouting. I thought about Stacee and her way of reaching whatever goals she had at the paper, comparing it to my own time as a green reporter. I had spent my first two years up in Bakersfield covering a crime beat. And the first stories I took on at the *Express* weren't glamorous. Pet vaccination clinics, shopping center openings—and lots of crime stories, everything from break-ins to paramedic stories. If it was really juicy, they gave it to a veteran—which is how I met O'Connor. He had chosen me to work with him after I had paid some dues.

Now, at the time when maybe I would have picked somebody out on my own, I was going to be stuck with double-e Stacee. Hell if I was going to take responsibility for thrusting her career forward.

But as I thought about it, a little smile began to form on my lips. There were lots of ways to pay dues. I was going to run her ass so ragged she wouldn't have enough time or energy to warm Wrigley's bed. God, what a great way to pay Wrigley back.

That decided, I called the Montgomery campaign to see what I could learn. I asked for Brady Scott, Montgomery's press manager.

"Irene! What a pleasant surprise!" An unsolicited call from the local press. He was gushing all over himself.

"How's it going, Brady?"

"Very well, very well. Monty will make a great D.A."

"Any special reason for all of this optimism?"

"Oh, just faith in the voters," he said, and I could hear the note of caution creeping into his voice.

"Come on, Brady. Word on the street is that you've got a nasty hit planned on the Henderson campaign."

"Monty is running a clean campaign." Maybe it wasn't caution. Maybe it was—naw, these guys are never ashamed of anything.

"Who's saying he isn't?"

"Look, you know how it is. As any campaign gets down to the wire, people pull out the stops. It's already happening and you know it—our opposition is doing the same thing. We found out something we think the voters ought to know about, and we're going to tell them."

"If the voters ought to know about it, tell me. It's practically your civic duty, Brady."

"Well . . ."

As he hesitated, I heard the muffled voice of someone else in the room with him. I couldn't make out who it was.

"Look, that just wouldn't fit into our plans right now. I promise you that I will be available for you if you've got any other questions. Are you coming to the coalition meeting tonight?"

I hadn't planned on going to this particular "Meet the Candidates" night, but just at that moment I saw Stacee cross the room to the City Desk, and I got a flash of inspiration.

"No, Brady, but we're sending someone else there."

He sounded a little disappointed, but I didn't owe him anything.

"Sorry you're clamming up on me, Brady. I thought by now—well, call me if you change your mind, okay?"

I hung up. So some kind of hit piece was planned. But they were definitely keeping it under wraps. I tried calling a couple of other people who were close to the campaign. Nothing.

I started plowing through the mass of paper that had accumulated on my desk since yesterday. I was making some headway when I noticed a shadow across my desk. I looked up to see who was darkening my reading light. It was Stacee.

"It's not polite to read over people's shoulders," I said.

She blushed and said, "I'm sorry. Didn't mean to. I guess I'm just curious."

"Not bad to be curious. Just practice reading things on people's desks when you're *outside* the newsroom, and you'll make more friends here."

"I don't seem to have many."

My heart was breaking. Gee, Stacee, I thought to myself, don't you wonder why? But aloud I said, "Sit down. I was going to try to talk to you later today anyway."

She sat there dutifully, mooning at me. Christ Almighty, I thought—it won't work with me, kid. I tapped my pencil. What was I going to do with Wrigley's little princess?

"I understand you want to work on political stories."

"Yes, I do."

"What makes you think you can cover politics? Have you done it before?"

"In college, I covered student elections."

I looked up at the little holes in the ceiling tile above me. The answer to my prayer for patience was not there.

"I mean," she said, in a meek voice that made me want to kick her, "I know it's not the same thing."

"No," I said. "Just tell me why. Why political stories?" Why me? I thought, but I didn't say it.

"I really want to work on something that's important."

I looked over to the City Desk, where a group of general assignment reporters were gathered around Lydia Ames, assistant city editor and a friend of mine since grade school. She was busily handing out the day's less glorious assignments.

"Who do you know around here who *doesn't* want to work on something important?" I said.

"I know I haven't had much experience. But how am I going to get any experience if somebody doesn't give me a chance?"

"Same way the rest of us got it—pay some dues."

She looked crestfallen. I felt a little twinge—I refused to believe it might be guilt.

"Look, if you expect me to hand over a major story to someone who's as green as—"

"I don't expect that," she protested. "I don't mind hard work. It's an honor just to be helping you. I've always admired your writing, Miss Kelly. I want to be like you."

Where are the hip-waders when you need them? On second thought, she was laying it on so thick, it was more than hip-deep. I needed a steamshovel. She must have seen my doubts, because she grew very serious and said quietly, "I mean that."

That twinge again. "Well, if you mean it," I said, "then thanks. But understand that I'm doing this as a favor to John. I don't know you well enough to have picked you out to work with me."

"I understand. But I still appreciate the chance."

"We'll see. Here's what you can do for starters. Go down to the morgue and read issues from June on—

anything you can find related to local politics. When you've got at least that much background, we'll go from there. And tonight there's a meeting of the Las Piernas Coalition for Justice. All the major candidates will be speaking there. Go to it."

"Tonight?" she said, looking uncomfortable.

"Yes, tonight. You do want to cover politics, don't you?"

"The Coalition for Justice will be meeting on Halloween?"

"Yes," I said, and I pulled out a flyer to prove it to her. "You weren't expecting nine-to-five hours when you got your degree in journalism, were you?"

"Oh, no."

"Well, I can see this isn't going to work out," I said, trying to keep the glee out of my voice. "You've obviously got a hot date or something. I'll ask Lydia to put one of the more experienced general assignment people on it."

"No—please. I'll go. I'm sorry—I'll cancel my other plans. Thanks for giving this to me."

Maybe she would last a week, I thought. "No problem. Try to read up on the candidates before you get there."

"I've been reading all of your stories—I clip them out."

"What?"

She looked sheepish. "Like I said, I admire you. I've clipped out all your stories since you came back to the paper. I used to read your columns when I was in high school and college. Then you left the paper. When you came back, I didn't know how long you were going to stay, so I started clipping them. You know, starting with the ones you did on Mr. O'Connor."

I must confess I was flabbergasted. And embarrassed. And, yes—well, flattered. "Really?" I managed to choke out.

"Really." God, she looked so sincere, I wanted to believe her. But I thought about what was going on with Wrigley and fell back to earth.

"Well, you still need to reread anything you've read about local politics—any story by anyone."

"Okay."

"Take this flyer. And let John know if you can't make
it for some reason—he may want to send someone else."
That was baloney, of course. This meeting was only one of
a hundred, and whatever would be said tonight would be
repeated at ten or twenty other meetings this week. The
candidates were running around to every civic group they
could get their hands on. Oh sure, they'd tailor tonight's
speeches along the more liberal side, to fit the coalition.
Tomorrow, at the Veterans of Foreign Wars meeting,
they'd tailor to the more conservative side. If she was serious, seeing them in each camp would provide good experience.

Before she left my desk, I told her about the VFW
meeting and she noted the time and place. She thanked me
again and I waved it off. I was going to be furious with
myself if I started trusting all of her gratitude and flattery
at face value. I reminded myself again that she had been
crawling into Wrigley's bed to get what she wanted. I
shivered and went back to work on my pile of papers.

Afternoon rolled around and I called Casa de Esperanza
to make sure there wouldn't be any problem meeting there
with Sammy and Jacob. The woman who answered wa-
vered a bit, even though I told her I wasn't planning on
writing anything about the shelter. She wasn't moved to
commitment by my saying I had once worked at the shelter, either. Finally, I dropped Mrs. Fremont's name as a
reference and doors opened—suddenly I was a welcomed
guest. "Mrs. Fremont should be here any time now," the
woman said brightly. I thanked her and told her I would be
there in about twenty minutes.

I tidied up a few things, still feeling like it was unnat-
ural for this desk to be so clean—O'Connor had always
covered it in mountains of loose papers. As I made my
way out to my car, I was concerned about going into this
meeting without having spent at least a little time trying to
get some background on witchcraft or on any previous
news of local cults. Hadn't I just given Stacee a big speech
on being prepared?

And all I knew about witches came from a little background on what went on in Salem three hundred years ago and a few episodes of "Bewitched."

"Eye of newt and toe of frog; Wool of bat and tongue of dog," I mumbled, drawing a look of apprehension from a passer-by. I doubted the incantations from *Macbeth* were going to be of any help either.

Oh well, I thought, climbing into my car, I'd just have to keep in mind that I was meeting with Sammy to confirm Jacob's purpose for being at a certain gathering—a political story. Not a witchcraft story.

I left the parking lot with those good intentions. By the end of the day, I would be wondering if I was on that famous road that is paved with good intentions.

| Five

I got to Casa de Esperanza before Sammy and Jacob arrived. The place was all decked out for Halloween. Inside, it didn't look much different than it had fifteen or more years ago—I had to stop and do some math—right, fifteen years ago. The music groups on the posters which adorned its walls had changed, except for one for the Doors. I tried to do a little more math, working out how old Jim Morrison would be today, when a clean-cut, muscular young man came walking toward me. I was wondering if all the runaways looked so well-adjusted these days, when he said, "Irene Kelly? I'm Paul Fremont. My grandmother has often spoken of you."

As I took the offered hand for a vigorous handshake, I tried to absorb the shock of realizing this "kid" was a twenty-one-year-old college student, not a runaway. "Hello, Paul. Your grandmother has told me a lot about you. She's certainly very proud of you."

He looked at me a little oddly, I thought, but I didn't have time to figure out if I had embarrassed him or if he just didn't believe me, because at that moment the grandmother in question appeared at the scene.

"Why, Irene! Mrs. Riley told me you'd be coming by this afternoon. And now you've met my grandson, Paul. Good, good. Let me show you around, dear. This part of the house hasn't changed since you worked here, but we've been busy out in the back." She took hold of my arm and led me off. Paul nodded in understanding and went into a small office.

Mrs. Fremont was right. The place had changed. A recreation room had been converted out of a garage. There was a deck and a beautiful garden, including a spot where the residents grew some vegetables. There was some indefinable something that inwardly itched at me about the garden. I knew it wasn't because I remembered it; the last time I had been in this yard it had just been dirt and grass of dubious parentage.

"Frank and a friend of his built the deck and did all of the landscaping for us," she said.

I looked at her in surprise, then smiled. "Now I know why something about it seemed familiar."

"Yes," she said, returning the smile, "I'm not sure his friend Pete enjoyed the work so much, but Frank put his heart into it. He's a keeper, Irene."

"A keeper? As in, 'my brother's'?"

She laughed. "No, as in, 'one you shouldn't throw back into the pond.' " She became reflective for a moment. "Come to think of it, Frank is the kind you mention as well. His brother's keeper. Yes. He certainly isn't afraid to get involved or lend a hand."

I looked out at the garden again. She was right. Frank was a keeper by either definition. The *Express* and the LPPD be damned.

This warm fuzzy moment of ours was rudely interrupted by the sudden blare of a stereo and the simultaneous ruckus that can only be raised by a group of teenagers. I was cringing at the loudness, but Mrs. Fremont was looking at me with laughing eyes. "I've lost some of my hearing," she shouted into my ear. "Probably from when people who were in high school with you used to sit around here and play records by the Who and Pink Floyd at full blast. I count my blessings."

Judging from the noise inside, Mrs. Fremont had about twenty blessings in tow; but when we got back inside the house it turned out to be about half that.

I looked the group over and didn't see Jacob; I figured Sammy wasn't here yet either. I was trying to take in this boisterous sea of energy, released from the school day and excited about a Halloween party to be held that night, when it dispersed in varying directions almost as soon as it had arrived. Some of the residents took over the bathrooms, some headed down the separate wings of the house to their rooms, a group went out into the backyard, and a couple of them tried to raid the refrigerator. Mrs. Fremont moved off into the kitchen to chat amiably with them—the generation gap we had talked about in my day narrowed to a sliver.

Paul walked into the front room and reached for the volume control, cutting the decibels in the room in half. He winced as he turned to me and said, "My ears can't take it as easily as Grandmother's."

"Believe me, I'm with you," I said.

"Don't ever let any of the residents know, but I prefer classical."

"Your secret is safe with me."

At that moment, the front door burst open with such fury it bounced off the wall and almost closed again on the thin young woman who entered the room. She marched past me, pausing long enough to give me an angry look before heading back into the women's wing. She was pale, dressed totally in black, and had long hair dyed to a dark, raven color. This spidery young lady had to be Sammy.

Quite a few of the other residents I had seen earlier were wearing black, and some had that same look of bravado over pain as well, but something about the creature who had just flown past me made her a better candidate for a witches' coven. I had just figure out that part of this impression came from a cloying fragrance that still hung in the air—she had smelled strongly of some kind of incense or spice oil—when the door opened a second time, more gently.

Jacob looked at me and blushed to the roots of his hair. "Sorry, Miss Kelly. I told you she was dramatic."

"Yes, you did. That was quite an entrance. Do you think she'll talk to me?"

"Oh yeah. Are you kidding? She loves the idea of being interviewed by the newspaper. I think if we just wait outside, she'll come out again."

He spoke with the easy assurance of one childhood friend discussing another. He knew Sammy. I wondered if she deserved such loyalty. I shrugged and followed him out to the deck. We sat on some patio chairs surrounding a table. From the recreation room we could hear a game of Ping-Pong in progress.

Jacob chattered excitedly about his afternoon at school. He had gone in to see the journalism teacher—Michael Corbin, an old friend who had gone to college with me, and who was, as Jacob said, "way cool." Michael had told him that he could add the class, which was about four days in progress for the winter quarter, and wrote a note to that effect for Jacob's counselor. The counselor had been obliging as well. I smiled at Jacob's enthusiasm—a day of conquering potential hurdles of adult permission-giving had his spirits soaring. A different kid from the one I had seen in the morning. I wondered if Michael and the counselor had seen that, too. I'd have to give Michael a call.

Jacob had predicted Sammy's mood swings well. As he reached the end of his tale about the class, she appeared at the back door, and made her way over to us as if nothing had happened fifteen minutes before. She sat next to Jacob and favored me with a long glowering stare. A summer as a camp counselor had taught me all I needed to know about the likes of Sammy.

"Well, Jacob," I said starting to rise from my chair, "I guess I'd better go. Sorry about your dad's campaign and all that. I know it means a lot to you." It was a mean thing to do to Jacob. I hated myself when I saw the look of hurt on his face. But it worked like a charm on Sammy.

"Hey, wait a minute," she said. "I thought you wanted to talk to me."

I took my turn staring, then said, "You haven't indicated to me that you're really up for that, and I don't have time to sit around and coax you."

I started to turn again, and she fairly shouted, "Wait!"

I faced her.

"I'm sorry," she said, shocking me—I hadn't expected an apology. She turned to Jacob, but kept speaking to me. "I'll talk to you. Jacob says you're okay."

I sat back down again, and tried to give Jacob a quick reassuring look. "Okay, Sammy—want to tell me the story of this witches' coven?"

She looked around nervously. I wondered if it was real nervousness or more drama. "Will my name be in the paper?"

"This whole thing may never actually reach print. I'm just trying to be ready in case something breaks. And for that matter, I don't even know your last name. What is it?"

"You won't contact my parents?"

"Not my business."

"Garden."

Holy Mary. No wonder the kid had problems. Anyone who had been given a handle like Gethsemane Garden had an uphill battle. I tried not to let my face reveal that I knew what Sammy stood for.

"Okay, Miss Garden, why don't you tell me about the coven?"

"Don't call me Miss Garden. I hate my name. I'm going to change it. Anyway—call me Sammy, okay?"

"If you'd prefer that, sure. Look, Sammy, I'm not here to cause you problems. Tell me about this group you're in."

"Well, last Friday night our coven gathered, and I went and Jacob came by and tried to get me to leave. End of story."

"Not quite. What kind of group is this? Satanist?"

She rolled her eyes. "No. Satanism is a different thing altogether. We're not Satanists, no matter what that moron Montgomery says."

"So what are you?"

She sighed, and looked over at Jacob. He just watched her silently, but his eyes were willing her to keep talking. She turned back to me.

"We're into what you would probably call paganism. It's a very old religion. It's a religion of the earth. That's what we worship—the earth and her creatures are holy to us. It's a very female thing. Satanism is a very male thing."

If any of that bothered Jacob, he didn't show it.

"So these witches met last Friday. Are they male and female, even though this is a female thing?"

"We don't discriminate."

"So what happened that night?"

"Jacob came along and he asked me to leave with him."

"Jacob didn't participate at all?"

"No."

"What would participating include?"

"I told you, he didn't participate."

"And I asked what participating includes."

She stewed for a moment. "I can't tell you."

"Sworn to secrecy? You take some blood oath or something?"

"No! I mean, yes, I am sworn to secrecy and no, it is not a blood oath. Look, this is like my religion, okay? I won't tell you what we do. It's between the members of the coven; it's not for outsiders."

"If what Jacob tells me is true, at least one other person not only knows what you do, but has taken photographs. Don't you want to tell your side of the story?"

"I can't tell you that. Besides, I left with Jacob on Friday."

"Really? Does that put you on the outs with the group?"

She shifted uncomfortably. I decided to take a stab at something.

"What are you afraid of, Sammy? Has someone threatened you for leaving that night?"

"No!" she said, betraying herself with her vehemence, and catching herself at it. "If anyone could scare me, would I be sitting out here talking to you?"

"You're not even afraid of the guy in the goat's mask?"

She turned white, a startling contrast to her hair and clothing. She turned to Jacob, her eyes brimming with tears. "You told her that? You asshole! Don't you ever speak to me again!"

She jumped up from the table and would have run into the house, but I was quicker and stronger—I grabbed her by the wrist.

"Let go of me, you bitch!"

"Apologize to the guy who may be the only real friend you have, and maybe I will."

"Fuck you."

"Look Sammy, if you want to have a cuss-out, you should know you're up against a pro. You're not going to shock me—not with bad manners, witchcraft, tantrums—and not at all with foul language."

I hadn't noticed that Jacob had moved up out of his chair. He put an arm around her. "Please let her go," he said to me.

I shrugged and let go. She crumpled up into his arms, crying on his shoulder. Twice in one day, I thought. Maybe I really was the meanest reporter in town.

"I'm sorry, Miss Kelly," Jacob said quietly. "I owe Sammy an apology, too. This whole thing was a bad idea. I never should have bothered you."

"Jacob, Jacob, Jacob," I said softly, shaking my head. "It wasn't a mistake. Sammy, you need to figure out who your friends are. Jacob needs your help. Seriously. Believe me, I don't get up and jump every time there's a troubled teenager somewhere. I'm sorry if I scared you or bullied you. It's just that if I don't know at least as much of the story as whoever is feeding Montgomery his information, then I can't present a balanced view of whatever happened. I'll get one side of this story from the Montgomery campaign. I need your help to get the other side."

She sat back down in the chair, her face a mess from crying. I pulled out a couple of tissues and handed them to her.

"The . . . person you were referring to . . . that person

wasn't there that night. It wasn't that kind of gathering. That's all I can say."

Looking at her, I could see that the fear she had of the character in the goat's mask was not feigned. It didn't seem to me that we were going to get much farther. I took out a business card and scribbled my home phone number on the back. I handed it to her.

"If you think of anything more, give me a call."

I stood up and started to go. Some movement inside the house caught my eye. I remained still for a moment, then realized that the curtains on one window were swaying slightly, as if someone had been watching us. This seemed so strange—we were off to one side of the activities of the recreation room, but surely it would have been easy for someone to have planted themselves within earshot. Why hide in the house, where he or she would be unable to hear us over the music?

I looked back at Jacob and Sammy. He was saying good-bye to her. We left together, and I offered him a lift home. He hesitated only a moment and then accepted.

"Jacob," I said, when we were in the car, "do you think there's any possibility that Sammy is in real danger?"

He turned his face away, staring out the window, but answered, "I don't know. I guess I must think that she is, or I wouldn't want her to stay away from the coven."

"Do you know any of the other members of the coven?"

"Yeah—a couple of the other kids at the shelter are into it. Sammy was hanging out with them at school at lot. That was before she got kicked out of her house. Now I kind of feel like it's my fault."

"Why?"

"She wasn't really very into it until she got kicked out. Then I mentioned the shelter, not knowing these kids lived there, and then she really got seriously involved in it. I never should have mentioned the shelter. I should have talked to my mom about it more than I did. I asked if Sammy could live with us, and she said no, but I didn't really—you know—beg and plead with her or anything. Now look."

"Sammy is your age?"

"A little older. She's seventeen, I'm sixteen. I won't be seventeen until January."

"She's free to make her own choices, even bad ones, Jacob. Don't feel guilty. There are other kids at the shelter she could have chosen as friends, and you said yourself she was already into it before she moved there."

"Yeah, I guess you're right. I just wish there was something I could do."

"Keep her occupied with other interests, other friends."

"You probably saw why she doesn't have too many friends."

"You saw through it—other people can, too."

He was quiet until we pulled up in his driveway.

"Thanks, Miss Kelly. Thanks for trying, anyway." He walked back into the house in the same glum mood I had seen him in first thing that morning. I was, at that moment, happy to be heading toward forty after all. I wouldn't be sixteen again for anything.

I stopped by the store on the way home and bought some candy and a pumpkin. Pickings were slim by then, but I did manage to find a bag or two of not-too-unpopular candy bars. At the checkout stand I had an inspiration and bought something for Frank.

I opened my front door cautiously, and found myself battling the fear that always overtook me when I was home alone. I lived in a little 1930s-style bungalow in a neighborhood that threatens to become more upscale, a relatively peaceful area. But the violence of the previous summer had been brought to my doorstep, and try as I might, I could not yet feel safe in my own home. The window blasted out by gunfire had been replaced, the locks improved, the wall replastered—even my grandfather's chair had been repaired and reupholstered. I was the only item that was still damaged.

Wild Bill Cody, my gray, twenty-pound tomcat, heard the door open and came bounding in, scolding me loudly when he reached my feet. I picked him up and scratched his ears; he closed his eyes and purred loudly. "It's your own fault, Romeo," I said. He clawed my arm in response. I dropped him on the floor with a yelp. We were even.

He trotted after me, following me into the kitchen. I opened a can of some foul-smelling stuff he was fond of. I rinsed the cat food can and put it in the recycling bin. He was already chowing down, but he looked up and blinked his thanks.

I watched him with affection. Lately he had been shuffled around like an orphan, traveling between my place and Frank's. At first he was a terror to transport, employing a vast array of tricks for fighting the car carrier, and wreaking havoc on Frank's house when we got there. Frank learned to catproof his place and Cody learned— after two or three times of being left by his lonesome— that if he was going to make a stink about it, he'd be left behind. This time he had refused to come when I called for him, so I had left some dry food and fresh water near his cat door.

Outside of shredding the newspapers I put down to shield the kitchen table, Cody didn't interfere with my pumpkin-carving efforts. He made the biggest mess he could with the papers, decided he didn't like the smell of pumpkin pulp, and took off. After a minute, I wondered what he was up to, and found him chewing on a candy bar. It was one that had a mint flavor—a particular weakness of Cody's. I took it from him and got a nice scratch for my efforts. I was going to have to watch that candy bowl like a hawk.

The trick-or-treaters started arriving, and kept me busy for the next few hours. It is not a good idea to rest your hopes for the next generation on what they choose for Halloween costumes. While I knew that the boys probably wouldn't *all* end up being mass murderers and leaders of evil space empires, I couldn't help but feel dismayed about the number of princesses and ballerinas I was greeting. Just when I feared that there were no tomboys left in Las Piernas, a little girl came trundling up the steps carrying a sword, a black buccaneer's hat perched atop her head.

"You're a pirate!" I said.

"I'm a pirate *captain!*" she corrected.

I gave her six times as much candy as the usual ration, and told her to be sure to thank her parents for me.

Frank called as business was slacking off, at about 8:30, saying he wouldn't be free until after 11:00—could I wait? I told him I'd have a snack and wait for him to get back for dinner. I air-popped some popcorn and curled up on the couch to listen to a Kings game in progress. Cody strolled over and settled on my lap. He smelled suspiciously of mint, but I didn't see a half-eaten candy bar anywhere.

During the second period break, I packed up my clothes for work the next day. Frank and I were alternating between houses—one week at mine, one week at his. It was an arrangement that had already grown tiresome, but neither of us had broached the subject of moving in together. Or whatever it was we were going to do next. I was happy to keep packing clothes and cats for a while.

On my way back to the living room to listen to the second period, I stepped on something soft—Cody's candy bar. I bagged up the remaining candy and stuck it in the freezer. What worked with Frank would work with Cody. After that I was completely absorbed in listening to the hockey game. The Kings won in overtime and I was jumping up and down whooping for joy when the front door burst open, scaring me clean out of my wits.

Frank and I stood looking at one another with startled expressions.

"Are you okay?" he asked. "I heard screaming."

"I'm fine," I said sheepishly.

The announcer was saying, "So the Kings win it with thirty seconds left in overtime . . ."

"I should have known," said Frank, coming over to give me a hug.

I looked up at him. "You're tired. Let's just go over to your place and I'll fix you something there."

He seemed tempted for a brief moment, then said, "No, I promised you dinner out tonight, and that's what we're going to do."

I frowned. It was easy to see that he was exhausted. He

had worked long hours all week, and the case he was on now—the murder of a four-year-old girl—had been especially hard on him. He was usually able to distance himself emotionally from the grisly business he had to deal with at work, but this case had bothered him. He bottled up most of his agitation over it, but it seemed to me that effort was wearing him down as well, and from time to time I caught glimpses of how much it had disturbed him.

On top of the strain of this case, the last few weeks had been rough ones for another reason: Frank wasn't getting along very well with his new lieutenant, Dave Carlson. Lieutenant Carlson was an ambitious man, and I suspected he was somewhat jealous of Frank's popularity with both the other cops and their captain, John Bredloe. Carlson and Frank had already had a couple of minor run-ins, and Bredloe had backed up Frank both times. That didn't score him any points with the lieutenant.

"I'm willing to take a raincheck on the evening out," I said.

"Get a sweater, it's cool outside."

Okay, so he wanted to go out. We went to an all-night cafe, Bernie's, which is not far from my house. The food was good, but despite the fact there wasn't much of a crowd, the service was pathetically slow.

"I talked to my mom," Frank said. "She doesn't have a problem with having you join us for Thanksgiving."

That didn't sound quite the same as boundless enthusiasm, but maybe he was too tired to convey her level of interest in having me there. Besides, I had made up my mind about it anyway.

"Great, I'll be happy to be with your family for Thanksgiving. Thanks for inviting me."

His face went quickly from puzzled to pleased. With a little food and coffee in him, Frank perked up a bit, but we were both ready to head for home. I looked around. If our waitress was in the room, she was wearing a cloaking device.

"You know, Frank, I have thought about our growing old together—I just didn't think we were going to do it in Bernie's."

"Yeah, I wanted dessert, but I'm afraid to order it; we'd be here 'til I'm pensioned."

"Don't bother," I said, reaching into my bag and pulling out a Snickers bar—the little gift I had bought for him at the checkout stand. "Have at it, sweet tooth."

He grinned in appreciation. "You know, Irene, I think I might satisfy one other craving tonight as well."

"You taking up smoking?"

"One more guess."

The waitress chose this moment to reappear.

It was about 1:30 in the morning by the time we got back to my house. We captured Cody and I grabbed my clothes and overnight bag. We decided to go to Frank's place in one car—he would bring me back in the morning.

As we made our way up the walk to his house in the early hours of All Saint's Day, we both saw something that made us stop and stare.

Mrs. Fremont's lights were on, and her front door was wide open. Even from where we stood, we could see the crudely drawn goat's head on the door.

| Six

"Stay here!" he said, running across the lawn to Mrs. Fremont's house.

I thought of following him anyway, but just then Cody gave a pitiful yowl from his cat carrier, and I realized Frank had set it down near the driveway.

I heard Frank calling Mrs. Fremont's name, and I turned back to see him pulling out his gun before going into the house.

I quickly put Cody inside Frank's house, then went next door. "Frank?!" I shouted at the bottom of the steps, not wanting him to mistake me for an intruder. Something told me that whoever had been here was already long gone, and that Frank wasn't likely to find anyone in the house. I was half-right.

From the doorstep, I could see Frank at the end of the hallway, bent over something in an odd way; he hadn't responded when I called. As I walked toward him he looked up suddenly, an expression of anguish on his face. Before him, on the floor, Mrs. Fremont lay face down in a pool of blood. On the floor next to her, someone had drawn a circled pentagram in blood.

"Don't touch anything," he said, his voice strained. He stood up, and I saw that she had taken some kind of crushing blow to her head. As I stared down at the body, Frank reached over and turned me away. "Let's go home—I've got to call this in." I held on to him and somehow we stumbled back to the house.

I sat numbly while he went to the telephone. He was visibly upset, but he took a minute to regain his self-control and was able to put the call in without betraying emotion of any kind. He stood there, staring at the phone for a moment, then walked over to me and took my face in his hands. "Please stay here. I'll be back as soon as I can," he said.

I felt unable to do anything but nod. He seemed so calm, but something in his eyes hurt to look at. For a moment, he looked as if he were ready to say more, but he dropped his hands and turned and left quickly.

Cody found me sitting on the couch, and jumped up into my lap. I thought of Mrs. Fremont and the conversations I had with her not twenty-four hours ago, of how alive and vibrant she was then. Endless questions crossed my mind, questions without any possibility of being answered at that time.

The goat's head and the pentangle made me think of Sammy and her coven of witches. Was Satanism on the rampage in Las Piernas? Could Sammy's routine about paganism versus Satanism have been a cover-up of some kind? She had been afraid of the man in the goat's mask.

Wasn't that connected to Satanism? What did Sammy really know?

I saw the reflection of the blue-and-red lights of police cars on the walls, soon followed by the crackle of radios. I looked out and saw Lieutenant Carlson pull up. I sat back down, sad and suddenly weary, but not feeling as if I could sleep.

To my surprise, about half an hour later, Frank came back home. I got up to greet him, but something in his walk warned me to keep my distance. When he was close enough for me to see his face, the coldness there came at me like a blow.

"What's wrong?"

He walked past me and over to his liquor cabinet. He poured himself a large scotch and downed it quickly.

"What's wrong?" I asked again.

"Carlson won't let me work on it. He basically ordered me to leave."

"Why?"

He shrugged his shoulders, poured himself another scotch, and downed it as easily as the first. I was wondering if he was going to stay up all night drinking, but he put the bottle away and said, "I'm going to bed."

I followed him into the bedroom and we got undressed in silence, Frank keeping his eyes averted from me. We got into bed, and he turned away from me. I reached to rub his shoulders, but he pulled away, moving his large frame to the edge of the bed. You don't have to call Western Union for me. I got the message.

I rolled over so that we were lying back-to-back, and turned out the light. The room was bathed in pulsing lights from the police cars next door. Doors opened and closed, voices carried on the night air. My muscles ached with tension.

"Irene?"

I turned back, thinking maybe he wanted to talk after all. There was a long silence.

"What, Frank?"

Still more silence. I was about to give up when he said, "I think we should take a few days off from each other."

I didn't answer because I couldn't answer. My throat was constricted and I could feel tears welling up. I rolled away on the off chance he would turn and look at me. I lay there for a long time before I was able to breathe normally.

Before we started sleeping together in that bed, I had spent a number of years living alone. My friends and family always worried that I was lonely then. But in all those years, I was never as lonely as I was that night, lying less than three feet away from Frank Harriman.

| Seven

Between my emotional state and the noise next door, I didn't sleep at all that night. The two triple-sized scotches had apparently done the trick for the bastard next to me, although I noticed he was restless even as he snored away.

I went from feeling extremely sorry for myself to being extremely angry with Frank. I was pissed at myself as well, for not having a car to make an escape in. I considered calling a cab. Maybe because it was a Holy Day of Obligation, I prayed for strength.

At dawn, watching Frank and wondering if I would ever watch him sleep again, something like sympathy found its way past my anger. I remembered how upset he had been earlier, how close he had been to Mrs. Fremont. I thought of the helplessness he must have felt when Carlson took him off the case. I didn't like the idea that withdrawing from me might be his way of dealing with his own emotions, but I concluded that like it or not, I was going to have to give him the time alone he wanted. I reminded myself that he had said "a few days," not "I never want to see you again."

I'd been around too long to feel much comfort in this last thought. I hated being in the position of waiting to see if he still wanted me.

I decided the answer to my problems was to busy myself with the election and to do what I could to find out about occult groups in Las Piernas. If the paper raised a stink about it, I figured I could argue reasonably that I wasn't working on a crime story—after all, I had already been contacted by someone who indicated a connection would be made between Satanism and the D.A.'s race. Besides, who knew how much longer I'd be bedding a cop? It might only be a few more minutes.

Sometimes my own sense of humor backfires on me.

I decided that the odds of Frank waking up and taking me in his arms and murmuring, "Darling, how could I have been so wrong! I can't live without you . . ." were slim to none. So I carefully slid out of bed and went down the hall to the bathroom and took a shower. Okay, so what if we usually took one together? That was just water conservation, right?

I was in a really foul mood by the time I dried off. Frank wasn't awake yet. I carried my clothes into the bathroom and got dressed there. I was too restless to stay in the house, so I went out on to the patio. That wasn't such a great idea. It made me think of standing in the backyard of Casa de Esperanza, hearing Mrs. Fremont tell me Frank was a keeper. Well, I apparently hadn't set the hook properly—he was wriggling away.

I heard him moving around inside the house; heard the shower and later, kitchen noises. My own appetite was running around somewhere with my ability to sleep. I couldn't take looking at the garden anymore, caught between the loss of Mrs. Fremont and the distance from Frank, so I left the yard through the gate. I walked past Mrs. Fremont's house without more than a glance at the yellow police barricade tape that sealed it, and headed for the beach. It was only a short walk from the house.

I stood at the edge of a walkway that led down to the beach. The Pacific stretched out in dark gray, the autumn sky cloudy to match. As I stood there, it worked its magic, the rhythm of the waves breaking on the shore easing away my tension.

By the time I walked back to Frank's house, I was calm. I had decided not to push him, and not to make too much of what he had said in bed. I had plenty to do between now and whenever he wanted to see me again.

I went into the house. I could hear Frank washing the dishes. I avoided the kitchen and gathered my things together from his bathroom and bedroom. That left Cody. When I walked out into the living room, Frank was holding him, scratching his ears. "We'd better go," I said.

Frank put Cody in his carrier, then picked it up and came over to get my bag. "I can manage," I said. He looked at me for the first time since the night before. He looked unhappy, more sad than angry, but he said nothing. We walked out to the car in silence.

The drive to my house was silent as well. He helped me bring Cody in, not trying for the bag this time. As he set the carrier down, he looked at me. I couldn't stand the thought of him just driving off.

"Why?"

He looked away. "It's not you."

"If it's not me, why are you shutting me out?"

"Just give me a few days."

"Fine."

He finally looked at me again. "I don't want to hurt you, Irene."

To avoid shouting "Too late!" into his face, I bent down to let Cody out of his carrier; by the time I stood up, Frank had left.

I looked out the front window; he was sitting in his car. He hadn't started the engine. "Please come back," I whispered.

He drove off.

I went into the office taking deep breaths and internally chanting something that went like this: I will not take it out on the people who work with me.

I met Wrigley on the staircase.

"Well, good morning, Miss Kelly. Just wanted you to

know I took Miss Martin off that ridiculous little assignment you gave her last night. She had more important things to do."

... Eight ... Nine ... Ten. Still pissed. Remembering the chant, I said, "You're not doing her any favors."

He laughed and shoved his way past me. I resisted the strong temptation to kick his double jugs down the stairs.

Just as I reached the newsroom door, Stacee Martin came flying out. She looked at me and burst into tears, then ran off down the hall.

For a moment I debated whether to follow her or mind my own sordid business, and decided that maybe John had given her a hard time about not covering the story. As I walked into the newsroom, a group of people were standing around John. Suddenly there was a burst of laughter, the kind of laughter you hear when a joke has been made at someone else's expense. I decided not to join them, and walked over to my desk.

"What's wrong with you, Irene?" one of the reporters called out.

"Police brutality," another yelled, and there was more laughter. It was a stupid, worn-out remark, and usually I would have met it with a comeback of my own. I could see from the look of anticipation on most of the faces that they were waiting for just such a repartee, but I was too far out on the edge of my ability to keep my temper to respond. I glanced at John, and saw a worried look on his face. I turned and walked back out of the newsroom. As the door closed behind me I could hear John yelling at everyone to get back to work.

I went into the morgue, away from prying eyes, and used the computer there to open the file on the Gillespie murder. That was the case Frank was working on. I'm not sure exactly why I reviewed this particular file, except that I knew the case was bothering Frank; maybe I just wanted to try to understand what was going on with him. I realized that as busy as I had been with the election, I hadn't paid much attention to this case. I did remember that Mark Baker, the reporter who covered the story, had been pretty shaken up by it.

Megan Gillespie was a beautiful four-year-old girl, the only daughter of Joseph and Elizabeth Gillespie. She had disappeared from a city park, where she had been attending a children's birthday party one Saturday afternoon in late September. Her body had been found in a trash bin in an industrial park a week later, now about three weeks ago. She had been sexually molested. Cause of death was strangulation.

I closed the file with a shudder. Although Las Piernas was big enough to have its share of crime, including homicide, this type of case was rare. I didn't need to read more of the file to know that although the case was being worked on actively, no suspect had been charged. The level of fear in the community, especially among people with small children of their own, was palpable. The pressure on the police was tremendous, but I didn't think that was what bothered Frank. He had lived with that before. It was more likely that the very nature of this particular case had upset him.

"Excuse me, Miss Kelly?"

I know I must have jumped. When I managed to find my voice, I said, "What is it, Stacee?"

"I'm sorry, I didn't mean to frighten you."

"I'm okay. What do you need?"

"I just wanted to apologize. I wasn't able to cover the coalition meeting last night."

In view of what I had just read, I couldn't have cared less. "I know," I said.

"You know?"

"Yes, Wrigley stopped me on the stairs to gloat over it."

"Oh." Her eyes misted over.

I wish I could tell you that I was moved, but I wasn't; I was just angry. The day was going lousy and I just didn't have patience. But I held my tongue, because I remembered my chant.

Finally, she said, "Well, I apologize anyway. It won't happen again."

"Why should I believe that?" I said, nasty in spite of myself.

"I guess you don't really have any reason to. I wanted

to tell you that I learned a lesson—I really don't think I want anything more to do with—well, I'll just say Mr. Wrigley has made a first-class fool of me and I deserve it. If you'll give me another chance, I won't disappoint you."

I was too tired and frazzled to argue with her, and God knows I didn't want her to sit there and confess all the lurid details of her liaison with Wrigley. "I'll see what I can come up with for you. Are you here to do more research?"

"Yes, I am."

"Good. Come by my desk later and we'll talk it over."

She smiled a little and said, "Thank you, Miss Kelly."

I logged off the computer and headed back to my desk. Compared to the pain the Gillespies were living with, I guessed I could cope with my little aches. I remembered O'Connor quoting something to me once. "Irene," he said, "if everyone in the world could put all of their troubles in a basket, we'd each still want to pick our own problems back out of it."

I'd take mine over the Gillespies' any day.

| Eight

As I walked back into the newsroom, I could feel some tension, but no one came anywhere near me. I sat down at my desk and tried to shake off the cloud of depression that threatened to settle on me. There were three phone message slips waiting for me. The first was from a Julie Montgomery. No message, no number—would call back later. Monty Montgomery's wife was named Nina. He had three daughters and a son. I pulled up a file on him on the computer. Yes, one of the daughters was named Julie.

The second was from Jacob Henderson. Will call back later.

The third was from Sammy Garden. Same routine.

Damn. While I was in the morgue listening to Stacee, half of Las Piernas High School was trying to get in touch with me.

I wondered if Sammy had tried to reach me at home. I'd been too distracted that morning to check my messages. I called my home number and entered the code to get the machine to play back to me.

"Miss Kelly? Are you there?" The voice on the tape sounded frightened. "This is Sammy. Look, I've got to talk to you. I'm leaving the shelter. Something awful has happened. I've got to go. I'll try calling you at work tomorrow."

I had a feeling in my bones that the "something awful" was the murder of Mrs. Fremont. If Sammy wasn't in danger before, she probably was now. Where on the streets could she hide out? What place that other runaways wouldn't know about?

I paced around my desk. I couldn't leave—I couldn't afford to miss a call from any of these kids. I started thinking about Julie Montgomery. She was about seventeen or eighteen. I remembered Jacob's blush when I had asked him about his source inside the Montgomery campaign. Could Jacob and Julie be friends? More than friends? Considering the bitter rivalry between the two candidates, it didn't seem likely. But it wasn't impossible.

My thought were interrupted by Lydia, who was walking toward me with a piece of paper in her outstretched hand. "Have you seen this?" she asked. "It's being hand-delivered to the homes of most registered voters today."

"Stop Satanism in Las Piernas," I read aloud, sinking into my chair. There was a dim photo of Jacob Henderson, dressed in black, his face lit by firelight, talking to a woman in a dark robe—she looked like Sammy, from what I could see. They were in a circle of other robed figures. The spiel below the photo was pretty much as Jacob had predicted. It didn't look good.

"The phones have started ringing off the hooks," Lydia was saying. "Looks like Henderson has had it. I think it's going to get worse; the Fremont murder story has been on the radio, and Wrigley wants to tag it 'The Satanist Murder.' "

I could see Mark Baker, who covered crime stories, starting to make his way over to me. The phone on my desk rang. I picked it up.

"Irene?" It was Pete Baird, Frank's partner.

"Yeah, Pete."

"I'm worried about Frank. You have a fight?"

"Not really. He's upset—look, let me call you later, okay? I'm in a crowd here."

"Okay, but let me call you instead. We're on our way out."

I hung up, noting the expression of extreme curiosity on Baker's face.

"Was that Frank?"

"No," I said, glad to be able to tell the truth. "What's up?"

"It looks like there may be some tie-in between the D.A.'s campaign and the murder of the Fremont woman. You got anything that might help me?"

I was spared answering by John Walter's booming "Kelly!"

"If I'm alive when I leave his office, I'll find you, Mark."

He nodded in sympathy, and I walked toward John's office. Even though I could see John turning red, I stopped by Lydia's desk on the way.

"Lydia, there are three people trying to reach me." I handed her the message slips. "If any of them call, please get me out of John's office."

"Are you nuts?"

"Please, Lydia."

I must have sounded desperate, because she nodded her head.

"Don't let me interrupt your busy day, Kelly!" John bellowed.

I straightened up and said, "I appreciate your understanding, John."

He turned on his heel and I made haste to follow.

I closed the door and sat down. He glowered at me.

"You know what, Kelly?" He held up a copy of the Montgomery flyer and waved it back and forth. "I've got an itch somewhere that tells me you knew something about this hit piece of Montgomery's yesterday."

"Almost right, John. Jacob Henderson met me yesterday morning, asking to talk to me off the record. He told me he had heard from someone in the Montgomery campaign that this was going out. He tried to explain why he was at this gathering in the photo. I spent yesterday morning trying to find out if there was going to be a hit, but although it was pretty clear some kind of mudslinging was going on, I couldn't get anyone to confirm the nature of the piece. I spent the afternoon trying to confirm Jacob's version of the story. He claims that he was there to talk a friend into leaving, and that he's not part of the coven. I talked to the friend, and she backs him up."

John stewed for a minute or two, then apparently decided that I had done my job. "You believe the kid?"

"Yes. I'd like to talk to other kids in the coven, but it's going to be hard. My connection to them—Jacob's friend—has run away. She left a message on my machine saying she'd call me again. I don't know if she will, but I asked Lydia to come in here and get me if she calls."

He scowled. "This is all a bad business. I suppose you know our esteemed editor's ideas on tagging the Fremont murder 'Satanist.' I don't like the idea of playing right into Montgomery's hands."

"Wrigley's just thinking of how many newspapers he can sell. It will help him sell them all right—at the expense of the Henderson campaign."

"You're going to write something up about the Henderson kid's version of the story?"

"As much as I can. It will probably be pretty thin unless I can find somebody else who was there."

He grew pensive again. He was watching me in a way that made me uneasy.

"Irene, what was wrong this morning?"

I looked away from him. "It's a list of things, John."

He waited.

"Mrs. Fremont was Frank's next-door neighbor. He found the body. I was right behind him."

"Jesus."

"Frank really liked her, and it was pretty rough on him. It wasn't too much easier for me. I had talked to her a couple of times yesterday. I didn't sleep at all last night, I walk in here and Wrigley sneers at me, then Stacee runs past me in tears. I just wasn't in the mood to take any crap about Frank from the laughing boys in the newsroom."

"You okay now?"

"Not really, but I'll survive."

"You say you saw the body?"

I could see the wheels turning in John's mind. I nodded.

"Cops wouldn't let anyone past the door last night. But you were inside the house?"

"Yes," I said, thinking of the pool of blood.

"Tell me what you saw."

I could feel my hackles rise.

"Go to hell, John. If I can't cover crime stories, fine. But don't turn around and try to get me to be a spy for you or to compromise Frank. One way or the other—not both."

"Goddammit, Irene, I'd ask any witness the same thing."

"I'm not any witness."

He was back up to the boiling point. "You're biting the hand that feeds you, Kelly! You'd better give some thought to who signs your paycheck."

"I'm not ready to make a whore out of myself for the lousy sum on that check."

"Get out of here!"

"Gladly."

I stormed out, only to be met by Lydia frantically waving me over to the phone. Would there be no relief?

"Kelly," I snapped into the phone.

"Irene Kelly?" It was a young woman's voice.

"Yes."

"My name is Julie Montgomery. I'm Monty Montgomery's daughter. I need to talk to you. Can I meet you somewhere?"

| Nine

This was going to be difficult. If I met her away from the paper, I might miss Sammy or Jacob. If I stayed, it was going to be hard to find privacy. I decided to try the storage room in the basement again. Even then, I wondered how I was going to sneak her into the building without anyone seeing us meet.

"Look, I can't leave here right now, but I don't think this is the best place for you to be seen, either. What are you wearing?"

She gave me a description. I described Stacee to her. "She'll meet you and take you to a room. I know all of this sounds like some kind of cloak-and-dagger operation—"

"No, I appreciate it. I understand."

We arranged to meet in half an hour. I corralled Stacee and found she was eager to be of help.

"Just meet her and take her to Danny Coburn. Have Geoff give me a call, then go on to lunch—don't come back upstairs and don't let anyone else know she's here. I mean that. Not anyone."

She nodded, obviously enjoying the intrigue. I called down to Geoff and Danny to warn them of what was going on. Then I looked around for Mark Baker. He was working at his computer, entering a story with lightning speed. I watched his long, black fingers flying over the keys. I always admire that kind of keyboard mastery. I don't exactly hunt and peck, but I'm no speed queen, either.

Mark looked up and smiled. "You lived!"

"Only a reprieve, not a pardon. John would like my head right now."

"Why?"

"Same reason you're going to, unless I can smooth-talk you."

He laughed. "You know I'm helpless before you, you silver-tongued devil."

"Bull. But thanks, my bruised ego needed that. Anyway, here's the deal. I suppose you know that I'm not supposed to be doing any kind of crime coverage?"

"Because of Frank."

"Right. Well, last night, in a purely personal capacity—not as a reporter—I followed Frank into the Fremont house—before the cops got there. He discovered her body. John wants me to tell all I know. My better self tells me if I had been there as a reporter, this would be no problem; but Frank was not dealing with me as a reporter."

"No kidding," he said with a grin.

"Mark, I need to talk this over with somebody who can avoid making double entendres out of everything I say."

"Sorry. I could tell you were upset this morning. I like Frank, you know that."

I nodded. "I suppose this rule on crime stories is set up so that I don't give Frank information on what the paper is doing, or try to write pieces that might end up being too pro-police or whatever. But I think it ought to be a two-way street. I don't think it's any more ethical for me to hand out information to the paper, if that information happens to come my way as a result of my relationship with Frank. It would be abusing our relationship. Am I wrong, Mark?"

"You're in a pickle, that's what you are."

"Very helpful."

He grinned. "I thought you had ink in your veins."

"Maybe so, but I have to pump it through a heart."

"No wonder Walters can't relate—don't think he has one."

"Oh, it's not John's fault. In fact, I see his side of it all too clearly. I don't like doing this. It really goes against the grain."

"He must have pitched a real hissy fit."

"To be honest, I don't know how long it's going to be before he really loses it with me. Anyway, thanks for listening. As for what I can tell you, I can give you some information, so long as we're talking as friends and no one has any wrong ideas about me getting involved in crime coverage."

"Why, Irene—I just figured it out. You're interested in this Fremont case, aren't you?"

"For a whole lot of reasons."

"I can imagine. Frank working on this?"

I felt myself wince, and saw him look at me with curiosity.

"No, he's not. He's busy with the Gillespie case. Anyway, you asked if there's a tie-in. The Montgomery campaign claims Jacob Henderson is a Satanist and published a photo. You've seen the flyer?"

He nodded.

"Well, first of all, we have nothing that really proves that the people in the photo are engaging in Satanism, witch-craft, or a weenie roast, for that matter. No credit is given for the photo, so we don't even know where it came from or who took it. No date or location. So I'm not saying right at the moment that the photo shows much of anything.

"As for the Fremont murder, there was a drawing of a goat's head on the door, and that's supposedly a symbol connected to satanic cults. There might be other reasons that a person would conclude that it was an occult group of some kind."

"So a certain person might have seen other signs of a satanic cult at work if she happened to see the inside of the house?"

"I'm not saying that at all, Mark. In fact, something really bothers me about this whole satanic business. I don't know, there's something not quite right about it."

"What?"

"Well, maybe Mrs. Fremont's death is the work of Satanists or some other offbeat group, but it could also be a pretty straight-ahead murder made to look like a ritual killing."

"Why Mrs. Fremont?"

"It's so hard for me to imagine anyone wanting to kill

her, I honestly can't give you much help there. But I think we should look at old-fashioned motives, not just bizarre cults."

"So is there a tie-in with the D.A.'s campaign or not?"

"Hard to say. There are apparently a number of members of an occult group of some kind living at the runaway shelter Mrs. Fremont started. They're kids, and I can't imagine why they would ever want to harm her, but you might want to see if you can find out more about the coven they're in—something tells me there may be some kind of offshoot group that's into the really weird stuff."

"How do you know about it?"

I told him about my basement conversation with Jacob and the talk I had with Sammy at the shelter. "Sammy has taken off from the runaway shelter. She left a message on my machine that sounded like she knew something was up last night. I'm worried about her, Mark."

"I can see why. Well, thanks, Irene. Maybe I can talk to some of these other coven members."

"That would be great."

"And I'll put in a good word with John—I'll let him know you've helped me out."

"Thanks."

I went back to my desk. A few minutes later, the phone rang. It was Geoff, letting me know my visitor had arrived, and that Danny was taking her to the same place I had met Jacob.

When I entered the storage room downstairs, the young woman who was sitting there waiting for me jumped out of her chair. She had that look one sees in those who have begun to lose their innocence, but who have not yet entirely relinquished their hold on it. No longer an angel, but not yet damned by any means.

"Miss Kelly?"

"Yes. Julie? Have a seat." I pulled the other chair up next to her. The presses were running, so it was hard to hear.

"I'm here because I have to do something to help Jacob."

"Does your father know how eager you are to come to Jacob's aid?"

"No. Well, maybe. I begged him not to put that flyer out, but he never listens to me anyway. He doesn't know I'm here, if that's what you mean."

"Are you and Jacob seeing one another?"

She looked down. "Off the record?"

"Jesus, Mary, and Joseph! You political brats are going to drive me wild!"

She looked so taken aback, I realized my lack of sleep was starting to affect my self-control. "Forgive me, Julie. I'm a little edgy today. Yes, okay, off the record."

"No one can know."

"It's hell to try to keep that kind of thing a secret."

"No kidding. But we've managed to keep it quiet for almost a year. We met at a Christmas party they held last year, for all the families in the D.A.'s office. Jacob and I talked, and it just seemed like we both had something in common—you know, our dads and all. Like you said, political brats."

"You have sisters and they don't know about it?"

"My sisters and I don't get along very well. They couldn't care less. In fact, most of the time, everybody in the family is so wrapped up in their own problems, they don't even notice whether I'm there or not."

It was hard to imagine anyone not noticing her. Julie Montgomery was a beautiful, dark-haired girl with large brown eyes. She had the kind of figure that causes morning traffic to slow down in front of high schools.

"You said you wanted to help Jacob. What did you have in mind?"

"I know he isn't a witch or a Satanist or any of those things."

"What am I supposed to do? Write that Jacob Henderson's anonymous girlfriend swears he's just not that kind of guy?"

She looked down. "We're going to tell our parents after the election is over. Right now it's impossible. I can't."

"What I'm trying to tell you is that even if you let me use your name, I have to have more than just your affection for him on the scale. I need something that will have a little weight with the public. Were you around the night the photo was taken?"

"No, Daddy took us with him on his rounds of meetings that night."

"Is that usual?"

"Not really. He brings us to the really big stuff—you know, fancy dinners and all of that—but mostly I think he wants us out of the way."

"Do you know any of the kids in this coven?"

"No, just Sammy. She knows about Jacob and me, but I haven't spent much time around her. She kind of—well, she hangs out with a different crowd. But she's been good about not telling anyone about us."

"Do you know who took the photo?"

She shook her head.

"Do you know how your father found out about this coven?"

Again, no.

"I'm sorry, Julie. I think it's great that you've risked talking to me and that you're trying to be of help. But I just don't see what it is I can learn from you that will counteract what's in that flyer. I like Jacob, too, but I can't just make things up; I've got to report the facts as clearly as I can."

For a moment, I thought I was going to be three-for-three in teenage crying jags, but she surprised me. Her disappointment couldn't be hidden, but she held back the tears. "Jacob really likes you," she said. "It's funny, he's all excited about being on the paper at school. I think it's the only good thing going for him right now."

"I suspect you're on the list of good things going for Jacob Henderson. As far as the flyer goes, I'd suggest you try not to take all of this on your own shoulders. It's something your fathers are going to have to fight about; it's not anything you have any control over. Just try to hang on until next Wednesday."

"By then the whole county is going to believe Jacob worships the devil."

"By then the whole county will have forgotten about it."

She shook her head. "I can't stand watching him get hurt like this. By my own father!"

Were the tears going to fall after all? No. Determined streak in this one.

She stood up and reached out a hand. "Thanks for meeting me."

"Thank you. Sorry to disappoint you." I pulled out a business card. "Give me a call if you think of anything or hear anything that might be of importance, okay?"

"Okay."

I led her out to the main lobby and watched her leave.

Not half a minute later, Mark Baker came running past me. He stopped at the door and turned toward me.

"SWAT teams are out down at the harbor. Couple of cops barricaded in a building with a suspect in the Gillespie murders. I think it might be Pete and Frank in there with him. Want to come along?"

Before I could answer, a voice boomed behind me, "She's got her own work to do, Baker. Get your ass down there!"

I turned on John Walters. All the fear that had hold of me a split second before had turned to a blinding rage. He saw it in my face. He mirrored it in his own. Just as I was ready to start screaming at him about finding a small, dark, lodging place for this job, a soft voice spoke up.

"Why, Mr. Walters, I can't believe you meant to say that. If it weren't for Detective Harriman, we wouldn't know who killed Mr. O'Connor. And I hate to think of what would have happened to Miss Kelly. You don't mean to keep her here while he's being shot at?"

It was Geoff. Blessed Geoff, who will someday inherit the earth. He somehow took the wind out of our sails.

John sighed. "Shit. Come on, Kelly. I'll take you there myself."

This was startling. John didn't go out on stories. I just stood there, feeling numb.

"Well, for godsakes, Irene, you don't think I'm going to let you go down there to face that alone, do you?" he said gruffly, taking my elbow and propelling me toward the door.

I turned and shot Geoff a look of gratitude, but the anxious look on his face made me suddenly feel the impact of every word I'd heard in the last few minutes.

I let John pull me out the door.

| Ten

Even press credentials couldn't get us very close to the center of activity down at the harbor. We caught up to Mark Baker. He told us that Frank and Pete had come down to the waterfront that morning to question someone who was seen in the park about the time the Gillespie girl had disappeared—a man by the name of Jerry Tanner.

A bystander had seen a green van leaving the parking lot shortly before the Gillespies started looking for their daughter; the witness hadn't been able to give a plate number. There had been a lot of people in the park that day, and tracking down those who had been near the site of the birthday party wasn't easy. But a neighbor of Tanner's had seen him there, and she knew he drove a green van. She had read about the van in the paper and called the police that morning. Frank and Pete had learned that he worked in a warehouse for an export company down in the harbor, a few blocks from where the body was discovered. They came down to where he worked to question him.

Apparently, Tanner saw them enter the building, and had taken out a gun. The other workers had fled, but he managed to pin down Frank and Pete in the building with him. Gunshots had been heard, but no one knew more than that.

Behind the barricade, Captain Bredloe was conferring with Lieutenant Carlson and the commander of the SWAT team, whose members were moving into position on surrounding buildings, some moving closer to the warehouse itself. I looked down and realized that my fists were clenched so tightly my nails were stabbing into my palms.

As we stood there, more shots rang out, and I felt my knees buckle as a sickening sense of fear ran through me. John grabbed on to me. Not long after, a man ran out of the building, motioning to Bredloe. It was Pete Baird. I saw him gesturing and speaking angrily with Carlson. This was interrupted by a single gunshot. The whole scene froze in place. Long moments later, the front door opened and I heard the click of readied weapons.

"Hold your fire!" Bredloe yelled.

Frank slowly walked out of the building.

Suddenly, there was a rush of people in uniform toward Frank and into the warehouse. Pete threw an arm around him, and I saw Frank give him a bewildered look.

I sagged against John, who held on to me. I wanted to run over to Frank, but there was no way in hell to get over to where he was. The SWAT team was moving back out of position. A public relations officer made his way over to the place where we were penned up with the rest of the press.

"Ladies and gentlemen," he said, "right now it appears that the suspect, Mr. Jerry Tanner, has taken his own life. As soon as we have more, I'll let you know."

I looked back over to see Frank slowly but deliberately walking off from an angry Carlson; Pete followed Frank. I couldn't make out any of what was being said, just Bredloe shouting Frank's last name. Frank turned, and said something back, then he and Pete drove off.

John talked to Baker for a minute and then guided me back to his car.

"He's all right, Irene," he said.

But something in Frank's manner as he walked out of that building, the arguing with Bredloe, the way he walked to the car, all said John was wrong. Carlson was a jerk, but Frank always got along very well with Bredloe; it wasn't like him to just ignore the man. That and, well, he just seemed dejected. Like he didn't care about anything. I remembered the look on his face when Pete had been so happy to see him come out of the building alive—as if he didn't know what the big deal was.

Something was really wrong.

John was quiet for a while, then he started talking to me about the D.A.'s campaign. I tried to focus on his questions, but I know I answered them woodenly.

As we pulled into the parking lot, he turned to me and said, "Snap out of it. Frank's okay, it was just a nasty scare. You'll be laughing about it over dinner tonight."

There was no way to tell John about the gulf of silence that lay between Frank and me, to say that no dinner or laughter was on the agenda for a while. But I saw John's efforts to comfort me; in fact, in the last hour or two he had been more gentle with me than I had ever seen him be with anyone. "Thanks," I said.

He noticed my mood though, and studied me for a moment.

"What are you working on this afternoon?" he asked.

"Following up on the Jacob Henderson story."

"Hmm. I guess you better stick with that. But unless you've got interviews lined up tomorrow morning, why don't you catch up on your sleep, come in a little later. Hard to keep your perspective when you're exhausted."

That really surprised me. "Maybe I will. You're right, I'm too tired to think straight."

"Goddamn right I'm right. Now get upstairs before you besmirch my reputation as an asshole."

I smiled at this and said, "You overestimate my abilities, John."

I stopped by the lobby desk and thanked Geoff, reassuring him that Frank had survived. He smiled and said, "I'm so happy for you, Miss Kelly.' I went upstairs and made some phone calls, getting reactions to the Montgomery flyer. I had hoped there might be a message from Jacob or Sammy. No luck. I forced myself to think about work, and not what had gone on at the harbor.

I suddenly felt exhausted, and knew it was a combination of delayed shock over the events of the afternoon and my struggle to overcome my reluctance to write up a story on the Montgomery accusations. In the latter case, I just didn't feel as if I had all the facts. I wondered if there was any other way to get in touch with these local witches.

Starting on the easy route, I pulled out a phone book and then thumbed through the yellow pages. The local phone company advertised them as the "Everything Pages," and I had to smile to myself at the notion of finding something under "covens," "hexes," or "spells." There wasn't anything listed under witchcraft, but I did find a heading for "Occult Supplies." I noticed with some amusement that it fell just below "Nuts—Edible."

Right here in Las Piernas, there was a shop called Rhiannon, named after a magical woman in Celtic lore, if I remembered my folktales. It offered "books, incense, oils, bulk herbs, athalmes, and crystal balls." I had to look up "athalmes"—witchcraft's ritual knives.

From the address in the phone book, I saw that the shop wasn't too far from the office—a few miles down Broadway, near the college. It was a district full of cafes that stayed open late, small bookshops, and artists' studios. A little rundown, but cherished by its residents. It was here that those who lived alternative life-styles of one kind or another could fairly well imagine that the world had grown accustomed to them. I wondered how long it would be before someone started buying it all up and converting it into a fashionable upscale hotspot.

Never, I hoped.

Any day now, I knew.

I had started clearing off my desk, getting ready to drive over to Rhiannon, when my phone rang.

"Kelly," I answered.

"Hi, it's Jacob. I was wondering if you know where Sammy is."

"No, I'm sorry. She left a message for me last night, but I wasn't home. She sounded scared and she said she was running away from the shelter. I was hoping you might know where she is."

"No." Even over the phone, I could feel the weight of the worry in that one word.

"Any ideas on where she might go?"

"I've been looking for her, but she's not in any of her usual hideouts. I left school early today. I looked all over. It scares me—I can usually find her."

"I guess you know the flyer is out."

"Yeah. My dad is going to kill me."

"You haven't talked to him?"

"Not yet."

"Jacob, I think your dad will believe you. He's probably under a lot of pressure right now, so don't judge him by his first reaction, okay?"

"I took your advice about changing my look. My mom about died. She said she hasn't seen me wearing this many colors at one time in years. It's an exaggeration. I'm just wearing blue jeans and a white shirt. At least she was happy with me this morning. By now they probably both hate me."

"I doubt it. They're probably angrier with Montgomery. Your dad won't like having his opponent pick on his family. In the meantime, I'm going to see if I can hunt down some other people from the coven. But I'm getting near deadline, so I'd better run. Are you going to be okay?"

"Yeah, sure."

I gave him my home number and told him to call me if he needed someone to talk to later. It wasn't going to be easy for him to face his family. I felt my resentment for this kind of campaign tactic rising.

For a moment or two, I sat there reminding myself that I had to stay more neutral. I left the office.

Something within me made me sit in my car for a while before I went into Rhiannon. Was it some childhood fear of witches? Or did my Catholic upbringing rebel at the thought of an encounter with this other belief system? No, I thought, I didn't feel that uneasiness about Islam or Judaism or Taoism. This was something different.

If I hadn't been up against a deadline, I might have driven off. Instead, I forced myself to get out of the car. The exterior of the store was painted black, which was no real surprise. In the display window were books, tarot cards, candles, and various other objects, some of which I

didn't recognize. Crystals—raw quarts and amethyst—
were suspended in the window.

"Double, double, boil and trouble," I said to myself, and
pushed the door open.

Eleven

The first thing I noticed was an overpowering sweet fragrance; some kind of spice or incense. It made me think of
high school, when many of my classmates and I burned
patchouli or sandalwood incense in our bedrooms, driving
our parents crazy. After some time away from the smell of
incense, I could see why it took a little getting used to.

Some sort of underwater bell-and-flute soundtrack was
playing in the background. I had to admit it was soothing,
but smiled remembering a musician friend of mine who
once pooh-poohed all "new-age" music as "hippie noo-
dling."

Apparently a new shipment of herbs had just arrived.
Boxes were piled in stacks here and there in the aisles.
The walls were filled with shelves, the shelves filled with
jars, the jars filled with all manner of things. I didn't look
around for any fillet of fenny snake; it was clear that all
potions and remedies were from the plant kingdom or the
earth itself. Through the middle of the store there was a
sort of self-service set of small bins, each holding stones
or crystals that were carefully labeled for effect: this one
for inner peace, this one for easing menstrual cramps, this
for sleeping better at night. A large black cat with bright
yellow eyes stared at me from the counter where the cash
register was, as if guarding against shoplifting. For an
amused moment, I wondered if it was going to transform
itself into human form.

"Hecate, it's not polite to stare." The voice came from a back room, and I realized that someone had watched me enter from behind a thin curtain. Soon a large woman dressed in a flamboyant purple gown came out to greet me with a warm smile. If this was a witch, I had been needlessly frightened as a child. "Hello," she said. "Your first time here, isn't it? Don't tell me, don't tell me . . ."

I had no idea what it was I wasn't supposed to tell, so I obeyed.

"Capricorn!"

"Ah, no. I'm a—"

"Don't tell me, don't tell me!" She closed her eyes and pinched the bridge of her nose. "Aries!"

She was wrong again, but rather than standing there watching my deadline time get whittled down by the zodiac, I said, "Incredible! How could you know?"

She smiled a little smile of success and shrugged modestly.

"Your ad said you have books," I said, knowing I couldn't just ask for a directory of local covens.

"Yes, this way, this way. Anything in particular?"

"Well, a friend of mine is getting involved in learning more about the ancient ways," I said, getting this last phrase off the spine of a book in the "A" section. "She tells me there is a big difference between witchcraft and Satanism. Is that true?"

"Oh, yes! There most certainly is. Witchcraft is known by many different names in many countries, and has its own varied forms, but it is essentially a spirituality that respects the earth and her creatures. It is not destructive; it is in harmony with the natural world. Satanism is quite different. First of all, to worship a devil, you have to believe in devils. Satanism is a perversion of Christianity, not the paganism of your early ancestors."

"Yes, but aren't there people who combine the two?"

She sighed. "You can find people who will do anything, I suppose. There are always going to be people who use whatever power they have of whatever kind it may be to do evil. But there is no evil incarnate or devil in witchcraft. I would think of people who tried to combine them as Satanists trying to abuse witchcraft in the same way they abuse Christianity. I would not call such a person a witch."

I considered what she had told me, and decided to be straightforward with her. She was watching me, and maybe because of the atmosphere or my own uneasiness, I felt like I wouldn't get away with a lie. The zodiac business was bad enough.

"Have you seen this?" I handed her the Montgomery flyer.

She groaned. "Sweet Goddess, I'm going to have the Nazarenes picketing me again."

"My name is Irene Kelly. I'm a reporter for the *Express*," I said, and had her full attention. I pulled out a business card.

"Zoe Freespirit," she said.

"I'm trying to manage some balanced coverage over all of this—and believe me, it's hard. Do you recognize any of the people in this coven? I think they're mainly kids. I need to talk to them, if at all possible."

She glanced at the photo. "I wouldn't feel comfortable just giving out names even if I knew them. If any of these people come in here, maybe I could have one get in touch with you—if he or she wants to."

I must have looked defeated, because she said, "I'm sorry."

"Could you at least tell me if you've seen the young man whose name is already printed on the flyer? Has he come in here?"

She studied the photo now, and then began laughing. It was a rich, rolling laugh. "I don't believe it! Yes, he's been in here. Trying to discourage business."

"Was it in connection with the young girl next to him—Sammy? I've met both of them."

"Yes, yes. She was in here one day a week or two ago, with some other young people. Jacob came in and threw a fit. Tried to get her to leave with him. She wouldn't, and he started telling her off. Finally, I had to ask *him* to leave. Little snot waited right outside the door. Sammy saw him out there and I think she took pity on him—left her friends and went outside with him."

"You're certain he's the one?"

"Believe me, not a doubt in my mind. This kid is no witch. And the kids in this photo are not Satanists. Whoever made up this flyer doesn't know what he or she is talking about."

I looked at my watch. "Look, I've got to run if I'm going to make my deadline. But I appreciate your help. Maybe I'll come back some time and really do some shopping."

"You're welcome any time—but you're not an Aries, are you? You're a Leo."

I blushed and nodded. I left wondering if she had just made a lucky guess. I no more believed in astrology than the man in the moon. But there was still something unnerving about it all.

My speed on the computer keyboard that day nearly matched Mark Baker's. I put together as fair a piece as I could, still raising as many questions about the allegations as possible, and quoting Jacob, Sammy, and Zoe. I wondered to myself if the readers would have any faith in an assertion made by someone named Zoe Freespirit, owner of an occult supply shop.

With the story finished and at the mercy of the editors, I cleared off my desk, then found Stacee and went over a couple of things with her. I was going to let her try to cover some of the political events I knew I wouldn't make it to—there was just too much to follow up on at this stage.

I said good-bye to Lydia, who was on her way to dinner with Guy St. Germain, a former hockey player who had settled in Las Piernas. They had kept steady company since the summer. I bit back a moment's envy of them. I walked down to my car. The sense of depression I had fought against all day started to press in on me again. By the time I got home, I felt tired and ill at ease. I hadn't spent very many nights alone in my house since Frank and I got together. He knew my fears and helped me cope with them, while still letting me work out for myself how I was going to overcome them.

Cody's warm greeting helped lighten my spirits a little, and I decided that while sleep was needed, a short run would help my mood. It would be dark soon, so I hurried and changed into my running clothes.

I did some stretching and headed out for a tour of the winding streets in my neighborhood. The air was cool and autumn leaves crackled under my feet. With each step, I felt better. By the time I got back home, dusk was turning to darkness. I was on a much more even keel. I opened a can of cat food for Cody and went in and took a shower. I went back to the kitchen and made a bowl of soup from a can. I like making my own soup from scratch, but soup from a can is sometimes just what the doctor ordered. This was one of those times. I indulged myself with lots of crackers, some of which I floated in the bowl, thinking that I was glad Frank wasn't there to see me eating like a kid.

The phone rang, and when I went to answer it, I noticed the answering machine light flashing, indicating a message. I'd listen to it after the call.

It was Jacob.

"I just wanted to let you know I'm okay. My dad is mad, but I think he believes me. I couldn't stand it if he thought I was hanging out with a bunch of Satanists or something. He's worried about the election—oh, I probably shouldn't have told you that."

"That much I would have guessed, Jacob. By the way, I talked to the woman who runs Rhiannon today."

"Oh."

"Cheer up—she supports your story, even said that you're not in the coven and that she remembers tossing you out of the store when you tried to pull Sammy out of there. It should help."

"If people believe her."

I decided a change of subject was in order. "How's the journalism class?"

"Oh man, I love it! I mean, we don't do really exciting things like you—you know, it's just school stuff- but it's fun. I'll get my first story in Monday's school paper! I saw the proof copy. I wrote about this school play; not a review or anything, kind of an announcement—you know, where to buy tickets, that kind of stuff. But it was so cool to see my name on the byline and all."

I smiled, remembering my first byline—on a story about a game our high school girl's volleyball team had won. "It's quite a thrill, isn't it? When the paper comes out, save a copy for me. And don't forget to start a string book."

"A what?"

"A collection of all your published stories. Later on, you use it to show someone samples of your writing—an editor, or someone hiring you for another publication."

"Okay, I'll do it. Maybe I'll be showing it to you someday."

I laughed. "For my interest—don't ever look for me to be an editor. I wouldn't want the headache. I like what I'm doing now."

We talked for a few minutes more, and when I hung up, I felt good. There was something contagious in his enthusiasm. Given the way the rest of the day had gone, it's a wonder I didn't see the rollercoaster heading down.

I pressed the button on the answering machine to hear the message. It was Sammy, her voice sounding small and scared in the warmth of my kitchen. She had called while I was in the shower.

"Miss Kelly? Are you there? It's Sammy. I'm leaving Las Piernas. Tell Jacob for me, okay? I'm sorry I couldn't help him. I can't stay here. I've got to go. Bye."

Frustrated that I had missed a second call from her, I pushed the play button and listened to the message again. I couldn't help but feel uneasy. Something in her voice said the words not spoken: Help me. I'm in danger.

I paced around, unable to think of what I could do to help her. I would just have to pray that I was near a phone the next time she tried to call. It was useless to try to find her.

Her parents didn't seem to care what became of her, and I thought of how she must be aware of that. The people most children would turn to first had rejected her, thrown her out of the house. Sammy might have been a very difficult child to deal with, but could she have been that hard to live with? I thought of her out on the streets somewhere, possibly turning to the wrong people for comfort and aid.

It was only seven o'clock, but I was beat. John's suggestion about catching up on my sleep was looking better and better. I crawled into my bed, which seemed far too empty, even with Cody beside me. I both missed Frank and worried about him, but didn't know what I could do to remedy either feeling. When I wasn't thinking about him, I was feeling uneasy about being in the house alone or anxious about Sammy. I fell asleep despite my apprehensions.

I dreamt that Sammy was standing on the edge of a ravine. I was on the opposite side, telling her to stay there, that someone would be there soon to rescue her. It wasn't clear in the dream what she needed rescuing from. But instead of waiting, she reached out to me, and fell. The ravine turned into a bottomless version of the Grand Canyon, and suddenly I was falling down with her, a few feet away from her. As could only happen in a dream, she was talking to me as we fell. "You didn't catch me," she said.

I woke up, scared half out of my wits. It took me a moment to realize the phone was ringing. I reached for it clumsily and answered, hoping it was Sammy.

"I woke you up." It was Frank.

"Thank God you did. I was having a nightmare."

Silence. I felt a little irritation. Nothing like calling someone up at—I looked at the clock—eleven o'clock at night and then not saying a word. This passed quickly, though. I was remembering what it felt like to hear those gunshots down at the harbor.

"Do you want me to come over?" he finally asked.

"Yes, but only if you want to."

"I'll be there in a little while."

I know, I know, a stronger person would have told him

where to get off. Somehow, when it came to Frank, I wasn't sure I was above begging.

True to his word, he arrived on my doorstep not long after. I opened the door to his soft knocking. He looked miserable. He stepped inside, and we held one another in a long hug. I didn't mind that his hands and clothes were cold with the chill of the night air, that his shoulder holster was jabbing me from under his suit, that he was silent. I was too damn glad he had decided to be with me, too worried over what I had seen in his eyes.

He kissed me.

Cody made his presence felt: he greeted Frank by biting him on the ankle. I wanted to reach down and rid him of his pelt, but Frank picked the rascal up and held him in his arms. "Hello, Cody."

Cody purred loudly. My sentiments exactly.

"Hungry?" I asked.

Frank shook his head. "Tired."

He put Cody back down in ankle range and took my hand. I led him back to the bedroom, turning out lights on the way. I took off my robe and got back under the covers. I watched him undress. An incredible sight. If he had known what I was thinking, it might have made him blush.

He stood looking at me for a moment, then crawled in next to me. I could tell he was still feeling—what was it? Hurt? Sad? I didn't know. But he seemed a little less miserable than he had earlier. He kissed me again. I pulled him close, savoring his touch.

"Frank."

"Hmmm."

"I missed you."

His answer wasn't verbal, but I didn't mind. Not at all.

He fell asleep holding me. I stayed awake for a while, listening to him breathe, and wondering how I had come to feel such a need for the man. I had been so fiercely independent for so long, it was frightening to realize what a hold he had on me. Not that I was a simpering wimp or anything—I smiled thinking of some of the tests of wills

Frank and I had experienced in the last few months. And I knew that if it didn't work out, I would go on with my life. But I didn't want to think of what life without Frank would be like.

Still, his behavior since Mrs. Fremont's death had been odd; I hadn't seen this side of Frank before now. I knew he could brood at times, but there was an intensity in his current mood that was unsettling. He had come back across some of the distance he had put between us last night, but something in his manner clearly said he didn't want me asking him a lot of questions. And as much as my curious nature rebelled against that, somehow I knew not to force the issue.

We still had a lot to learn about each other, Frank and I.

Cody jumped up on the bed and situated himself in the curve behind Frank's knees. I laced my fingers into Frank's hand, and fell asleep.

| Twelve

I was alone in bed when I woke up the next morning. Frank had awakened a couple of times during the night; his sleep had been troubled. I supposed that at some point he had given up on it. I stretched and got out of bed. Maybe he had already left for work. I looked at the clock and realized that I had almost slept until noon. I didn't feel as if it were a case of sloth, though. Just catching up on my sleep.

I went into the kitchen and opened the refrigerator, finding evidence that Frank had not only been up before me but had also been to the store and back. I was quite pleased that I would not have to test the "seven-day freshness" guarantee on the older milk carton.

There was some fresh bread as well, so I made a grilled cheese sandwich for myself. When I got to the table with my plate and milk, I saw the note he had left for me.

"Irene—Thanks. Please be patient. Frank."

Please be patient. Translation: Please don't ask me what's wrong, please be ready for me at the drop of a hat, please put up with my moodiness. The damnable thing was, I would try to do just that.

He had also brought the paper in, and I was fortunate he didn't leave it in the kitchen, or I probably would have lost my appetite. The front page was splashed with the Fremont murder story, and the headline made my stomach tighten. "Shelter Founder Murdered by Satanists?" A question mark to cover a multitude of reporting sins. The byline was given to Dorothy Bliss. In the newsroom, our private saying was, "Bliss is ignorance."

Although the story itself was couched in careful terms that as much as admitted this was a guess based on the drawing of the goat on the door, by the end of the day most of Las Piernas would undoubtedly be convinced by the headline. While I wasn't sure Mrs. Fremont hadn't been murdered by Satanists, somehow seeing it in print brought about a reaction in me, making me want to find the flaws in the assertion.

Mark's story on Jerry Tanner and the harbor shooting didn't get the play it deserved, but it was reasoned, clear, and balanced. It's a good thing I saw it, because the next story I laid eyes on didn't make me feel any pride in working for the *Express*.

Not two inches away from the Fremont story, another headline proclaimed "Henderson Denies Son Is Satanist." It was my story all right, but the part that best defended Jacob was cut down to nothing and buried in the back half of the first section. I hadn't expected any of it to go page one and saw that being placed as it was would only make Henderson appear to be defending against a connection to the murder.

Damn Wrigley's miserable hide. This had his signature all over it.

I got dressed and made the most of what was left of Friday by working until about midnight, covering speeches and setting up interviews. Frank got off work about the same time I did, and stayed the night with me.

Saturday and Sunday were twin days. With the election so close, there was no such thing as a day off. There was a lot of work to be done, and Stacee actually proved to be of help. She and I ran around between various campaigns and political organizations, putting in long hours. Brian Henderson staunchly defended Jacob, but slid down in the polls as if they were greased.

Next to the Satanism charges, the big news was that definite physical evidence had been found in Tanner's home to link him to the murder of the Gillespie child. I thought that might have made a difference in Frank, but it didn't.

Sammy didn't call back.

I cam home exhausted each night, fed Cody, and crawled into bed with Frank, who still hadn't said more than ten words to me. But he held me close, and I was too tired to need more. At least he was sleeping better.

On Sunday night—or technically, Monday morning—I lay asleep in his arms when the phone rang just after one o'clock. It was Pete. I handed the phone over to a drowsy Frank. He had the phone in his hand about five seconds when he yelled "What?!" and sat up in bed, moving his feet to the floor. He ran a hand through his hair. Every one of his muscles tensed. After a minute he said, "Why?" He listened in silence to the reply. He thanked Pete for calling and hung up.

I was sitting up now. He was facing away from me. He sighed and said, "Monty Montgomery's daughter walked in a couple of hours ago and confessed to murdering Mrs. Fremont. Pete just found out about it."

"Julie?"

He turned and gave me a piercing look.

"Frank, she didn't do it. She's trying to protect someone."

The look didn't waver.

"It's true, Frank, she talked to me Thursday. Not about the murder, but about her boyfriend."

"What?"

I struggled for a moment with the problem of breaking Julie's confidence, but decided if she was going to do something as stupid as confess to a murder to help Jacob, I would face the consequences of telling Frank what I knew.

"She and Jacob Henderson are seeing one another. Secretly. She's been agonizing over the flyer her father sent out saying Jacob is a Satanist. She's doing this to get back at her father or clear Jacob or both."

"Pete says she claims that she's a Satanist. That she was given the mission of killing—" His voice broke and he looked away.

I waited. I resisted the urge to touch him. "She didn't do it," I said calmly.

"I've got to call Pete."

He made the call, telling Pete all I had told him. On a hunch, I caught Frank's attention and said, "Ask him if there was anyone from the *Express* there when she confessed."

He did, then waited while Pete asked one of the detectives who had been there. Frank listened, then said, "Mark Baker was there fifteen minutes before she showed up. He said he got an anonymous tip that there was going to be a big break in the case, that someone was going to confess. She walked in and announced her confession in a loud voice as soon as she laid eyes on him."

"How long ago did Mark leave?"

He asked Pete, then said, "He was gone about two hours ago."

I looked at the clock. "Shit. It will be in the paper tomorrow. She planned this. She confessed in time to get a late chase in, but not early enough to give Mark time to follow up much. If she's released, it won't be in time to counteract the damage to her father's campaign."

Pete and Frank talked for a few minutes more, than Frank hung up.

I called the paper, but anyone who could have made a difference was long gone. I realized that by now the story was in print and on its way to being distributed. Nothing could be done about it. As I put the phone down, I noticed Frank was sitting with his head in his hands.

I turned the light out. There was still enough light from the moon and streetlights to make out his features in the dark. I got in bed behind him, and reached up and rubbed his neck and shoulders. It was killing me to ask him the five hundred or so questions that I had been gathering together for the last three days. He started to relax a little, and reached up and took my hands. He pulled them around his chest and lay back down. He wouldn't look at me. I moved a hand up into his hair and stroked it gently.

"Frank?"

"What?" A whisper.

"I was there on Thursday, at the harbor."

He turned toward me suddenly. "What?" Not a whisper.

"I was there when—"

"Oh God, Irene." He sighed and turned on to his back, looking up at the ceiling. I waited, but he didn't say more. After a while, he took hold of my hand again and held it between his. "Now you really know what it's like, don't you?"

"What?"

"Being with a cop."

I thought about this for a minute. "No, Frank, that's not the problem. Yes, I'm afraid for your safety. I'm going to worry about you, but I can live with that. It's much more difficult to feel distant from you."

He was quiet for a long time. When he spoke, his voice was strained. "I just can't talk about it now."

I watched him lying there, tense and troubled.

Neither one of us slept much that night.

| Thirteen

"Manipulated by a sixteen-year-old kid. I'm about to become known as the man who changed the course of politics in Las Piernas county on a setup by a teenager." Mark Baker, usually one of the more easygoing members of the staff, was in a foul mood the next morning.

"You wrote it as fairly as you could." Even as I said the words, I knew they would be little consolation.

"I waited around as long as possible, and they were still questioning her when we hit drop-dead deadline. I had no reason to believe she'd be released. I never said she was charged. I was careful, Irene. But you know no one reads anything as carefully as you write it."

"Forget it, Mark. Every reporter has had something like this happen to them at least once."

"Aw, crap, I should have known. But nobody here wanted to wait on it."

"Understandable. Her timing was impeccable. She must have found out from somebody what time we . . ." An awful feeling came over me. I picked up the phone on Mark's desk and called down to Danny Coburn. Sure enough, she'd asked him about deadlines and printing schedules when she was here on Thursday.

Mark, who had heard only my side of the conversation, was furious. "You saw her here on Thursday? And you didn't say anything?"

"Hold on, hold on. I talked to her *after* I talked to you. And she wasn't confessing to murder then. That surprised me as much as it did you. And I sure as hell didn't know she had talked to Danny about our deadlines."

He wasn't completely mollified, but I didn't have time

to smooth his ruffled feathers. I went back to my desk and started working on election stories, which had now been made vastly more interesting by a couple of high school students. I thought about Julie. Monty Montgomery must have wanted to throttle her. In Jacob's case, he could go to his father saying he was wrongly accused. Julie was responsible for her own predicament; I couldn't picture her father being very understanding.

Not an hour had gone by when the phone rang. It was Pete, sounding frantic.

"Look, something's happened to Frank."

I let out a little cry, and he immediately knew what I was thinking.

"No, no, no—God, Irene—no, he's not hurt or anything. I'm sorry. Bad choice of words. But look, something's wrong with him."

"I know, but he won't talk about it."

"Damn. I was hoping he was talking to you. He seemed to be doing better until this morning."

"What happened?"

"He's been suspended."

"What?!"

"Bredloe suspended him for a couple of days."

"Why?"

"Well, he sort of punched somebody out."

"Sort of punched somebody out?"

"The guy had it coming. We're sitting around this morning and Frank walks in, and Bob Thompson makes a crack and Frank punches him." Pete laughed. "Knocked old Thompson flat on his ass. We had to hold them to keep them from going at it."

"Frank punched somebody? Another detective?" I was having trouble getting all of this to sink in. Frank is not someone who goes around punching people.

"Yeah," said Pete, more subdued.

"You said Thompson made a crack. What kind of crack did he make?"

"A wisecrack."

"Pete. Don't."

"Okay, okay. The guy made a crack about *you*. Satisfied? Some stupid remark about the paper not getting to bed on time."

"Oh no."

"Oh yes. And Frank would probably have let it pass any other day, but I'm telling you, since this Fremont thing, he's been impossible. Im-poss-i-ble. He's a powder keg. That's why Bredloe suspended him."

"Pete, why was Bredloe so angry down at the harbor?" There was silence for a moment.

"Shit, Irene, don't tell me you were there."

"I was there."

"You poor kid. Damn, that shook *me* up. Bredloe wasn't really angry, just concerned. He knows Frank isn't happy with Carlson, but he keeps hoping they'll work things out. Besides, Frank hasn't been himself lately."

"No, he hasn't."

"You can't really blame him. It would be too much for anybody. He's been bothered by the Gillespie case; he's let it get to him. I don't know if he told you, but he's done almost all the contact with the little girl's parents. Kid's father just sits in front of the TV, watching videotapes of her, crying. Hit Frank hard, I guess.

"And back on Halloween night, when Mrs. Fremont died, he was losing it—Carlson picked up on it and told Frank he knew her too well to work on the case, and that he had enough on his plate with the Gillespie case. So that was bad, but Frank seemed to take it okay."

"Not really."

"Well, he seemed like he took it okay at the time. The next morning he was wreck. That's when the call came in about Tanner. He moved a little fast on that, but I understood—no telling how long Tanner was going to hang around. Besides, at that point, we just thought we were going to be questioning someone who had been in the park; we didn't have much at all on the guy. We didn't expect him to be armed, but you always kind of have that in the back of your mind. The guy started shooting before we got anywhere near him. Carlson thought we had put a bunch of civilians in danger.

"Anyway, I told Carlson off about that. There wasn't

anybody else in the room—Tanner took off running, pulled out a gun, and everybody else ran outside. We didn't fire on him until he fired on us, and we were the only ones in the building by then. Frank did pull a stunt so that I could get out, but I'll be damned if I was going to tell that to Carlson. I'm telling you, Irene, Frank scared the living hell out of me in there."

I couldn't say anything.

"Sorry—I shouldn't be telling you all of this." He sighed. "The job might not even be what's eating at him. It's November, and that's Frank's bad month anyway."

"What do you mean?"

"You don't know?"

"Pete! Would I ask you if I did?"

"No need to get nasty, Irene."

"Sorry. Just tell me why November is a bad month."

"His dad died in November. Thanksgiving."

I thought back to what Frank had told me about his dad's death. I knew he had died about three years ago, from a heart attack.

"Frank has been upset every year in November for the last three years?"

"Well, it's always hard on him, but this year is the worst I've seen him. Maybe just too many other things happening. I don't know. I think he blames himself for his dad's death."

"What? I thought his dad had a heart attack."

"Yeah, well, I guess Frank had been talking to his dad, then he went outside to play with his sister's kid. He was only out there a minute when his mom started screaming. Frank ran in, and his dad was on the floor, clutching his chest. Frank did CPR, but his dad died anyway."

"Jesus."

"You know how many times I've told him there was nothing he could have done if he had stayed in that room talking to his dad?"

I sat there, suddenly not caring a damn about the election, the newspaper, or anything else. Except Frank.

"Where is he now, Pete?"

"Home, I guess. He won't talk to me. Could you try?"

"Sure. I don't know if it will do any good, but I'll try. Thanks for telling me all of this."

I found Lydia and asked her to call me at Frank's if anybody needed me. Then I located Stacee.

"Something's come up, Stacee, and I have to leave. Lydia knows how to get in touch with me." I listed some of the things I had planned to do that morning; she was excited to take on the responsibility. I was a little afraid to give her so much, but that Monday night would be busier than the day, with the last of election eve to deal with. The next night would be endless.

I raced down to Frank's house. He didn't answer the doorbell, but his car was in the driveway, so I pulled out my key and let myself in. I called to him as I opened the door, but there was no response. I kept calling all the way through the house, then saw he was sitting out on the back patio. A bottle of scotch sat next to him.

"A little early in the day, isn't it?" I said as I walked out into the backyard.

He didn't answer me or look at me.

I moved around to where I could see his face. He looked like hell.

I sat down next to him.

"If you're going to defend my questionable honor with your bare knuckles, the least you can do is look me in the eye."

"Pete has a goddamned big mouth," he spat, but at least he looked at me.

"How long do you think this would have been a secret, anyway?"

"With that bunch of hens, not long."

"Pete's just worried about you. So am I."

"I'm fine."

"Sure you are."

Silence.

"Look," he said angrily, "I don't need you to hold my hand every time I have a problem at work. Don't you have an election to cover?"

"A problem at work? Is that what this is? Face it, Frank. Something's really wrong and you know it."

"It's my problem."

"Our problem."

"No."

"Yes."

"Goddamn it, Irene, do you always have to have the last fucking word!?"

"When it matters, yes."

More silence.

"Go back to work."

"Talk to me."

He threw his glass against the wall of the house. I jumped, but I wasn't going to back down.

"Break every last piece of glass in the house if it makes you feel better. But talk to me, Frank."

"I told you, I can't."

"Bullshit. You won't."

He got up and walked into the house. I followed.

"Give me my key back," he shouted.

"No way."

"I don't want to be with you anymore, Irene. It's not working. Go on, get out."

"You are a lousy liar, Harriman. And I don't take orders from you."

"Goddamn it, get out of my house."

"Like I said, I don't take orders."

He drew his hand back and took a step toward me, but the action seemed to startle even Frank. He backed down immediately and sank to the couch, as if defeated. I sat next to him.

I lowered my voice, trying to ease things down a notch. "Wednesday morning, when I saw Mrs. Fremont, I told her you had invited me to Thanksgiving."

He put his head back and looked up at the ceiling. His jaw flexed with tension. I hated seeing him feeling like this, but not enough to let things stay as they were.

"I was worried about meeting your mother, feeling afraid that she wouldn't like me. Mrs. Fremont asked me if we loved each other."

He swallowed, but didn't say anything.

"You know, even though we've never said it to one another, I told her yes. Maybe I presumed something. Anyway, she said that if we did, then we had everything we needed in life, with or without your mother's approval."

I took his hand. He didn't pull back, but he let it lie lifelessly in my own, not responding.

"Was I wrong, Frank?"

He looked at me then, and after a moment he whispered, "No."

"Then let me hold you."

He did. I held his head against my shoulder, stroking his hair, not talking. He seemed to relax, and after a while I wondered if he was falling asleep.

"If I had listened to you, she wouldn't be dead," he said in a low voice.

"What?"

"You wanted to come here that night. I insisted on going out."

"And you think she wouldn't have been killed anyway?"

"I would have been here. I would have heard her."

"Frank, three other neighbors were home, they didn't hear a thing. and if we had been here, we probably wouldn't have noticed anything was wrong until the next morning. Because we went out, you were able to get an investigation started within a couple of hours of the murder."

"Lot of good it did her to live next to a cop."

"You're not God, Frank. You can't be everywhere, watching over everybody. And besides, it did do her a lot of good to live next to you. She was crazy about you. Bragged on you all the time. I saw her earlier the same day, and she showed me what you did for the shelter. She told me you were a 'keeper.'"

"A what?"

"A keeper, you know, a fish you don't want to throw back."

Unbelievably, a small, fleeting grin crossed his face. But in the next moment, his eyes clouded up. "She was one of a kind."

I laughed. "I'll never forget the first day she asked me

to go running with her. Here I am expecting to jog-walk, and I end up winded before she's warmed up."

In spite of himself, he laughed, too. We sat quietly for a while, remembering Mrs. Fremont.

"God, I'm tired," Frank said. Maybe he was commenting on his life in general.

"Come on, I'll tuck you in."

That earned another small smile. He washed his face, then met me in the bedroom. I undressed him and pulled back the covers. He crawled in, then turned and reached up, taking the nape of my neck in his hand and pulling me to him gently. He kissed me, then said, "What, no bedtime story?"

What the hell. My ass was in a sling at work anyway. I undressed and lay down beside him.

Like Mrs. Fremont said, we had everything we needed in life.

| Fourteen

"Well, well, well—I can guess what kind of emergency you had at home."

Lydia's comment made me blush to my roots.

She laughed and said, "The gods must be watching over you, Irene. No one noticed you were gone. John's been tied up in meetings about the Montgomery fiasco all morning, and Brady Scott called to say there would be a press conference this afternoon. Otherwise, all's quiet."

I allowed myself a sigh of relief. "I was sure this was going to be the day City Hall caught on fire."

We talked for a moment and then I walked back over to my desk. I looked over some notes that Stacee had left for me. I didn't like admitting that she was doing a good job, but she was. I wondered why someone with her brains and abilities would ever get next to Wrigley. She had talent, why use her skirts? I grinned to myself, thinking maybe that was a talent in itself.

I never have been much of a flirter. I don't consider myself an ugly duckling, but I'm not Miss America, either. I'm not the kind of woman who gets her way by batting her eyelashes. If I did bat my eyelashes, someone would probably hand me a bottle of eyewash. For a moment, I wondered if I might be jealous of the Stacees of this world.

Another moment's thought, and I knew I didn't envy her. She was going to have to put up with the attentions of the likes of Wrigley. When I had talked to her a few days ago, she had said something about Wrigley making a fool out of her. She would have to live not only with his whims, but with the kind of lack of respect from her coworkers that had made her run from the newsroom that day.

I sat back in my chair and looked up at the holes in the ceiling, imagining a self-help group called "Flirters Anonymous." "Hi, my name's Buffy and I'm a flirter. I once whored my way to the top of a large corporation, and woke up in the gutter." Murmurs of sympathy in the group. Flirters are featured on afternoon talk shows. Pretty soon, offshoot groups start—Adult Children of Flirters.

"What's so funny?"

I sat up so suddenly, I nearly rolled the chair out from under me.

Stacee was standing next to me, puzzled by my suddenly crimson cheeks.

"Nothing, nothing. How's it going?"

"Fine. I got some of those quotes you wanted on various people's predictions of the election outcome. Did everything go okay at home?"

Her obvious concern further shamed me. "Things are much better. I appreciate your taking over for me. Want to go to the Montgomery press conference with me?"

"Sure."

As further penance for my daydream, I asked her to join

me for lunch as well. We drove down to the Galley and ordered a couple of sandwiches.

"This sure is better than the deli downtown," she said, delicately biting into a chicken salad sandwich.

"Yeah, Frank turned me on to this place. Someday you'll have to try the pastrami. Out of this world."

"Is Frank your boyfriend?"

I cringed. I've never liked the term "boyfriend."

"He's the man I'm seeing now, yes," I answered coolly.

She was unfazed. "He's a cop?"

"He's a homicide detective." Don't ask me why I felt like I had to keep refining her vocabulary on the matter.

Her eyes grew wider. "Homicide?"

"Yes."

"That must be exciting!"

Good grief, she was starting to squeal. I was regretting my decision to bring her along. But you can't go back on your penance. Against Catholic Hoyle.

"I suppose sometimes it is exciting," I replied. "But it can also be pretty hard on a person. They see the handiwork of some very cruel people. Frank just finished working on the Gillespie case."

Her face fell, all the silliness of a moment ago leaving her. She swallowed hard and said, "The little girl?"

I nodded, and somehow, my appetite was gone. I pushed a dollop of potato salad around on my plate for a while, then gave up.

"I'm sorry. I've upset you, haven't I?"

"No, no—I just feel badly for the family. Crazy, really—I never met them, just read about them. And I could tell that this case really bothered Frank."

"I can see why. It must be awful, having to investigate something like that."

I didn't answer, just thought about Frank, how lost he seemed lately.

"Irene?"

I focused back on Stacee. "Yeah."

"I don't think you're being treated very fairly at the paper."

I had to laugh. "You don't, huh?"

She blushed. "I mean, the way people talk. And being taken off crimes stories. It doesn't seem right to me."

"I can handle it. A friend of mine once told me that having people talk about you is an indication of how much more exciting your life is than theirs." I smiled, thinking of O'Connor, who didn't hesitate to outrage the newsroom every now and then.

"Not necessarily," she said glumly, obviously aware that she was as much—if not more—the focus of newsroom gossip.

I wasn't going to pursue it. She had, so to speak, made her bed.

"Let's go," I said, and we made our way to the press conference.

The room was crowded. The accusations about Satanism and the high drama of the last twenty-four hours had attracted press from outside of Las Piernas, and many L.A. radio, TV, and newspaper reporters had shown up. I saw one of the photographers from the *Express,* and nodded to her. Brady Scott walked out and said that Mr. Montgomery and his daughter would be with us in a moment to read prepared statements. Following the statements, Brady would be available for questions, but Mr. Montgomery and his daughter would not. Mr. Montgomery had a very busy schedule to meet, on this the last day of campaigning, and he appreciated our understanding.

This sent a rumble of commentary through the room. Although I knew she had been released, I hadn't expected Montgomery to put Julie up to a public recanting of her confession. Apparently, my cohorts were equally surprised.

The room was suddenly filled with flashes and the sound of camera motors as Monty Montgomery and Julie walked into the room. Monty was all smiles. Julie, on the other hand, was solemn. She carried herself proudly, but she was pale and there were circles under her eyes to attest to what must have been a long night.

Montgomery spoke briefly, saying he regretted that the public had been given a false impression by an unfortunate childish prank on the part of his daughter. "The police have never charged her with any crime, and there is absolutely no reason to believe she was in any way involved in any cases under investigation by the Las Piernas Police. It would indeed be a travesty if the premature publication of a scurrilous report in the *Las Piernas News Express* influenced the outcome of the election."

He sat down, and Julie slowly made her way to the podium. She cast a quick look at me, then began to speak, reading from a text. "I apologize to the Las Piernas Police for misdirecting their time and energy, and appreciate their understanding." She stopped, and looked back at me. "I also owe an apology to certain people at the *Las Piernas News Express,* who became unwittingly involved in my— escapade." I could see Monty Montgomery and Brady Scott grow nervous at her departure from the text. Scott stood up and watched her anxiously.

"The text Mr. Scott has given me says that I'm to tell you that this was merely a prank on my part, of which I am ashamed. I do regret the pain it has caused my father. However, I could not condone my father's own prank, his lie that Brian Henderson's son is a Satanist. I wanted to even things out ..." By now Brady Scott had made his way over to the podium and turned off the microphone. Montgomery was right behind him, looking for all the world like a snake oil salesman who has had to swallow his own merchandise. Shouts and questions went up from the reporters, making it impossible to distinguish anything anyone said. Julie was ushered out by her father, and Brady Scott returned to the podium. He turned the microphone back on and motioned to everyone to sit back down.

"Miss Montgomery has a teenager's loyalty to her friend Jacob Henderson, and unfortunately lacks judgment. I apologize for her behavior here before you today. In light of what has happened here, we will not be taking questions. Good day."

Another chorus of shouts went up. I thought Brady was making a tactical error by not taking questions, but I have to say I was enjoying the effect it made on the reporters. He had frustrated them, and I could well imagine how this campaign fiasco would be served up in the media. Far from being his worst enemy, the back-pedaling *Express* would probably give Montgomery fairer treatment than the others. Not that I wasn't going to make the most of Julie's statements in my own write-up.

"Wow," was all a flabbergasted Stacee could manage.

"Come on," I said. "Let's get some reaction from Henderson." We ended up following a contingent of reporters that apparently had the same idea, and soon there was a good-sized group of us at Henderson campaign headquarters. By luck or design, Jacob Henderson was in his dad's office, and they walked out to meet the reporters together. I started to favor design.

Brian Henderson had been given word about the Montgomery press conference—obviously someone had called him. He put his arm around Jacob's shoulder, who was looking shy but not cowed by the sudden attention. I smiled at him, and noticed that he was wearing a long-sleeved light blue shirt and a nice pair of slacks. He didn't look preppy, but the effect was one which would make you think the best rather than the worst of this kid.

He smiled back at me, and I was happy to see that the photographer from the *Express* had come along—she caught the smile and started clicking away. That father and son took pride in each other was plain to see. A striking contrast to the Montgomery ordeal.

The questions came at them, and they calmly fielded them. No, Brian had never believed his son was a Satanist, and he was sorry Mr. Montgomery's daughter had felt compelled to take such a drastic action to draw attention to Jacob's innocence. He added that he thought she was, nevertheless, a courageous young woman. He said he laid the blame for her desperate act squarely on the shoulders of Mr. Montgomery, who was reaping the rewards of his dishonest campaign tactics. Jacob said that he was concerned for Julie and hoped people would not form bad opinions of her. He was proud to have Julie as his friend.

He explained again that the photo in the flyer was taken when he was trying to get a friend to leave the coven. This time, the attitude of those present was clearly sympathetic toward him.

As things wound down and reporters began to leave,

Jacob sought me out. I introduced him to Stacee, and was amused that he seemed immune to her charms, unlike 90 percent of the men who had been eyeballing her that afternoon. "Did you save a copy of the school paper for me?" I asked.

He looked sheepish, but said yes. "Have you heard from Sammy?" he asked.

I told him of the call on the machine Friday, but when I said I hadn't heard from her since then, his brows knitted together.

"I'm really worried about her, Miss Kelly. This isn't like her. She usually gets in touch with me every day. I haven't heard from her in so long. I'm kind of scared for her."

"Well, to be honest, I'm worried about her, too. I've got a friend or two with the Las Piernas Police. Maybe I'll talk to them about her."

"Do you think she's mad at me because I had her talk to you?"

"No, she wouldn't have called me if she was mad about that. You don't have any ideas on where she might hide out?"

"A few maybe. But I've gone by those places four or five times now, and there's no sign of her."

"Well, you've got enough to worry about. By the way, you look great. And you handled yourself very well with the reporters."

"Thanks. I kept imagining what it would be like to be the one asking the questions."

Just then, Brian Henderson walked over. "Hello, Irene. I understand you're the one who got my son interested in journalism."

"I hope you weren't planning to send him to law school. He seems to have been bitten by the bug."

"Whatever makes him happy. We're quite proud of him. You should see the story he wrote for the school paper."

He might as well have given the kid a million bucks.

We chatted for a minute or two about the election. His campaign manager came by and hustled him out the door to an appointment, and we took our leave as well.

* * *

"Who's Sammy?" Stacee asked when we were in the car, driving back to the paper.

"A friend of his. She ran away last Wednesday."

"On Halloween?"

She had asked a simple question, but it stayed with me, making me feel a chill down my spine.

What could scare a witch on Halloween?

| Fifteen

By the time I had finished writing my story, it was late afternoon. I called Frank and arranged to meet him for dinner, then sat thinking about Sammy. An idea came to me.

I called Mrs. Riley at Casa de Esperanza. Luckily, she remembered me. She told me that everything had been a little disorganized at the shelter since Mrs. Fremont's death, and she started crying.

I tried to calm her down and commiserated with her. She said the kids at the shelter weren't taking Mrs. Fremont's death very well, and there had been a lot of behavior problems as a result. She asked me if I was going to Mrs. Fremont's funeral the next morning, and when I told her I was, she broke up again. This didn't make what I was about to do any easier, but I went right ahead.

"Sammy Garden is going to be staying with me for a couple of days and she asked me to come by and pick up a few of the things she left behind." It was a bald-faced lie, of course. If she hadn't been coping with the aftermath of Mrs. Fremont's death, I've no doubt Mrs. Riley's suspicions would have been raised. Instead, she told me how relieved she was to hear that Sammy was safe and with someone who cared about her, and invited me to come on over.

I felt like a first-class heel as I drove over to the shelter, but I didn't see any other way to try and search through Sammy's belongings for some clue as to where she might have gone or what might have frightened her away.

As Mrs. Riley led me back to Sammy's room, she said she was about to leave the shelter to make a run to the grocery store, but Paul Fremont would be around if I needed anything. I wasn't necessarily comfortable with this news, because I wasn't so sure I could fool Paul as easily.

When we reached the door of the room, a tanned young blonde with a street-hardened look scrutinized me. Mrs. Riley introduced her as Sarah, and told her I was there to collect some of Sammy's things. If there wasn't such obvious animosity between Mrs. Riley and Sarah, perhaps the older woman might have caught the look of pure skepticism on the girl's face.

As soon as Mrs. Riley left us, Sarah closed the door to the room and leaned against it. "You're a liar," she said, giving me the kind of look that starts fistfights.

I ignored her and went over to the closet. "You might as well show me which of these things are yours, so I don't take them by mistake."

"If Sammy asked you to get her things for her, she must have told you what they looked like."

I shrugged and moved my face closer to the clothes and started pulling out some of the ones that smelled most of incense and herbal oils. I was careful to shield my bloodhound act from Sarah, and the look on her face as I turned around with Sammy's clothes told me I had appeased her to some degree.

"Where is the little bag of bones?" she asked, lighting a cigarette.

"Are you worried about her?"

"Are you kidding? She's a pain in the ass." But she started helping me gather shoes and underwear. I was glad I didn't have to sort Sammy's underwear out the way I had picked the clothes.

"Something tells me you *are* worried about her," I said.

She stopped what she was doing and gave me the eyeball again.

"You don't know where she is, do you? You made up some story so you could search her stuff. Are you a cop?"

"Reporter," I said, pissed to be busted by a smart-mouthed kid.

But Sarah had dropped the hard act and was looking at me in wonder. "You're the reporter she talked to? She told me she was going to get her name in the paper, but I didn't believe her." I watched as she reconsidered me in this new light. For all I knew, she could go running down the hall and·fink on me to Paul Fremont.

Instead, she said, "Where do you think she is?"

"I don't know, but I'm worried enough to come in here and lie to some pretty nice people in order to try and find out. Did she say anything to you?"

She shook her head, then said vehemently, "Sammy is such a fucking idiot!"

I knew better than to take that at face value. "She didn't mention anything that might have been scaring her?"

"She told me that something had gone wrong in the coven, that people weren't what they said they were. She was really upset about it. But I wasn't into her dumb witchcraft thing. You know what? I really thought she was gonna drop that bullshit. She even talked about it. Halloween night, she said she was going to get away from those nutcases and find new friends."

She wiped the back of her hand across her eyes and turned away from me. I didn't want to insult her by acknowledging that I saw she wasn't so tough, so I turned to the desk and looked through some papers.

"Hey! There's some personal stuff there—nothing of Sammy's."

I stopped and turned around. "Where's her journal?"

"What journal?"

I was banking on the hope that teenage girls still kept diaries and journals. Sarah had backed me down once; I wasn't going to let her do it a second time.

"You know what journal."

She shrugged and put out the cigarette, much to my lungs' relief, and flopped stomach-down on one of the beds. I thought she was just ignoring me, but then I saw she was reaching under the mattress. She tugged at something and brought out a small, spiral-bound notebook about the size of her hand. She held it out to me. "There's nothing in it about where she went. I already read it."

Just then there was a knock at the door, and she quickly sat on the notebook. "Who is it?"

The door opened as a voice said, "It's me, Paul."

"I asked, 'Who is it?' " she said angrily. "I didn't say, 'Come on in.' "

"Hello, Irene," he said to me, ignoring Sarah. "Mrs. Riley tells me you've heard from Sammy. That really is a relief. I've been worried about her. Of course, with everything else . . ."

His voice trailed off and he looked away. I felt awful. I wanted to just confess what I was up to—I couldn't do this to Mrs. Fremont's grandson. But before I could say anything, Sarah was up off the bed, and to my shock, embracing me.

"Everything's such a mess now!"

She was sobbing on to my chest. My hands were full of Sammy's clothes, and here I was being hugged tightly by this kid who, moments before, had been ready to spit in my face. It was only when I felt her slip the journal between the clothes and my chest that I realized what she was up to. I freed one hand and put an arm around her, and picked up my cue.

"There, there, Sarah, it's hard on all of us."

Paul Fremont was watching us, puzzled but immobile.

Sarah looked up at me and said softly, "Well, at least Sammy's safe." As she spoke, tears welled up in her eyes, so that by the time she turned to face Paul, she didn't have to fake her crying.

I studied him as he looked between us, but couldn't figure out why Sarah had reacted to him as she did.

"Paul, maybe you could find one of the other girls to comfort Sarah. I really have to be going. I can find my way out."

He nodded, but put a hand on my elbow as I passed him in the doorway. For a moment, my heart leapt into my throat, but he only asked, Will you be at Grandmother's funeral tomorrow?"

"Yes," I said, once again feeling shame for being so underhanded.

"And Frank, I hope?"

"Yes, of course."

"She thought so much of both of you. Thank you for looking after Sammy."

I couldn't look him in the eye, so I turned to Sarah. "Will you be all right?"

"Sure."

On the way out, I walked through a living room full of teenagers, most of whom watched me. Near the door, two tall, muscular young men that I hadn't seen on my last visit stepped out in front of me, blocking my way. They looked enough alike to be brothers. They were both dressed completely in black, and I noticed their left wrists were each tattooed with a chain of skulls.

I can't say I felt right at home with these gents. It wasn't so much the tattoos as the look in their eyes. I got the feeling I meant about as much to them as a pesky fly would, and might be dealt with in a similar manner. There was something more—ruthlessness? Yes. They would first pull the wings off the fly.

"Where do you think you're going?" one said. He was the taller of the two, and he was rolling a toothpick around in his mouth.

"Out. Let me by." No use bothering with please and thank you with this type. I became aware that the other kids were leaving the room. Great. I was going to face Heckle and Jeckle by myself.

"What if we say you're staying?" the other said. He didn't look as if he solved chess problems in his spare time.

I was about to come up with an answer, when I heard a voice say, "Let her go."

It was Paul Fremont, and his eyes were blazing with anger. They slowly stepped back, no less insolent, but at least they did as he asked. I thanked Paul and left.

Both Cody and Frank were waiting for me when I got home. "Hello, boys," I said as I met them at the door.

Frank looked with curiosity at the mound of black clothes in my arms and said, "Going for a new look?"

Before I could answer, he wrinkled his nose and said, "And a new fragrance?"

I wondered if he would forgive me if I told him I had hoodwinked Mrs. Fremont's grandson. I decided to delay telling him. I set the bundle down on the couch, where Cody immediately took a very strong interest in the new smells. I turned to Frank and gave him a kiss. "I'll tell you later. Right now, I'm hungry."

With a mischievous look in his eyes, he held on to me and said, "Damn, I'll bet you mean you want food."

"I wonder if Carlson would be willing to add a couple more days to that suspension."

"You may have a good idea there. But I've got a better one."

Okay, so we ate a little later than I had planned.

Over dinner, I told him about Sammy's disappearance and the stunt I had pulled at the shelter. As I spoke, he started to sit up in that way he does when the business side of him appears. All cop. He asked me a lot of questions, most of which I couldn't answer, about the coven and the kids she might have known at Casa de Esperanza.

"I don't like it, Irene."

"I don't like it either, but I didn't know what else to do."

"What if she's involved in Mrs. Fremont's murder? You've gone in and taken things that might be evidence."

"She didn't kill Mrs. Fremont."

"How do you know?"

"I know. I just know."

He sighed. "She disappeared the night of the murder, right?"

"Well, maybe. She talked to Sarah on Halloween night,

but I'm not sure when. At the most, I think she might know who the killer is. I think she's in danger."

"I don't suppose it ever crossed your mind to share these thoughts with the police?" The tone was sarcastic in the extreme.

"I *am* sharing these thoughts with the police."

"You know I'm not on that case."

"Well, then, goddamn it, Frank, tell someone who is. What am I supposed to do? Call up Robbery-Homicide and say, 'Jeez, guys, I'm worried about a kid who took off from a runaway shelter. She's never mentioned the murder itself, but I just have a gut feeling that the two might be connected'? Do you think they'll listen?"

"I'm listening, aren't I?"

I grasped my head in my hands. "Tell whoever you want to."

"Irene."

"What?"

"Don't be angry with me. You know you can't give me this kind of information and not have me act on it."

"I'm not angry, Frank. I'm just frustrated. Tired. I don't know, something. But not angry with you."

"Even if they look for her because they think she's killed Mrs. Fremont, at least they'll find out where she is."

"I hope so." But even as I said it, those hopes were sinking.

"Mind if I go with you tonight?"

I was surprised. "Do you have any idea how boring this last-minute grandstanding gets to be?"

He ignored that. "Which race are you covering to-night?"

"District Attorney. John put other people on the mayor's race and city council."

"Well, I have a real interest in who becomes District Attorney," he said with a grin.

"You're going to have to work with both of them anyway, and you know it."

"I just don't want to sit around by myself."

"Thank God you told me the real reason, Frank. I

thought you had lost your mind. I'd love to have your company."

We went to the Montgomery gathering, which was notice-ably subdued. Stacee had covered Henderson that night, and we met up with her later at the *Express* offices. Stacee took an immediate interest in Frank, who—damn his gray-green eyes—was not as immune as Jacob Henderson to her powers. It was all I could do to get her attention away from him long enough to talk about the business at hand. I wanted to strangle her.

I pounded on the keys as I wrote my story and noticed that whenever I looked up, Frank was watching her sashay hither and thither. He would feel my eyes on him some-how, and look down at me and smile. It would be a double homicide, I decided.

I stood up and cleared my desk, and left without so much as a "toodleloo" to Stacee. Frank got up and fol-lowed in my wake, puzzled.

When we got to the car, he said, "What's eating you?"

"Nothing."

"You're jealous."

"Don't flatter yourself."

"You *are* jealous!" The bastard was laughing.

I started up the car. "I am not jealous! I'm embarrassed that a man who is close to forty sat there and mooned over a twenty-year-old twit."

At this, he only laughed harder. I fumed silently.

Eventually he was subdued enough to find his voice. "Irene, she can't hold a candle to you."

My jaw was clenched too tightly to respond.

We pulled up in front of the house, and I looked over to see he was still very much amused, but was wisely main-taining silence. Outside the car, the air was chilly and clouds rolling past the moon threatened rain.

I stomped up the walk, but came to a halt about five feet from my front porch. There was blood on the steps. And there was some object on the porch itself, a lump. I felt fear clawing at me, taking me down into some welcomed oblivion.

As if from far away, I heard Frank moving up quickly behind me, felt him grab my shoulders, heard him say, "Oh, for Christsakes . . ."

The lump was a human heart.

Sixteen

My stomach churned and I ran to the side of the house, where I vomited. I heard Frank come up alongside me and ask if I was okay, but I couldn't answer. I leaned against the house, shaking. I reached down and turned on the garden hose, and rinsed out my mouth. I splashed some cool water on my face. I felt a little better. Frank held me. "I have to get out of here," I said, feeling as if I were in a small box instead of outdoors.

He walked me over to my next-door neighbor's house, carefully steering me away from any view of the porch. He rapped loudly on Mr. Hottlemeyer's door. Mr. Hottlemeyer and I had a nodding acquaintance—we were pleasant but anonymous to one another. I'm sure it was quite a surprise to have us at his door at midnight. He ran a hand through his rumpled gray hair and asked politely what he could do for us.

I heard Frank explain in his most authoritative voice that this was an emergency and that he needed to use the phone. He also said that I had received quite a shock and asked if Mr. Hottlemeyer would sit and talk to me while he called.

I know we had awakened him, but Mr. Hottlemeyer was as pleasant as he might have been if we had come to pay a Sunday afternoon visit. He brought me a small glass of sherry and sat down next to me. It's not my favorite drink, but it helped to steady my nerves. Frank came back from using the phone, and asked if I could stay while he waited at my house for investigators to arrive. Mr. Hottlemeyer was agreeable, and Frank left.

He made small talk, asking me questions about anything but what had happened next door. Did I have a garden? What sports did I enjoy? Had I seen the new comedy program on television last Tuesday night? At first I was irritated; invading images from the front porch made his questions seem inane. Soon though, I understood he was trying to distract me, and so I cooperated by forcing myself to concentrate on his voice and what he was asking me. I'm sure his efforts were all that kept me from becoming hysterical.

Soon we saw the flashing lights of squad cars, and I began to feel as if I were back at Frank's house the night Mrs. Fremont died. But Mr. Hottlemeyer was never out of questions for me. After what seemed like a long time, Frank came back and asked me if I thought I could handle going over to the house.

I felt panic, which had never been far away, rise within me. Frank took my hand. "They've taken it away," he said quietly. I bit my lower lip and nodded my consent to leave this neighbor's safe haven.

We thanked Mr. Hottlemeyer, who shrugged as if to say, "It was nothing." I knew better. To his credit, he had kept at bay any curiosity of his own about the events which had frightened me. For that alone I would be grateful for a long time to come. As we left, I wondered why I had not tried to get to know him better before that night.

Outside, before we crossed the yard, Frank held me for a long moment, then asked me if I was sure I was ready. I nodded, and leaving an arm around my shoulders, he led me back to the house.

In my front yard, several people were bending over the front stairs, and I felt bile rising in my throat again. I stopped moving.

"Irene?"

I shook it off. "I'm okay, Frank." And I started asking

him the questions that had been creeping up on my mind. "Is the rest of . . ."

"No. There wasn't anything else," he said firmly. He paused, then added, "It might not be a human heart, Irene."

I shuddered, but said, "It's human." Something told me Frank knew that as well as I did. "Is Cody—is he okay?" Horrible visions crossed my mind.

"I couldn't find him," he said. Feeling me freeze up, he added quickly, "I haven't really had a chance to look. If they had done anything to him, they would have made sure we could see him. All of this activity has probably scared him. I'm sure he's just hiding. Maybe you shouldn't do this yet."

"I want to look for Cody. I'll be okay."

Somehow I made it past the front steps. Once I was inside and away from where I could see that porch, I was better off. There were cops everywhere; I noticed Lieutenant Carlson talking to Jake Matsuda, one of Frank's friends in Homicide. Frank watched them, but didn't participate or comment. I wondered if it was hard on him, but he seemed to take it in stride. He told me they had found signs of a forced entry at the back door. So much for my new lock.

Matsuda walked over and asked me to look around to see if anything was missing. The first thing I noticed was that Sammy's clothes and journal were gone from the couch. I casually looked around the rest of the house before glancing over at Frank.

Reading his face, I knew he hadn't said anything yet about the clothes and journal, that he was waiting for me to give out whatever information I had on my own. He was trusting me. I was grateful.

"As far as I can tell," I said to Jake, "my cat is missing, and some items I had brought here from Casa de Esperanza earlier today. I went to the shelter to pick up some clothes and a journal belonging to a young girl who had been staying there. They've been taken from my couch. She ran off from the shelter a few days ago, but she's contacted me by phone twice. I wanted to try to find out where she might have gone."

Before Jake could ask me more, a startled look crossed his face. He turned and saw Captain Bredloe walking toward us. "Hello, Frank, Miss Kelly," he said easily. Bredloe doesn't usually get involved in investigations at this level, and so it was surprising to see him there.

I thought there might be animosity between Frank and Bredloe, but if there was, they weren't letting it show. "Don't let me interrupt," he said to Jake, who nervously glanced over to where Carlson stood talking to a forensics man, then back to me.

"You said some clothes and a journal belonging to a young runaway were taken tonight?" Jake asked.

I explained the whole Sammy story to him, starting with Jacob's contact with me and ending with that evening, leaving out only the fact that Frank had known about my activities for a few hours. He had enough problems with the department.

Bredloe exhaled loudly when I finished. "Why didn't you contact us about the girl? I suppose you're aware that what you've done isn't exactly legal?"

"Are you going to press charges?"

"I ought to."

"Well, go ahead then."

Bredloe shook his head. "I see what you mean, Frank. And I thought you and Baird were exaggerating."

Frank smiled until he caught my glare, then quickly tried to compose himself.

Bredloe intervened. "Don't be insulted, Miss Kelly. I can see you learned at the knee of the late Mr. O'Connor. If you should hear from the girl again, would you please be so generous as to give us a call? We'd like to talk to her."

"I would be happy to, Captain Bredloe," I said, my tone as falsely sugary as his own.

He ignored me, and turned to Frank. "Pete let me know you had called this in. I just thought I'd stop by. Everything okay with you?"

Frank nodded. "Thanks, Captain."

Bredloe seemed relieved, and turned to leave, then hesitated and looked back at me. "Don't press your luck, Miss Kelly. You had Detective Harriman with you tonight, but that won't always be the case. You'd be better off keeping us informed."

"Captain Bredloe—" I started huffily, but Frank was squeezing my elbow in a plea of mercy. "Thank you for your concern," I finished, although I hadn't been able to keep the acid out of my voice.

Bredloe looked from Frank to me and back again. He grinned and said, "Good luck, Frank," then walked away from us.

My anger with him managed to snap me out of the state of fear I had been in since coming home. Carlson left on Bredloe's heels, not saying a word to either one of us. As the last officer left my house, I turned to Frank and said, "I've got to find Cody."

Most of Cody's favorite hiding places are in my bedroom, so we walked back there. Frank searched the closets while I got down on the floor. Two almond-shaped eyes blinked back from the far corner under the bed. I started crying. "He's under here, Frank," I managed to say. Frank got down on the floor as well, and started to reach for Cody.

"Don't—he'll scratch the hell out of you. He's scared."

"I suppose I've got to get something from the refrigerator for him," he said, standing up and absently reaching his hand to a place on his face where Cody had once clawed him.

He came back a few minutes later with a piece of steak. "Steak?" I said. "Isn't there something cheaper in there?"

Frank ignored me and got down on the floor again, and started coaxing Cody with the meat and cooing to him. For some reason, it amused me. Cody's stomach will always conquer his fear, and he was out from under the bed after allowing himself the bare minimum amount of proper cat obstinacy.

I held him up to my face for a kiss, and realized he smelled like Sammy's clothes. Frank was still on the floor, looking under my bed.

"Yes, those are dust bunnies," I said. "And no, I don't clean as thoroughly as you do."

He was trying to reach something under the bed, and I groaned to think of what pair of underwear or old pantyhose I might have tossed there during a look-who-just-dropped-by-to-say-hello rush clean-up operation. He got up and crawled over the top of my mattress and reached down, grunting as he pulled his hand free from the tight space between the wall and the bed.

In that hand was Sammy's journal.

"Hiding treasures, Cody?" Frank asked with a triumphant grin.

Cody continued his post-steak wash-up without so much as a pause to reply.

"I suppose we should call Carlson or Bredloe and tell them about this," I said, plopping down next to Frank on the bed.

"Of course," Frank said, opening it to the first page, and holding it so that I could read it with him.

| Seventeen

We lay there reading Sammy's cramped script, prying into thoughts too personal for a best friend's ears. The first entry was made on February 14—Valentine's Day. That fact, taken with the opening sentences, made me acutely aware of how isolated Sammy was.

> *2/14*
> *RM talked to me all day about how happy he is with JC. It's killing me, of course. I've loved him so much for so long, but I don't think I'll ever be more than a "kid sister" to him. I guess I should be happy*

*for him and not wait around for them to break up
any more. I didn't like her at first, didn't think it
would last. But now I see I was wrong. I must have
known this a long time ago to give them those nicknames.*

I hate Valentine's Day.

*I can't blame him for choosing her. She's pretty
and smart and popular. I'm ugly and skinny and I
don't know how to make friends. Besides, no one will
want me now. No one good.*

*The Bastard wanted me tonight. I told him I was
on my period. I want to die. It's Valentine's Day, he
should be with the Bitch. I wonder if they do it anymore.*

"Do you know who any of these people are? RM, JC,
the Bastard?" Frank asked.

"RM and JC have got to be Jacob and Julie, but I don't
know how she came up with the initials—must be the initials for the nicknames. No clue as to the Bastard or
Bitch."

He looked as if he was going to suggest something, but
changed his mind. We read on. Disturbingly, it became
clear that the Bastard and the Bitch were her parents. It
was obvious that she stayed away from home as often as
she could. She wrote of nights hiding out on the streets.
No wonder she had left home. Pages venting her anger,
fear, and sense of betrayal passed before we reached any
mention of the coven.

3/24

*I met some kids at school today who seem really
cool. After school, they invited me to go to the park
with them. They were really nice. They're into witchcraft. It's pretty interesting. I think we get along because the other kids think they're weird, too. I
admire them for sticking to what they believe in. Not
like my parents, who are the biggest hypocrites on
earth.*

We read of a gradual bond being forged between Sammy and her new friends. Against the previous passages of isolation, she now wrote of acceptance, the thrill of participating in something forbidden, the feelings of power that came with her act of rebellion. There was the sense of belonging and devotion to other group members that being in this secret society engendered. The allure of magical power was also drawing her closer to the coven. In more than one passage, she wrote of rituals and incantations.

> *4/15*
>
> *Learned some really great spells and chants from some books I bought at Rhiannon today. I really like the air spells. You can raise the wind by whistling three times. There's a spell to get rid of fear. You have to light a candle and let the flame take your fear away from you, then you take the candle outside and when the wind blows out the flame, the fear is gone. So you have to raise the wind before you start the part with the candle. I'm going to try this.*
>
> *This one books tells about all kinds of things you can use—stones, water, knots, feathers, even mirrors. It's all natural and from the earth. It doesn't harm anyone. There is so much power in it, but it's good power. Well, some people might try to do some black magic, but they'll be sorry. If you misuse it, it will come back on you. That's not what my coven is into. We practice an old religion—wicca. It makes me feel as if there is hope after all.*

"Romeo and Juliet," Frank said.

"What?"

"The initials for the nicknames stand for Romeo Montague and Juliet Capulet."

"Have you been thinking about that all this time?"

"No, I've been reading. But I kept trying to figure it out while I waited for you to catch up with me at the end of the page."

"I read fast," I said.

He only shrugged and pretended to go back to the journal, but he had a smirk on his face.

"You are most clever, Mr. Speedreader. I don't know if I would have figured that out."

The smirk became a smile. "Yes, you would have."

"Excuse me, I better read. Don't want you to fall asleep between pages."

Between tales of learning chants and working magic, the sections on the coven revealed that there were apparently a number of loosely connected groups in the area. The one she was in seemed to be based more on a "feminist spirituality" that had been revived in the 1970s than on anything even remotely satanic. It was nature worship, and if it was alien to my own traditions, it was nevertheless gentle and nonviolent.

> 9/1
>
> *Haven't had time to write anything in this journal for a few days. Things have been crazy. The Bitch found my altar and ruined it. She was screaming her head off at me, telling me I was possessed by the devil and a bunch of other bullshit. I told her I didn't believe in God. I asked her, if her God was real, why didn't He protect me from my own father? She told me I was lying again and screamed at me to get out. I told her she was the one who was going to burn in hell, and my dad would roast right next to her, then I left.*
>
> *I spent a couple nights at my friend's houses, then RM told me about this shelter, so I came here. KS and MB live here. So far, it's okay. Met Mrs. Fremont. She's ancient, but nice.*

"It's the only time she's written out a name," Frank said.

"Maybe if you're ancient, you get special privileges."

He flipped ahead a few pages.

"What are you doing?"

He ignored me, found what he was looking for, and

started laughing. He placed a finger on the page he had turned to, right under "Miss Kelly."

"Speak to me, oh ancient one."

"Shut up."

He kissed me lightly on the forehead. "Remarkably well-preserved."

"So glad you think so. But you know what? This old lady is tired."

"Want to go to sleep and finish this in the morning?"

I thought about it. "I don't want to stay here."

He ran a finger over my eyebrows. "Okay. I'll pack up Cody while you get your things together."

"Thanks."

We went to his house. Both of us were beat, but a couple of cups of coffee and our interest in the journal kept us going. We sat next to each other at the kitchen table, nearing the end of the entries.

9/25

> *Things are changing. I don't like it. Two guys who joined our coven are ruining it. DM and RA are just bullies, as far as I'm concerned. They push people around a lot and keep trying to change what we are all about. Things are getting really weird.*
>
> *Every now and then, they bring this guy who wears a goat's mask. It covers his whole head and he wears a long robe, so we never see anything but his hands. That's how I know it's a man—they're man's hands. He never talks. He just gestures, and DM and RA claim to be able to tell us what he means.*
>
> *I guess some people think he's really cool. I don't like it. It doesn't fit in with what we've been doing. I think some people were getting bored. Maybe it's because we're all a little afraid of these guys.*
>
> *I don't think I want to stay in this coven. I'm going to ask Zoe about getting into another one. Maybe if we all quit this one at the same time it wouldn't be so bad.*

I have a new roommate, SL. She acts tough all the time. Who needs it?

"Sarah? The one who smuggled the journal to you, right?"

"Right."

"How much do you want to bet that DM and RA are the characters who gave you a hard time?"

"You may be right. I was thinking the same thing."

I was starting to yawn, but we kept reading.

10/16

The Goat is very strange. Everyone is playing a game with this now, instead of doing what we are supposed to be doing.

I went to Rhiannon to ask Zoe about another coven, but RM showed up and made a scene. I was so humiliated. I mean, it's great to know he cares about me, but I don't need him to treat me like a child, especially not in front of my friends.

10/30

Almost sure I know who the Goat is. His sleeve caught on a branch and I saw his arm. He covered it really fast. I pretended I wasn't looking, but I definitely saw it.

People keep leaving the shelter. I guess it's normal, but I hardly get to know someone and they leave. SL is the only one of the girls I've known very long now. She's pretty easy to talk to—I've told her a lot of things I've never told anybody, and she's told me a lot of stuff, too. But sometimes I'm not sure she really wants to be friends with me. It's strange.

10/31

Met a friend of RM's today. She's a newspaper reporter. Her name is Miss Kelly. At first I thought she was a total bitch, but I think now maybe that was my fault. I've been really edgy lately. I wasn't very nice to her, and she is trying to help RM. He really trusts her. I don't know if I trust her so much yet.

Tonight is suppose to be a big deal, being Halloween and all, but I feel really down about it. There is some sort of group within our coven. They keep secrets from the rest of us.

Later—

Things are worse than I thought. DM and RA are up to no good. The Goat is the worst one of all. I'm really scared of them. I guess I'm no better than the others.

Maybe Miss Kelly was right. I think I'll call her. Maybe she'll know what to do. Maybe I can just hang out with SL and RM and JC. I've got to get out of this place. I'm going to get SL to leave, too.

It's supposed to be safe. It isn't.

It was the last entry.

"I failed her, Frank. She was looking for one adult she could trust, and I failed her completely."

"Let me see, now. Not long ago, someone was telling me that no more applications were being accepted for the position of God."

"It doesn't stop you from feeling helpless, does it?"

"No," he said, putting his arms around me. "You were right this afternoon. Neither of us can go back and change what happened Halloween night."

"Want to take an ancient newspaper reporter to bed?"

"Come along, Granny."

After I swore to him that I could get ready for the funeral the next morning in half an hour, he set the alarm for ten o'clock. We fell asleep almost as quickly as we lay down.

Eighteen

The alarm seemed to go off immediately. I felt like I was made of lead. Frank practically had to shove me out of bed and into the shower. He propped me up under the spray and eventually I seemed to be fully conscious, if not energetic.

We got dressed and drove to St. James Episcopal Church. I felt close to being right at home. After a night of reading about wicca rituals and chants, the rituals and chants inside St. James would be infinitely more familiar and comfortable. Not so hard for a lapsed Catholic to follow.

We had no sooner sat down near the back row than Pete Baird and Rachel Giocopazzi arrived and sat down next to us. I was surprised to see Rachel, as was Frank. She's a homicide detective from Phoenix; she and Pete met on a case the previous summer and had been carrying on a long-distance relationship since then. They must have been racking up the frequent-flyer miles.

Pete leaned over to Frank and asked in a whisper if Episcopalians gave out holy cards at funerals. Frank shook his head "no." As a lapsed Episcopalian, Frank would have to serve as the guide for the three of us. He was tense. He was doing his cop thing of observing everyone and everything in the room, and I noticed Pete and Rachel were doing it, too.

During her lifetime, Mrs. Fremont had been very generous to Las Piernas, not only with her money, but with her time as well. She had served on a number of community boards and organizations. Her work on behalf of young people had earned her many friends. The church was packed. In the front pew sat Paul Fremont and a man I didn't recognize, but who had a rather striking appearance, even when seen from the limited view I had of him. He was about the same height as Paul, but he was wearing a black leather jacket with chains on the shoulders. His head was shaved and he wore an earring in one ear.

"Who is that next to Paul?" I whispered to Frank.

"Jack Fremont. Her son—Paul's father."

The service was short but moving. Unlike some others I had been to, this one was performed by a minister who actually knew the deceased. When he spoke her full name, Althea Fremont, I realized that even though I had heard her first name before, we had called her "Mrs. Fremont" for so long that it seemed like "Mrs." was her first name. Althea. It was pretty and old-fashioned and I liked it.

The minister was able to make the congregation recall something of the spirit of Althea Fremont and why we were so fond of her. If a memorial service can be said to be upbeat, this one was.

I knew that Frank had been asked to be a pallbearer, but he had declined. I got the impression that he wanted to grieve as privately as possible, away from the eyes of the other mourners. By the end of the service, he was visibly upset, but trying to hold himself together. Pete offered to drive us over to the cemetery, and we accepted.

Outside, the sky was a dark gray, threatening rain. As we made our way in the long procession of cars, we took our minds off what we were doing by asking Rachel about Phoenix, her flight, her plans for this visit. She was taking three weeks of vacation, she said, returning near the end of the month. Pete was going to take some time off, too, but probably not until close to Thanksgiving.

Time off. It sounded great. Especially when I realized how long this day was bound to be.

Our attention was forced back to the funeral as we pulled up at the cemetery and made our way over to the graveside.

Frank, although dry-eyed and silent, held on to me and leaned against me from time to time, grieving for her in his own, quiet way. When the graveside service was over,

Pete and Rachel moved off toward the car, Pete signaling me to take our time. Soon, only Jack and Paul Fremont were standing there with us. They walked over to us. Jack had an arm around his son's shoulders. He extended his other hand to Frank. "You meant a lot to my mother," he choked out. "She thought the world of you, Frank."

It was odd to see grief on this man's hardened face. A long white scar ran from the corner of his right eye to his jawline.

"She was so happy when you came back home, Jack," Frank answered. "I'm glad you reconciled before . . . this happened."

The gray mist was becoming a light sprinkle of rain. We turned away from the graveside and walked toward the cars. It was then I noticed the black limo parked at the curb. A tinted window rolled up and the car started and drove away as we approached.

"Do you know who that was?" I asked.

"No," said Frank, but I could see that, like me, he had taken a good look at the license plate. Once Jack and Paul had walked off, I reached into my purse and jotted the number down twice. I tore the paper in half and handed a copy to Frank.

"Thanks. I'll have to give this to Pete."

Just as we got into the backseat of Pete's car, it started to really rain. I felt that numbness that I feel after funerals settle over me. We rode in silence, though Pete kept looking at Frank in the rearview mirror. Frank held my hand tightly and looked out the car window with an unseeing gaze.

As we pulled up to the curb in front of the shelter, where the mourners were gathering, Frank turned to Pete and said, "I'll be okay, Baird."

"I know you will, Harriman, 'cause you've got so many guardian angels."

| Nineteen

"No, other than telling me that Frank saved his hide, Pete hasn't said a word about what happened at that warehouse."

Rachel and I sat on a sofa at the shelter, comparing notes.

"When are you going to move out here?"

"Who said I will? It wasn't so easy to make detective in Phoenix, and I'm not ready to come here and be a meter maid just to warm my bones next to Pete."

"A meter maid. Sure."

"Well, I'd be back in uniform. No doubt about it. Look what happened to Frank. Even though he had made detective in Bakersfield, he had to go back to being in uniform here. Every department is like that. Frank managed to make detective here in record time, but that's rare—I can't depend on the same thing happening for me."

Frank walked up to us just then. "You'd get there just as quickly, Rachel."

"No, Boy Wonder, I don't think so," she said glumly.

Frank leaned down toward my ear and whispered, "Excuse us for a moment, ancient one—police business."

I rolled my eyes, but let him drag Rachel off toward Pete, because Sarah had just plopped down next to me. She sighed with all the weight of the world on her.

"Everybody worth a crap is gone from here now."

"It's stopped raining; let's go outside and talk," I said. "We can sit under the patio roof—in case it starts up again."

"Okay, I could use a cigarette anyway."

We made our way out to the backyard, and away from

the crowd inside. She lit a cigarette and took three or four drags off it.

"Why are you living here, Sarah?"

"'Cause my old man thinks that if he slaps me around hard enough, I'll listen to him. But he hasn't said anything worthwhile since my mom died. He fell into a bottle five years ago and hasn't crawled out since. I just got tired of it, that's all. What's *your* sad story?"

"Someone left a heart and a lot of blood all over my front porch last night."

Her eyes widened. "No shit?"

"No shit. I need your help, Sarah. But first—this is important—you've got to find somewhere else to stay. Is there anywhere else you can go?"

"Oh, I get it. You read the journal. Listen, Sammy is paranoid. Comes from reading all that hoodoo jive she's into."

"Please think about it."

She took a few more drags off the cigarette, watching me through half-closed eyes. "Man, I guess if I was you, I'd be pretty freaked out, too. I got an aunt in San Diego. My mom's sister. Maybe I'll give her a call. What kind of help you need?"

"For starters—the initials."

"Wasn't that just too dumb? I mean, like we're not going to figure it out. Gee, 'my roommate, SL'—who would ever guess that stood for Sarah Landry? Big secret code. That Sammy sure can be a dumb shit."

"I don't know the cast of characters like you do. To me, it is a code."

She gave me a look that said I ranked right up there with Sammy in her estimation, and ground out her cigarette. She reached in her jacket and pulled out another one. I waited while she lit up and got it going.

"Well, let's see. RM is Jacob Henderson and JC is Julie Montgomery. God knows why she decided to give them phony initials. It's still obvious who she's talking about. RA is Raney Adams and DM is Devon Morris."

"Heckle and Jeckle," I said.

"Who the hell are Heckle and Jeckle?"

"Old cartoon characters—before your time. Couple of crows with a bad attitude."

"Oh. Yeah, Devon and Raney do look like they're auditioning for 'The Raven'—you know, the poem by Edgar Allan Poe?"

"Yes, but I never would have figured you to be a fan of his."

"Love him." She smiled over at me and then proceeded to flawlessly recite the first two verses.

"Bravo!" I said, applauding. "I'm impressed. I can't make it past the 'weak and weary' part."

She laughed. "My favorite is 'The Tell-tale Heart.' "

I winced.

"Oh, sorry, forgot about your porch. Where were we? Oh yeah, Raney and Devon. You ask me, those two are definitely twisted. Something not right in those two boys."

"What about KS and MB?"

"Katy Stewart and Mary Brennan. They don't live here any more. They took off not too long after Devon and Raney showed up. I think they're still in town somewhere, though. Someone told me Katy is turning tricks, but they say that about every girl that leaves."

"Sammy too?"

"Even old skinny bones herself." She paused and took a long drag, and I could see her debating whether or not to tell me something. "I don't believe people who say Sammy's turning tricks. I don't think she likes guys, except maybe Jacob. She told me her old man used to have sex with her—can you believe it? She hated it. That's really sick if you ask me. And then he acts like some holy roller or something. Shit, I'd rather live with my dad. All he ever did was hit me."

"I misjudged her. The more I've thought about what she went through—I don't know if I would have been as brave about it as she was."

Sarah shrugged. "You do what you have to do to survive."

We sat there quietly for a while.

"Paul kicked Devon and Raney out yesterday," she said.

"What?"

"They were assholes. They were really mean to everybody. Beyond mean."

"Is that why Paul kicked them out?"

"Yeah, he said he was tired of them hassling everybody. They didn't seem heartbroken about it or anything. Hey—why should you care? You seem kind of down about it."

"Oh—no, I'm glad he kicked them out. It's just that now I don't have much to go on; four of the names in the journal were connected with the coven, and all four people are gone from the shelter."

"Oh, yeah. I guess it's five if you count the Goat."

"Do you the Goat is somehow connected to the shelter?"

She was thinking about this when a male voice made us jump out of our skins.

"What are you doing out here?"

It was Jack Fremont.

| Twenty

"You two are going to catch cold—it's starting to rain again. Come on back inside."

We followed him in, but not before exchanging a look that said we would try to talk again later. Once inside, Sarah took off for the dessert table, leaving me with Jack in the kitchen.

"I'm surprised Frank doesn't keep a tighter rein on you, Irene," he said with a grin.

"I'm not exactly broken to the bit."

He laughed. "I'll just bet you aren't. Well, nothing wrong with that. Not at all. I like a woman with spirit."

Great, I thought. But the man intrigued me. I never would have imagined Mrs. Fremont's son to look anything like Jack. It wasn't that he didn't resemble her—he looked quite a bit like her. But she just didn't seem the sort to raise a scarfaced, biker son.

He appraised me as well, and made no attempt to hide the fact. Feeling a little nervous, I started cleaning off dishes that had piled up in the kitchen. Without a word, he took off his leather jacket and started filling the sink with hot soapy water.

"I'll wash, if you'll dry," he said.

"It's a deal."

He immersed his arms to his elbows and scoured away. As he handed me the first dish, I noticed a colorful tattoo on the inside of his left arm. It was of a horned goat's head, with the inscription "Satan Rides Again."

He saw me staring at it and laughed. "Merely a token of my misspent youth, Miss Kelly. And nothing to worry over now."

"Sorry, I didn't mean to stare."

He washed a few more dishes, then turned to me and said, "I scare you, don't I?"

"I just don't know much about you. For example, how do you know my name?"

"Oh, I asked Paul all about you the first time I laid eyes on you. He seems to think Frank Harriman has a corner on the market."

I didn't reply.

"Oooh—that serious, huh?"

"At least that serious."

"Okay, okay. I'll back off," he said, laughing. "Let's see now. You've still got that curious look in your eye, even though I've made you mad. Now, what does Irene want to know? Let me guess." He rinsed a stack of dishes and handed them to me. "She wants to know, 'How could this ratty-assed biker be my friend Mrs. Fremont's son?' Am I right?"

I blushed. He laughed again.

"I am right! Okay, here goes. Life story of Jack Fremont, prodigal son of Althea and John Fremont, Senior. I barely remember John Senior—died when I was five. Left us well off, though. So I became a much doted upon, rich spoiled brat—the apple of my mother's eye. And totally uncontrollable.

"You might say I had been something of a surprise. She was told she couldn't have children, and at forty, found herself pregnant with yours truly. Dad was fifty, so I'm sure he felt like quite the old rooster. But as I said, he died not long after. Heart attack. Have this impression of a big guy holding me on his knee while he smoked a cigarette and drank a gin martini. But I couldn't have known what a gin martini was when I was five, so who knows where that comes from."

He looked over at me, as if to see if I was still interested, and went on.

"So much for the early years. As I got older, I got wilder. Got mixed up with what every parent in Las Piernas knew was the wrong crowd. Hell, I was one of the ones that made it the wrong crowd. And at fifteen, I got a girl pregnant. Cindy Larabee. Seeing a chance to have her marry into money, her daddy all but pulled out a shotgun. My mother made sure I did the honorable thing."

"You were married at fifteen?"

"Yep. My mother supported us, of course. Old Cindy had me by the balls then, and she knew it. She knew that all she had to do was have that grandchild and Althea Fremont would take care of her for the rest of her days. I mean, the minute I said, 'I do,' the woman was transformed into the meanest thing on two feet. Cindy was a bitch. No other word for it."

He paused while he rinsed off a plate and then reloaded the sink with dirty dishes.

"Well, all this marriage and pregnancy stuff scared the hell out of me. Nothing like feeling your life has come to an end when you're fifteen. So I ran off; baby wasn't even born yet. Mom found me and hauled me back. She did it again and again.

"When Paul was born, I stuck around for awhile. It was really exciting to me at first, but I couldn't stand playing house with Cindy for long. She made my life miserable. So when I turned eighteen, I took off again, and this time I was too old to haul back home.

"I wandered around for about twelve years, dropping by every now and again. Caught glimpses of my boy growing up. Mom hated me then.

"I even tried to get back together with Cindy when Paul was in high school, mainly because I'd started thinking that I was his age back when he was born. I wanted to know my son."

He stopped washing, but didn't look up at me. He seemed to tense up for a minute. Just when I was about to ask him what was wrong, he started washing again and went on with his story. But his sarcastic tone was gone now.

"It was a big mistake. I didn't have anything to offer either one of them. Cindy was still a nasty-tempered little shrew, and a drunk to boot. The night I left, she went on a bender. Died in a car accident—only good part of it was she took out another drunk.

"Anyway, if Paul didn't hate me before, he surely did then. He was really messed up by the whole deal."

He stopped washing again, staring off into space. His voice, when he continued, was much quieter.

"Kid even tried to kill himself." He shook his head. "When my mom told me about that, I really felt like a piece of shit. I thought to myself, 'Jack, you should be the one to kill himself. The world would be a better place. You've given your mother and that poor boy nothing but grief.' But I don't know, self-destructive as I've been— and believe me, I've pulled some dumb stunts—that just isn't the way for me."

He drew the back of his hand across his forehead, then looked over at me, trying to read something in my face. I suspected he wondered if I had passed judgment on him in some way. I've never been qualified to cast the first stone, so I was merely waiting for him to go on.

"Paul decided he wanted to live with his cousins, and did for almost a year. Boy, is that bunch something. Cindy's sister can't keep her pants on long enough to button her fly. She had five boys, all by different fathers. Married and divorced a couple of them. I think she figured that my mom would give her money for looking after

Paul, and when that didn't happen, out he went. My mother took him in again.

"So anyway, here I am, six years later. Been back in Las Piernas four months. I've learned that my son has grown into a fine young man, much better than his dad." His voice grew quiet. "And I made peace with my mother before she died. I guess that should be enough for anyone who's been as irresponsible as I have."

He didn't look as though it was enough. He seemed tired.

"What brought you back?"

He looked at me and grinned. "Well, well. So you are a little curious about me, even after I've told you my life's story. Good sign.

"Let me see. What brought me back to Las Piernas? I suppose if I tell you it's the only place I *ever* come back to, you'll say I'm hedging. So what's the answer? Hmm . . ."

He dried his hands on a towel.

"Well, in a roundabout way, a knife fight brought me back. I don't kid myself that you haven't noticed the scar. But like they say, you should see the other guy. Only he's dead. Mom's lawyers got me off and Mom's doctors patched me up. And without boring you with a lot of details, I'll just say I realized then that I wasn't going to live forever. Ironic, isn't it? Her doctors said she'd live to be a hundred, and they didn't give me a snowflake's chance in hell. But here I am, and she's gone."

We had finished the dishes. He looked completely worn down, and his weariness changed him in some way I couldn't quite name. There was something charming about this maverick. I was thinking that just as the guy with the corner on the market came walking into the kitchen.

Frank gave me that look of his that says he's just taken something in, some observation that he wants to chew on for a while. But all he said was, "Pete and Rachel want to leave. Are you ready to go?"

"Sure." I turned to Jack and shook his hand. "Thanks for talking to me."

"My pleasure," he said with a grin.

Frank was looking between us when the door opened again. It was Paul Fremont.

"Frank," he said, "you can't leave yet. Grandmother's lawyer wants to know if we can have the reading of the will now. Would that be okay?"

Frank was openly puzzled.

"I'll take you and Irene back to the church to get your car," Jack offered. But seeing Frank's look, he added, "Didn't you know? My mother named you in her will. You're a beneficiary."

"No, I didn't know," he said. It was clear that he was totally surprised. He looked uncomfortable in the extreme. As if to find an out, he turned to me and said, "I guess you need to get to work, don't you?"

I nodded, and seeing his lost look, wished I could stay longer.

"Let me just walk Irene out to Pete's car," he said. "I'll be right back."

"Okay," Paul said, then added, "By the way, Irene, I meant to ask earlier—how's Sammy doing?"

I had no choice but to keep weaving my tangled web. "She never showed up. I'm quite worried about her."

Frank steered me out of the room before I had to dig myself in any deeper. We decided to exchange car keys—I'd take his car from the church, which was not far from work. He'd get a ride home from Jack and use my car if he needed to go anywhere.

We went outside, where the rain had become a fine drizzle. He put an arm around my shoulder and walked me toward the car.

"Frank, if you need me to stay—"

"I'll be okay. Really. I just wasn't expecting this. Don't worry about me. You've got an election to write about."

"Want to meet me for dinner?"

"Okay. Where will you be?"

"Let's see. At first, probably at the Montgomery campaign gathering. At the Cliffside Hotel. Can you meet me there around seven? Not much will be going on until after the polls have been closed for an hour or so."

"Okay. I'll call the dining room at the Cliffside and make reservations for us. And I'll feed Cody."

"What more could a woman ask for?"

"You could probably think of something if you tried." He gave me a quick kiss when we reached the car, and I left with Pete and Rachel.

In the car, I reached into my purse and pulled out Sammy's journal. I handed it over the seat to Pete.

"This the missing kid's diary? I told Frank that Bredloe would never believe that story about the cat hiding it."

"Yeah, well, it's the truth. Remind him that this is the cat that once landed a set of scratches on the face of his fist-fighting detective. Even if he's mad at Frank, he'll believe you."

"You got him all wrong, Irene. Bredloe likes Frank. He's going along with the suspension for Frank's benefit— give him a chance to cool off a little. By the way, I don't know what you said to him, but I think he's doing better today."

I smiled, thinking of what Frank and I had said to one another.

Rachel saw me and grinned, thinking something else entirely, I'm sure; but after all, she was close. Pete looked over at her. "What? What did I miss out on?"

"Who knows? It's just nice to see Irene smile, so I smile."

He wasn't satisfied, but said, "Well, Miss Cheshire Cat, I suppose you want me to call you about the plate number Frank gave me."

"Right," I said.

He shook his head.

"Oh, so what's the big problem?" Rachel chided. "It's not like she couldn't track it down—it would just take her a little longer."

"I didn't say I wouldn't do it," he growled.

"Via, non t'arrabbiare."

"If you're going to start speaking Italian to one another, please provide a translation."

"I told him not to get mad. I think Pete feels like we

gang up on him when Frank's not around to even things out."

"Damn right I do. I feel outnumbered when I'm around either one of you—even one at a time."

"*Caro,* you can't mean it," she said in a honeyed tone.

He turned bright red. I wondered when he would take Rachel home to meet his Italian mother.

We reached St. James and pulled up next to Frank's old Volvo.

"You be careful, Irene," Rachel said as I got out of the car. "Frank told me about last night. Call if you need us— don't go wandering around on your own, okay?"

I thanked them and said good-bye. As they drove off, I could see them through the car's rear window, having one of their typical conversations—both talking at once, gesturing to one another. It's a wonder they didn't wreck the car.

| Twenty-one

When Pete called me that afternoon, I was working on two different versions of the election story. In one, Montgomery won; in the other, Henderson. I left a couple of open paragraphs at the beginning for victory or concession speeches, vote tallies, and quotes. But the rest of each article would capsulize what had been written about the race in the last few months: background on the candidates, highlights of the campaigns, analysis of their areas of support.

"Got the registration on that limo," Pete said. "Our boys were interested in this too. It belongs to Malcolm Gannet Enterprises. Carlson will not be thrilled if he finds out I told you that."

"Malcolm Gannet. Well, what do you know." Gannet was a real estate developer. His group had changed the skyline along Shoreline Boulevard, and he had made a mint doing it. Mrs. Fremont had been actively antidevelopment, fighting a largely hopeless battle to preserve some of the examples of the 1920s and 1930s architecture of downtown Las Piernas.

"Something else, Irene."

"What?"

"I talked to Hernandez about the little door prize you got last night."

I braced myself. Dr. Carlos Hernandez was the coroner. "And?"

"And it's definitely a human heart. Human blood, too."

"Oh. Well, I guess I knew it would be."

"Sure. But the logical conclusion is, whoever it belongs to ain't doing so hot right now. So until we figure out who put it on your doorstep, you better watch out. Are you listening to me, Irene?"

"I've heard every word."

"Yeah, but I know you. Hearing is not enough. Listen, for once. I know you want to get nosy about this, Irene, but it just isn't smart. We can handle it."

I didn't say anything.

"Look, you don't see me walking down there and trying to be a reporter. So don't you go trying to be a cop, okay?"

"They're just trying to scare me, Pete."

"So be scared, would you?"

"It makes me angry."

"Crimeny. You got anger? Go see a shrink. And while you're there, ask him why you don't have the sense God gave a rabbit!"

"Via, non t'arrabbiare. Did I say that right?"

"Pronunciation needs some work," he said grumpily. "So you want it in Italian? *Ti sto avvertendo!*—I'm warning you!"

"Okay, thanks."

"Shit. I'm wasting my breath."

"Probably."

"Shit."

"Bye, Pete. I'll be careful."

I went back to my stories. Stacee and I also put a piece together on GOTV or "get out the vote" workers. Those folks who call you two dozen times on election night to make sure you voted. We were covering the system, from the professional campaign consultants to the leagues of volunteers who do everything from going door to door over a precinct or two to driving people to their polling places. We filed that story in the late afternoon.

I had some time to kill before going down to the Cliffside, so I tracked down our real estate editor, Murray Plummer. Murray is the Clark Kent of real estate writers. With his baby face and oversized glasses, he looks like he just got out of a high school physics class. But he always manages to keep up with—if not one step ahead of—the wild and woolly world of commercial real estate in our town. He has published stories about deals before the principals have finished reading each other's faxes. I've often wondered how well his abilities could be used in other kinds of reporting, but he will have none of it. He loves his work.

His section comes out three times a week, so when I found him, he was finishing up material that would run in Thursday's paper.

"Hello, Irene. Where've you been lately?"

"Election time, Murray. You know where I've been."

"I guess I do, and I don't envy you. Take a look at this copy—what do you think? We're featuring the Sheffield Project on Thursday."

"That's the one someone wants to put up over by the cliffs? Where the old Sheffield Estate used to be?"

"Yes, they plan a luxury hotel."

"Is it a done deal?"

"Not by a long shot. There will be a hue and cry that will keep City Hall busy for a couple of years and make certain lawyers and consultants very rich."

"I'll want to read it. Listen—what can you tell me about Malcolm Gannet?"

His eyebrows went up behind the rim of his glasses.

"Malcolm putting some money behind someone? He may be a gambler, but he's usually pretty sure of his prospects when it comes to city council influence."

"Maybe," I said, realizing he assumed I was investigating a political story.

"Well, let's see. You know what he's done downtown, and he certainly doesn't need to worry about what he can get approved there, so you're probably more interested in the Lower Shore Project. I hope they come up with a better name for it, don't you?"

"Yes," I said, bluffing along.

"Okay, so from the boardwalk to the pier, he's been buying up properties. Life will be easier for him now that poor Althea Fremont is gone."

"What do you mean?"

"Oh, she fought him like a tiger on the Planning Commission. He was able to get past her on downtown, but when it came to the beach properties, she really organized her neighbors. Lots of people down there think it's too crowded as it is, and they didn't want to be looking at Gannet's high-rise condos where they now have an ocean view. And a lot of beachgoers like things as they are.

"But you know, even if she had lost every vote, she still had old Gannet over a barrel. Her husband, John Fremont, bought up all kinds of beach property ages ago, when it could be taken for a song. Even after John died, she never let go of an inch of it. It's in a patchwork with the Gannet properties, so between her and some of the others, he can't get a large enough parcel together to build like he wants to."

"So why did he keep on trying?"

Murray laughed. "You don't know Malcolm Gannet. He believes in getting his way. It was a standoff. Two old buzzards waiting to see who'd go first. I guess it was Althea, which is too damn bad. Not that I'd blame whomever she's passed it on to for selling out to Malcolm. You could retire on what five percent of that property is worth now."

"Strange thing is, I saw Gannet—well, I saw his limo—at Althea Fremont's funeral today."

"Really?"

"Yes. It was odd. He didn't seem to want anyone to know he was there. I mean, he wasn't exactly hiding, but he didn't come out of the car for the graveside service."

"Ah, that's Malcolm all over. Mr. Mysterious. I know very little about him personally. Just the odd rumor, probably spread about by some of his vanquished rivals."

"What kind of rumors?"

"Oh, nothing of importance. Petty, really. I was told he gets around in the limo because he doesn't know how to drive. Spends a tremendous amount of time on a yacht, when he doesn't know how to swim or sail. He has an able crew around him, though, so I suppose it doesn't matter. Same is true in business. He knows how to use the talents of others to get where he's going." He frowned for a moment, then shrugged. "As for the funeral, who knows? Maybe he was there to gloat."

"Over a murder victim?"

"Hmm. No, you're right. Well, sorry, I can't help you out there."

"Well, I've learned a lot anyway. Thanks, Murray."

As I turned to leave, I heard him chuckle softly.

"I knew they'd never keep your nose out of crime stories."

I turned back to face him. "Murray, please—"

He crossed his heart and put a finger to his lips. But this was a newspaper after all, full of people who couldn't resist telling the news about one another as much as anything else. I walked off feeling certain that John Walters would be chewing me out by the next morning.

I made my way down to the lobby. Outside in the darkness, rain was beginning to fall again. Voter turnout was bound to be low. I wasn't sure who that would help out—Montgomery, probably.

By the time I drove over to the Cliffside Hotel, it was pouring. I realized I had left my umbrella in the Karmann Ghia. By the time I made the dash into the hotel, I was fairly drenched. Frank was standing in the lobby, equally wet. We took one look at each other and started laughing.

"Well, at least we know *you're* no witch. You didn't melt."

"We witches fool everybody with that old trick, Frank."

"Are you hungry?"

"And curious."

"So what's new. I'll tell you about the will over dinner."

The Cliffside has a classy restaurant. We ate in a candlelit room overlooking the ocean. The room was paneled in beautiful dark wood, and the chairs were comfy and highbacked. It was too dark and rainy to make much of the view that night, but it was still a romantic place to share a meal. There was a big fireplace at one end of the room, and espying our wet hair, the maître d' seated us near it. We ordered a scotch for Frank and a Myers's and o.j. for me, which arrived posthaste, and we settled back to admire one another for a while.

"So tell me what happened after I left," I said.

He shifted around in his chair a little. "Mrs. Fremont changed her will about a month ago. The lawyer was not subtle about his unhappiness with the new one. She gave a lot of money to the foundation that supports the shelter and other charities. She left Paul enough to finish college. She gave Jack all of her beach properties, and she gave me some mountain property—a cabin and some land with a couple of weekend rentals on it."

"Jack got all of the beach property?"

"Yeah, I suppose she figured Paul would get it someday and that in the meantime Jack would fight against getting it developed."

"Pete tell you about Malcolm Gannet?"

"Yeah, something's not right there. I don't know. Something's not right about any of it. It bothers me. I wish Bredloe would let me in on it."

"It sounds like Pete's keeping you informed."

"But he gets everything secondhand, so by the time it gets to me, I can't ask the questions I want to ask."

"Such as?"

He took a long sip of scotch, then sat forward. "Okay. Why no signs of forced entry? No struggle? Beyond finding the pentagram and the drawing on the door, why blame a cult? I think about what happened at your house last night, and *that* seems like something Satanists would do.

You've been nosing around about someone who might have been in a satanic group, or who at least might have knowledge of one. And they leave a calling card—a human heart. But when Mrs. Fremont was killed, it was fairly straightforward, as murders go. Just one blow to the head. And why would Mrs. Fremont be a target for Satanists?"

"She was connected to the shelter," I said. "Maybe she knew as much as Sammy. Or suspected something. Maybe they didn't have time to do more at Mrs. Fremont's house. Maybe something scared them off. Maybe they heard us drive up."

"Maybe. But how did they get inside in the first place?"

"Don't you think the people assigned to the case will ask those questions?"

"Yeah." He stared into the fire.

"So tell me about this mountain property."

"Huh? Oh. Well, it's up near Pine Valley Lake, off by itself. A place called Pine Summit. Overlooks the valley and the lake. Very peaceful. She used to give me the keys and tell me to go up there whenever the job was getting to me."

"Are you happy about it?"

He shook his head. "No. I didn't want anything from her. Must make her family feel bad."

"Did Jack or Paul seem upset?"

"Not at all. They were very gracious about it. Paul said he had some things up at one of the rentals and I told him to take his time picking them up. I've never used the rentals, so I don't care if he uses one of them." He drained the last of his scotch. "It was still damned awkward."

I took his hand. "It was a place she knew was special to you. She didn't know this was going to happen this way. She was in good health. She thought of you and wanted to give you a place where you could be happy."

He shrugged.

The waiter arrived again and took our order, and we accepted his offer to bring us another round. Frank sat looking into the fire. When dinner came, he looked over at me and gave a little smile.

"Quit worrying about me," he said. "I'm just trying to sort things out."

"Can't help but worry about you, Detective Harriman."

" 'Mister' or 'sir' will do. And I'm okay."

"Yes, sir."

"I could get used to the sound of that."

"It would be a shame if you did, because it would mean you'd found another woman."

"Don't want one. Got all I can handle now."

We chatted about lighter subjects through dinner, which was excellent. When the last plate was taken away, he ordered a couple of brandies.

"Hey, take it easy. I'm not driving for a while, but I am working."

"Mind if I hang around again tonight?"

"No, so long as you promise not to flirt with Stacee."

I should have known that would get a laugh from him.

"Easiest promise I've ever had to make."

"We'll see."

The brandy came and we raised a silent toast to one another. It was smooth stuff.

"Irene?"

"Hmm."

"Move in with me."

"What?" Smooth stuff or no, I choked on it.

"Live with me."

"In sin?"

He laughed. "What would the Pope have to say about what we've been doing so far?"

"Easy thing for an Episcopalian to ask."

"Well?"

"I don't know, Frank."

"Why not?"

"I don't know. I've just always been able to go back to some place of my own if I needed to. And as I recall, you wanted your key back from me not forty-eight hours ago."

He looked down. "I recall being told I was a lousy liar—even at the time, you knew I didn't mean that. I want to be with you."

"What if you change your mind about that?"

"You think I'm not committed to you? That I'm not serious?"

"No. It's not that."

"So?"

"You are persistent."

"You want to keep living where you are now?"

Throughout the day, in idle moments at work, I had been thinking about this a lot. "No, I don't think I'll ever be able to feel safe there again. It makes me madder than hell that it's come to this, but when I think of being there by myself for even a few minutes—well, anyway, no, I don't. I'm probably giving up too easily. But it's just something I don't want to struggle with. I need to feel safe in my own home."

"Do you feel safe with me?"

"From everybody but you, and that's a kind of danger I can live with."

"You can bring your grandfather's chair and Cody's scratching post."

I laughed. "I'll think about it. I don't know. Maybe."

"Say yes."

"Maybe. And don't press your luck."

He grinned.

I knew that meant he thought he had won. He probably had. But I wasn't going to let him know that right away.

We finished our brandies and went into the room where the Montgomery campaign was holding its victory party. Of course, at this point, they were all victory parties. A band played old standards but no one danced. Not many people had shown up yet—still early in the evening.

Gradually, tired campaigners came through the door. I thought Frank would be bored, but being an observer by nature, he kept himself busy watching the various characters and their interactions.

Something about Frank attracts women who are over seventy. I had noticed this before. I supposed they thought he was a gentleman—well, where they were concerned, he certainly was. His manner toward them was always polite and attentive. That night, there were never less than three of them paying court at one time. While he was cornered, I picked up comments from Brady Scott and other members of the campaign.

I called the office every so often and found out that the race was running very close. It was going to be a long night. Why didn't I pick the races that were decided by eleven o'clock? I looked across the room and saw Julie Montgomery. Well, yes, this campaign was far more interesting than the sure things. I walked over to her.

"How are you doing, Julie?"

"Fine, thank you, Miss Kelly. Glad you're still speaking to me. I thought everyone on the *Express* would hate me."

"Well, I'm not crazy about your tactics, but I think I understand why you did what you did."

"Sorry if I got you in trouble."

"I'm always in trouble anyway. You might want to give Mark Baker a call, though. As for me, don't worry about it."

"Thanks."

"Your dad feel confident about tonight?"

"No. And he's blaming me. I think I'm going to go home before he finds out one way or the other."

"I envy you. I'm here or at Henderson's for the duration."

"Good night, Miss Kelly. And if you see Jacob, will you please say hello for me?"

"Will do."

I finally found Monty Montgomery and got an all-purpose quote or two from him. I had a feeling that no one would be conceding in time for the morning edition.

Frank was leaning back in a chair, looking like it was all he could do to stay awake. I sat down next to him.

"Why don't you go home? At least one of us can get some sleep."

"Don't want to leave you wandering around at night by yourself."

"Sooner or later, Frank, I'll have to be out at night by myself."

"Not yet. I'll get some coffee."

"Tell you what. Follow me over to the Lafayette. That's where the Henderson campaign is." Knowing Frank's long legs don't fit very comfortably into the Karmann Ghia, I exchanged keys with him.

The Lafayette is one of the grand old hotels that were built when Las Piernas was a thriving resort. Although the hotel itself is very posh, the neighborhood around it is struggling. The last time I was at the Lafayette, I parked on the street and my car was vandalized. I'm still too cheap to go the valet route, but this time I decided to spring for a space in the hotel parking lot.

We arrived there just before midnight. As I suspected, no one was conceding anything. The tally was too close. We walked up to Stacee, who made goo-goo eyes at Frank, but he walked over to the coffeepot after sparing her only a polite hello. Of course, as I watched him over her shoulder, I saw him make a little halo over his head with his hands. I put two fingers up behind my own head, making Stacee look between us like we were nuts.

"What do we do if it isn't decided by late deadline and no one concedes?" she asked, covering up a yawn.

"I phone in a noncommittal story with a couple of quotes from the candidates. It's looking like that's the way it's going to be anyway. Why don't you go on home?"

"Thanks, I think I will." She gathered her things together, went over some notes with me, and left.

She was back five minutes later. Frank and I were sharing a cup of coffee when she walked up to us, soaked to the bone.

"My car won't start."

Frank looked at me.

"I'm sure Detective Harriman would be happy to help you."

As he started to get up, I leaned over and whispered, "Don't forget your halo."

Jacob spotted me a few minutes later and walked over. "Hi, Miss Kelly. Long night, huh?"

"Yes. Julie says 'hello,' by the way. She was headed home for the night."

"How is she?"

"I don't know. I think things will be rough for her for a while yet. But you'll be there for her, right?"

"Yeah. I just wish there was something I could do for her. She's done so much for me."

We were interrupted by the return of Frank. A sopping wet Frank. He looked like he had fallen into a river. I introduced him to Jacob, who didn't seem sure what to make of him. He asked Jacob to excuse us for a moment, and led me out to a balcony. The rain was falling in loud torrents, but the balcony was covered, so I stayed dry.

"Her battery has been stolen. That's why her car won't start."

"Take her home then."

"I don't want to leave you here."

"I'm okay. In another hour I'll be so close to the last chance to make tomorrow's paper, I'll have to turn something in and come home anyway."

"But Stacee—"

"I trust you. I was kidding before. Sort of."

He laughed and took me into his drenched arms and gave me a long kiss. "Come straight home."

"Home, huh? Okay. Now get going before I leave Stacee here to drown."

"Straight home," he said again, "as soon as possible."

"As soon as possible," I said.

Later, when I had a long time to consider this conversation, I thought about how, for once in my life, I should have done what someone told me to do. I also thought about how "as soon as possible" could be a very long time.

| Twenty-two

I called the office and got an update—the storm had caused some power outages, and the registrar's computers had been down for a while. They were counting some precincts by hand. I read off a "no declared winner" paragraph and told them I'd hang around for another hour just in case something changed.

Not long after that, Jacob came over to talk to me again. He asked me about newspapers and reporting and told me more about his school paper. I enjoyed his enthusiasm.

At about 12:30 or so, a pimply faced young man in a hotel uniform came up to me and asked if I was Irene Kelly. I didn't think a process server would go that far, so I said yes.

He said he had an urgent phone message for me and handed me a folded note. I tipped him and opened the paper. Jacob read over my shoulder—a sign that he would make a good reporter.

> Miss Kelly,
> Please meet me at the corner of Falcon and Briarcrest.
> I need your help.
> Will wait until 1:00.
>
> Sammy

"I'm going with you."

"Jacob, your father would never forgive me."

"Detective Harriman wouldn't like it if I let you go there alone."

"Ask your dad."

I waited while he walked over to Brian Henderson, who listened to him then waved and nodded "yes" to me. I grabbed my coat and Jacob left with me. Later, when I thought about it, I suspected Jacob had said something like, "Can Miss Kelly take me home, since it's a school night?" to his dad, but I was in too much of a hurry and lacking too much sleep to question it at the time. In all honesty, when I was a teenager, I had pulled the same kind of stunt myself. More than once.

I looked up the intersection of Falcon and Briarcrest in my map book. It was in a residential area of Las Piernas, a few miles from the hotel. At one time, its stately wood frame homes made it the most elite neighborhood in town. But it had fairly gone to seed in the last twenty years, being too far from the water to attract the kind of money that could afford the upkeep—especially the kind of dollars needed to restore such large houses.

The wind picked up, drumming the rain loudly against the cloth top of the Karmann Ghia. The defroster wasn't working right, and I could barely see out the windshield.

"Open the glove compartment," I said to Jacob. "Try to read the map by the lamp."

As he opened it, a couple of white business cards with detective shields embossed on them spilled out. Jacob picked them up. "Detective Frank Harriman," he read aloud, "Robbery Homicide Division . . . why do you have these in your car?"

"Uh, Frank must have left them there. He borrowed my car today."

When it comes to looking skeptical, teenagers have it all over adults.

"Okay," I admitted, resisting an urge to tug at my collar. "If I'm pulled over for speeding in Las Piernas, I make sure I have one of those next to my registration or my driver's license. Do not—repeat—*do not* tell your father about this."

The look I got for even suggesting that he would break a confidence was far more scathing than skepticism. But after a moment he asked, "Does it work?"

"Not with the Highway Patrol," I said glumly, but noticed he discreetly pocketed one of the cards.

He called out directions, checking the map by the dim glow of the glove compartment light.

Suddenly the streetlamps went out, and houses all around us were darkened.

"Great, a power outage."

"We've got to hurry," he urged. "She shouldn't be out in rain like this—especially with no streetlights."

I drove as fast as I dared under the conditions. I got out at one intersection and went to look at the street signs up close—they were impossible to read from the car under that dark sky. My umbrella was nowhere to be found, so I had to dash over with my coat over my head. We were on Falcon.

I followed it until we finally found the corner at Briarcrest. We parked on Falcon. It was a vacant lot, covered with shoulder-high weeds. No sign of Sammy. I looked at my watch. It was 12:50 A.M.

"Where is she? I don't see her!" The kid was frantic.

"Stay here," I said, "I'm getting out to look around."

"I'm going with you."

I didn't want to waste time arguing. If he wanted to get soaked, fine. I stepped out of the car into a rain that was coming down so hard it stung. It bounced off the pavement so high, it fell twice. We walked up and down the corner in each direction, and never saw her. I looked into the field and was about to start calling out for her, when I saw a place where some of the weeds had been matted down. There were water-filled footprints leading into the field.

Jacob followed me as I squished and squashed along the same direction as the prints. I heard him sneeze a couple of times as we made our way. Between the rain and weeds, I couldn't see more than a few inches in front of my face. I was about halfway into the lot when I tripped over something. As Jacob rushed over to help pick me up, I heard him half-shout, half-wail, "No!"

I had tripped over a leg. The leg of Sammy Garden. Or rather, her corpse. Jacob kept repeating his keening, one-word lament, clutching a corner of her muddied skirt as he knelt next to her. Her blouse was torn over a gaping wound in her chest. The rain ignored our shock and disbelief, and pelted hard against us.

My concern for Jacob kept me from giving into my own fear and sense of failure. I grabbed him by the shoulders and turned him away from the figure on the ground. He held on to me, sobbing. I led him back to the car. He was shivering, wet and miserable.

"Jacob, listen to me. You've got to try to push that out of your mind."

He sneezed, but didn't answer. I wondered what Brian Henderson was going to do to me for letting his son catch pneumonia. Jacob sneezed again.

"It's raining on her," he said, as if that somehow was a final indignity that he couldn't bear to have her suffer.

Oddly, I found myself in agreement. I handed him the keys. He took them with a clumsy grasp and looked up at me.

"Get in the car and pop the trunk open for me," I said. "I've got a tarp in there. You stay here and try to dry off."

He stopped crying and stared at me, but I could see he hadn't really heard me. I couldn't blame him.

"Jacob, please. Get in the car and open the trunk. I'll put the tarp on her, but nothing can hurt her now. Nothing. Not even the rain."

He squeezed his eyes shut, then nodded and did as I asked.

I heard him start the motor up as I closed the trunk. I looked through the windshield at him. He was looking down into his lap, his forehead leaning against arms crossed over the steering wheel.

I made my way over to Sammy's body and spread the tarp, then bent down to anchor the edges. I forced myself to slow my breathing and to think about Jacob and getting out of the rain; I tried not to think about what lay beneath the tarp. Would the folks in forensics consider this disturbing the scene or protecting it? I didn't suppose they'd be happy about it.

I thought I heard Jacob driving off and stood up. I

peered through the darkness. The wind was still whipping rain into my face, but it wasn't falling quite as hard. The Karmann Ghia was still at the curb, engine running. I had walked about halfway back to it, when I noticed a Blazer parked along Briarcrest. I knew it hadn't been there long, or we would have seen it when we first looked for Sammy. I was just starting to feel fear climbing up the back of my neck when I was tackled from behind.

I fell face first into the mud and grass, the wind knocked out of me. Before I could react, my arms were pinned behind me and my attacker pulled me roughly to my feet. I saw Jacob climb out of the car. "No!" I shouted. "Get out of here! Go!" A big, gloved hand came over my mouth. I struggled against it, panicking as Jacob hesitated. But in the next moment, he seemed to look back toward Sammy, then got back in the car and drove off.

My attacker's grip tightened. I lifted one foot and brought it down hard on his instep. The ground was slippery, as was the top of his boot, so I didn't land as much force on it as I wanted to; but he yowled in pain and released me with a hard shove, causing me to fall again.

Someone was on top of me almost as soon as I hit the ground. This time, the barrel of a gun was pressed to my temple, and a voice said, "I wouldn't try anything like that again."

I was yanked up to my feet, and I became aware that I had two escorts for the evening; the sight of the second one and his gun must have been what convinced Jacob to leave.

Although they both wore dark ski masks, the newcomer wore no gloves. I recognized the chain of skulls tattooed on his left wrist.

"Well, if it isn't Tweedledum and Tweedledee," I said.

The one with the gun said, "You think you can tie her up this time, Devon? Gag her, while you're at it."

"The bitch almost broke my foot," Devon whined, but he took pleasure in tying both the gag and the rope around my wrists as tightly as possible. They carried me over to the Blazer, and propped me up against it while they opened the door.

"I owe her, Raney."

"You think I care? Go ahead. But make it snappy; that kid may already be at a phone."

Devon wasted no time. He brought his booted foot down like a hammer on my right ankle. When I stumbled forward, they caught me and shoved me into the back seat, face first. They climbed into the front seat, Devon taking the driver's side. They pulled off their masks. Raney turned back to me and said, "Tweedledee and Tweedledum, huh?" and brought the barrel of the gun down on the back of my head.

| Twenty-three

I came to in a cold, dark room. In pain.

My head and ankle throbbed in unrelenting, independent rhythms. I could hear voices, but passed out again before I could make sense of them.

The next time around I was able to concentrate better. Three shafts of light were coming into the room from small windows at the top of one wall. Turning my head caused the room to swim. I fought off a wave of nausea.

I tried to focus on my surroundings once again. I was lying on a thin, bare mattress, the kind you might find on a very old foldout couch. No, more like a bunk bed at summer camp. About an inch-and-a-half thick. It was musty-smelling and had skinny black-and-white stripes on it. It was on the floor. A bare wooden floor.

The room was small, about eight by ten feet. There was one door, beneath which a thin line of light crept in. A metal bucket sat in one corner. My toilet, I supposed. Nothing more—the bucket, the mattress, and me.

The gag was off and my hands were no longer tied. My

mud-soaked coat was gone, as were my shoes. My right
ankle was the size of a softball. I was still wearing my
blouse and slacks. I reached up to feel the knot on the
back of my head, and was shocked to realize that my hair
had been cut. Shoulder-length before my captors took up
barbering, it was now cut into odd-shaped clumps. The
loss of my shoes and coat, even the pain of my injuries,
did not upset me nearly as much as this discovery. Why
cut my hair?

My mind began to fill with questions, most of which I
didn't like the answers to: Where was I? I didn't know. I
would make a project of trying to find out, but right now,
I didn't know. What day was it? Wednesday? How long
had I been out? I didn't know. What did they want with
me? I didn't know. Something to do with Sammy? But I
barely knew her. Why not take Jacob?

Why had they let me see their faces, hear their names?

That question made my stomach tighten into a hard
knot. The answer to that one came a little too easily: because they didn't plan for me to live long enough to tell
anyone else. I kept from panicking only because I couldn't
afford it. Still, I had to tell myself to get a grip about a
dozen times before I could breathe normally.

So why was I still alive? They wanted something from
me. Maybe. Thought I knew something. Maybe. Were they
going to bargain with me? For what? Doubtful that I could
gain them anything. But maybe.

Why had they cut my hair? To humiliate me, I decided.
As with the shoes, the bare mattress, the stark room: to
make me feel demeaned and helpless. To let me know who
was in control. When I thought about this, the actual effect
was to make me angry. I resolved to keep that anger burning, to not give them the pleasure of seeing me cringe before them.

The "how" questions were not so hard. I had been set
up, pure and simple. I berated myself for falling for their
trick.

At least Jacob was safe. I wondered how long it had
taken him to summon help.

My mind turned to Frank, and I suddenly felt overwhelmed with emotion. He would be worried. If I were hurt or killed, he would once again feel that he had failed to protect someone. And it wasn't his fault at all. It was mine. Straight home. As soon as possible. God forgive me.

The sound of voices and approaching footsteps made me push these thoughts away. Survive. Survive. Survive. I repeated the word silently, again and again, and closed my eyes. I wasn't sure it would be wise to let them know I was conscious yet. I willed my fear away as the door creaked open.

"Naw, still out cold. You hit her too hard, Raney."

"You're the one who screwed up by letting her kick the shit out of you."

"She didn't kick the shit out of me."

"Shut up, both of you." This third voice came from near the mattress. There was something familiar about it. I heard cloth rustling next to me. I tried to keep my breathing even and slow, to retreat into myself as I heard him kneel down next to me. He reached over and pulled my left eye open. Jesus God, I thought, how does an unconscious person's eye look? I stared straight ahead. Suddenly my field of vision was filled with an elaborate, garish goat's mask. I prayed my face did not reflect the rising panic I felt.

But apparently this goat-masked man either saw what he expected or didn't know any better than I did what to look for. He let loose of my eyelid.

"I want to work on her myself. You understand? She's mine. You can come in here and play the dice three times a day. Ask her who has the witch's journal. I've got to know how much she knows and who she's told. But you just do the preliminaries. I want to do the work— understand?"

"She can't see you, man. Why don't you take that weird fucking mask off?" Devon's voice.

"She could regain consciousness at any time."

"So what? She's dead meat anyway. All that Satan stuff was good for scaring the crap out of a bunch of kids, but I don't think it will work with her."

I heard the man stand up and move away from the mattress. "Okay, okay," I heard Devon whimper.

There was the sound of a blow, followed by a small cry. "Don't try to think things out, Devon. You're no good at it."

"You didn't have to do that."

"I'll do as I please. You both need me. Don't forget that. Raney, I expect you to keep him in line." He paused, and I heard his footsteps along the opposite wall. "You did a good job on the windows, Raney," he said. "Call me just like we planned. This will all be wrapped up soon. I'll be back on Friday. You'll be out of here before the weekend."

His footsteps moved across the room, pausing near the door. "Keep in mind that I reserve certain privileges. You can play the dice. But she's mine. Remember that, Devon—she's mine."

He left the room and the other two slowly followed. They talked in the room beyond the door, about food and supplies. I heard them go outside of the building, their voices coming through the outside wall and windows now, rather than from within the room beyond the door. From their conversation, I gathered I was locked in a storage room of some sort.

I opened my eyes and tried to force myself to a sitting position. I was too queasy, too sore. I fell back on the mattress, staring at its stripes, feeling my head pound. I heard a car start and drive off.

I mentally played back the conversation I had just heard. They were worried about what might be in the journal. How long before they learned the police had it? My head was throbbing, and I could hardly keep one thought connected to the next. The identity of the Goat. Satanism. Phony Satanism. Something Frank had said about that— but I would have to set that aside. Back to the Goat. Sammy mentioned seeing something on his arm.

I fell asleep, dreaming of goats and fields of rain.

The room was a little warmer when I woke up. Not warm, but not the bone chilling cold of before. My head still beat like a bass drum, but I could move it without such a strong feeling of nausea. I tried stretching out of the stiffness I felt.

I rolled off the mattress again. Any movement or pressure on my right ankle produced searing bolts of pain. I took deep breaths and crawled over to the bucket. I managed to turn it over and pull myself up on to it, leaning against the wall. I was breathing hard. I had broken out in a sweat and felt shaky, but I smiled. It seemed a wonderful accomplishment to be able to sit on an upside-down bucket.

I could hear water. Moving water. A river? No, a creek or a stream. The thought of water made me realize how thirsty I was. I would have to live with it. I kept listening while I caught my breath.

In the next room, Devon and Raney were arguing loudly about which radio station was the best. Both were grousing about not having brought tapes up here, where they couldn't pick up any stations worth listening to.

Up here. Out of radio range. A place with a creek or a stream. The mountains. But which ones? If I hadn't been unconscious for more than a few hours, then this was Wednesday. Less than a day's journey from Las Piernas. But being a few hours from Las Piernas could put me in mountains anywhere from Santa Barbara to San Diego.

Using my arms and left leg, I slid my back up the wall. It was a slow process, but I was finally able to stand up. I was dizzy, but it passed. Standing up. Another small goal. But my objective was a look out the windows, and I was still three inches below the lower sill of the closest one. Looking up, I could glimpse pine trees and a roofline. I curled my fingers on the sill and pulled myself up until my left foot was on top of the bucket. I straightened up and took my first look outside.

I was in a small, woodframe cabin. The Blazer and a black four-wheel drive pickup truck were parked on a drive not far from the building. The cabin was surrounded by tall trees. There was snow on the ground, melting away. I couldn't see the sun, but the way shadows fell led me to believe it was early afternoon.

The windows of the room were nailed shut. On the

outer side of each were heavy-gauge, wire mesh screens of the type used to discourage rock-tossing vandals. The windows themselves were only about seven by twelve inches each. Unless I could use one of Sammy's spells to turn myself into a hamster, I wasn't going to escape through the windows.

There was no stream or creek in sight, but I had heard it through the other wall, and imagined it ran behind the cabin.

Before long, I had to give up my view. I could hear Devon and Raney moving around in the other room, and my efforts had left me dizzy. I hopped down from my perch, nearly losing my balance, but held to the walls and made my way along them. The door opened just as I lay back down on the mattress.

"Well, look who's up." Raney had a grin on his face I didn't like. "Tie her up, Devon. If you think you can handle her."

Devon scowled. Behind him, through the open door, I could see a kitchen. He closed the door and came over to me. He rolled me on to my stomach. He tied my hands together behind my back, then roughly pulled me up by my shoulders and on to my knees. The room swayed before me; I had trouble focusing.

Raney moved in front of me. He held up a pair of dice between his fingers. "You get a choice. Talk, or we play dice. Where's the journal?"

My mouth was dry, so I could only speak in a rasping whisper. "You boys are being taken for a ride."

He punched me hard across the mouth, and I fell over.

Devon laughed. "That counts as one, Raney."

Raney laughed as well. The fall to the mattress brought me close to passing out, and a blinding pain raged in my head.

The dice rattled in Raney's hand. "Hear that? Hear that, bitch? That's your fate rattling around in my hand. Let's see what it's going to be." He continued shaking them, watching me. "Look at her, Devon. She doesn't have a clue, does she? It's the last time you'll see that look. After this, she'll know."

He threw them. They tumbled to the floor and came to rest at the edge of the mattress. A five and a three. I was beginning to get the picture even before Devon hauled me to my feet.

"Remember, Raney—it's seven now," he said.

"One last chance," Raney said. "Where's the journal?" I didn't reply.

"That ankle don't look too good," he said, and kicked it. I felt the cold sweat cover me, felt the color go from my face, felt my knees give—but I didn't make a sound. They were laughing.

"Bend her over the bucket. She looks like she might puke."

"If she does, you're hauling it out of here."

"Fair's fair. Moderation from here on out, then."

He landed six more blows, one to my right eye, the rest to my ribs. They untied me and left me hanging on to the bucket. I hadn't wanted to give them the satisfaction, but I got sick into it anyway.

They laughed again. I fought off my sense of shame. It was difficult.

Devon stood next to me, and I was expecting it to be his turn, but to my surprise, he very gently lifted me off the floor and set me back down on the mattress. He got up and went into the kitchen and brought back a glass of water. He pulled the bucket over next to me and propped me up.

"Rinse your mouth."

I did. Raney walked out with the bucket.

Devon held me, softly stroking my forehead and hair. When he spoke, his voice was soothing and quiet. "It doesn't have to be this way, you know. You're so pretty, but he'll ruin your face. I don't like it, but he will. You should talk to us. I know you don't want to yet. But you already know you will. Save yourself the pain, Irene."

It was the first time one of them had used my name.

It's just a trick, I told myself.

I should have been repulsed by his touch, but the small kindnesses of those few minutes brought me closer to tears than the blows had. I made myself retreat farther inside myself.

It's all part of their method. Survive.

Raney came in with the bucket and a metal bowl with a handle on it. He set it next to the bed. It was some kind of broth. He looked down at us and laughed.

"Jesus, Devon, next you'll be feeling her up. Come on, leave her alone."

Devon eased my head back down to the mattress and they left. The aroma of hot chicken broth came from the bowl. I moved myself over to it. I drank it, maneuvering the bowl around my now tender and swollen lips. It was warm and good. I lay back and let the tears fall, but made no noise. I would not let them hear me. I fell asleep crying.

| Twenty-four

I awoke to hear them arguing loudly. The room was darkening, so I figured I must have slept about three or four hours.

"Look, he knows what he's doing. When they sell the old lady's land we'll all be rich." Raney, losing patience with Devon.

"I just don't like waiting around. What if he just takes off and calls the cops on us? We're sitting ducks."

"Nah, then we spill our guts to the cops. Even the Pony Player would go down then, and they know it."

Pony Player? I wondered who this new nickname referred to. Was this another name for the Goat?

"I still don't like it," Devon said. "I don't care who his mother was, it pisses me off when he hits me like that. I don't like taking crap off him all the time. 'Devon, don't think. I'm the Einstein around here.' Well, what have we got to show for it? A murder rap, that's what."

They were quiet for a moment, apparently brooding over that possibility. I lay there, wondering about what they had said, when I heard Raney's voice again.

"Don't get yourself all wound up like this, Devon. What's that you're reading?"

"It's about cancer. I picked it up at this clinic on my way back from the store."

"What clinic? And why the hell are you reading about cancer?"

"Place where they take skiers who break legs, stuff like that. Old geezer runs it. Told him I knew someone with cancer and I wanted to get something to read about it. He gave me this little booklet."

"Christ, Devon, you are un-fucking-believable! We're supposed to be lying low. We're not supposed to make any trouble in town or get ourselves known around here. What the hell is wrong with you?"

"I just wanted to make sure it wasn't contagious."

"Shit, Devon, I could have told you that. You worry about the weirdest shit, man. You think I'd ever let you catch something like that from somebody? I look after you, don't I? How come you didn't just ask me?"

"'Cause you ain't no doctor. How would I know you were right?"

"Oh man—I can't believe the stuff you come up with sometimes. Don't let him know you did this. Please, Devon—I don't like it when he hits you, but you keep pulling this kind of shit and he'll be all over your ass."

"I don't care! I don't care! There's nothing wrong with it!"

I heard one of them storm out the front door, slamming it hard. Devon, I thought. It was quiet then.

I lay there thinking of a plan to escape. Then I thought about Frank, wishing I could send messages to him by mental telepathy, to let him know I was alive. Silly really, but I wanted to talk to him so badly, I felt a hollow ache over it. Finally, I fell back to sleep.

* * *

It was dark when they came into the room again. Light spilled from the kitchen through the doorway, where one of them stood in silhouette. I could hear the dice rattling.

"Irene."

It was Devon. I didn't answer.

"Irene, tell me where the journal is."

Raney stepped in behind him carrying a propane lantern, which cast long shadows on the walls and ceiling. He had something in his other hand—I couldn't see what it was.

"Tell me, Irene. You know I don't want to have to do this. Don't make me do it, please don't. Come on, Irene, tell me who has Sammy's journal."

This man is not your friend, I told myself. Say anything and they will kill you. Stay alive.

Stay alive, I repeated to myself, as he squatted down next to me.

"Irene, tell me. Where's the journal?"

I thought of them putting Sammy's heart on my front porch.

He rolled the dice. I didn't look.

Raney laughed. "Five." He set the lantern down and handed something to Devon. I saw then that it was a piece of rubber hose. Devon tapped it in his hand.

Raney picked up the soup bowl and moved it by the door. The whole time, I heard the hose tapping. Raney grabbed my wrists and pulled them over my head. He rolled me over.

The tapping stopped. I heard the hose whistle and then, as if coming from someone else, heard myself cry out as the first blow landed between my shoulder blades.

He waited.

Tap, tap, tap. "Come on, Irene. Tell me. Where is it?"

I didn't answer.

By the time they left the room, I was drenched in sweat and trembling. Sleep was impossible now.

I wondered how much more I would be able to take. I also wondered if I would be able to force myself to do whatever would be necessary to escape. I remembered what Sarah had said to me—you do what you need to do to survive.

Sleep still eluded me, although I would have welcomed it. I was quickly learning the importance of keeping my mind occupied. Left to wander, it concentrated on my injuries, on emotions I was holding in check, on all that was hopeless in this situation.

So instead, I thought about a sequence of events in Las Piernas that seemed to fit together: Jack Fremont shows up in town, and is reconciled with his mother and son. Shortly after this, the coven changes under the influence of a mysterious stranger and his two assistants.

Mrs. Fremont changes her will. She's murdered.

Sammy sees the Goat's forearm. She's murdered.

I'm seen taking some of Sammy's things from the shelter—no, I'm still alive. Start over.

No matter how I looked at it, things changed when Jack Fremont came back to Las Piernas. "I don't care who his mother was," Devon had said. Could he mean Jack? No one had benefitted from her will as much as Jack. Murray had told me the property was worth a fortune.

"She's mine." I thought of the way he had flirted with me in the kitchen.

I allowed my thoughts to go back to Frank. I realized that even my pride could not sustain me much longer through this ordeal, but my desire to be with him again would. Some small article of faith was left in me: I would live. My life with him was not over. I would endure this. I slept at last.

I don't remember the nightmare that made me wake up screaming. Maybe the pain had just finally had its way with me.

The door opened and Raney entered with the lantern. He stood there awhile before I was awake enough to realize he was pointing a gun at me. Devon pushed past him and knelt beside me.

"She's just had a bad dream, Raney. Put the gun away."

Raney put the lantern down, smirking at me. He picked up the bucket and carried it out, leaving Devon with me. Gradually, I gathered my wits enough to calm myself.

Devon knelt there, staring at me. "You're so pretty," he said.

I hadn't seen my reflection, but I could imagine what I looked like—hair chopped off, face bruised, fat lip, and one eye swollen shut. I laughed. It wasn't much of a laugh, but he heard it.

He seemed offended. "I'm not making a joke. Even like this," he said, stroking a finger under my chin, "you're still pretty." He kept staring at me, and I felt fear tugging at me again.

Raney came back in with the bucket and picked up the lantern. "Leave her alone, Devon, or he'll have your hide."

"Fuck him," Devon muttered, but he stood up.

"Next time," Raney said, "you get the bucket. I've done it twice now while you sat around getting a hard-on for that bitch."

They left the room. My mouth felt dry and I couldn't seem to make myself breathe normally. My mind kept burrowing down into my fears. So I concentrated on my ankle, on my back. It was easier. Pain had an edge to it, a place where it began and ended.

I had not forgotten that the Goat had said to play the dice three times a day, so it was not a surprise when they entered the room again later that night. At least, I told myself, it will be the last time until morning. Raney's turn again. The bastard rolled double sixes.

| Twenty-five

It was cold the next morning, and I awoke stiff and sore, but the swelling in my right eye had gone down a little, so that now I could see out of both eyes. The knot on the

back of my head had gone down some, too, and I wasn't
dizzy. I still hurt all over, but once I got past the first few
minutes, I felt a little comfort in waking up at all. I had
made it through a day.

I heard Raney tell Devon that he would be right back,
heard the front door open and the sound of the truck or the
Blazer driving off. I worried about being left alone with
Devon, then turned to more constructive thoughts. I tried
moving around the room as much as I could, trying to
warm myself. I moved along the walls, still hopping, since
I learned that I couldn't quite force myself to put any pressure on the right ankle. I was going to stay off of it or risk
passing out. I felt better as I moved. I even managed another look out of the window, and discovered Raney had
taken the truck. I decided I would try to learn the difference in the sounds the two vehicles made. It might not
help me in any way, but it was another distraction from
captivity.

Before long, though, I was worn out, and made my way
back to the mattress. I had a plan, but I would need more
strength to make it work. I would be hard between dice
robbing me of sleep and nothing more than a bowl of
chicken broth to eat.

Raney came back. He stomped into the house. As usual,
they made no attempt to keep me from hearing what they
had to say—I was, after all, expendable. A temporary di-
version.

"We're fucked. Just plain fucked."

"What happened, Raney?"

"He has a tail on him."

I felt hope rising. Catch him, I prayed. If I die, at least
let them catch him.

"Shit!" Devon swore and paced. "I tell you, Raney—we
ought to do her and just get the hell out of here now."

"I don't know. I don't know. Let's think about it." They
were quiet for a moment. Raney's voice was cool and even
when he spoke again. "Maybe it's time for an insurance
payment."

"Which one?"

"I say we go for the big boy. Put the blanket right under the Pony Player's nose."

I listened more closely, puzzled.

Devon snorted in derision. "It doesn't have to be under his nose. He'll find it before the cops do. It really reeks. It's got that witch's blood all over it."

"No, he won't find it. Keep it wrapped up in that garbage bag. Put another one around it just to make sure. Besides, even if he finds it first, he's not home free. We've got the knife."

"What does Einstein say about the tail?"

Einstein, I knew by now, was the Goat.

"He's got some plan where I go down and pick him up tomorrow morning. He doesn't want to take his car anywhere. He thinks we can pull it off. He's probably right, but like I said, I want some insurance," Raney replied.

"The knife would be better."

"Don't worry about that now. Leave that to Einstein. He'll figure out a good place to hide it."

"I don't know . . ."

"Look, Devon, let's face it. He's smart. We wouldn't have thought of cutting the Pony Player, getting his blood on the blanket and the knife."

So the Pony Player was not just another name for the Goat, I thought.

Devon laughed. "That scared the shit out of the Pony Player. He's not so tough."

"No, and our boy knows it. Like I said, he's smart. Now—you know where to find the Pony Player?"

"You want *me* to do it?"

"Think about it, Devon. I have to make the phone calls. If I don't, he gets suspicious. He never asks for you or has you make the calls. You told me he pisses you off—well, now you can show him what happens when he ignores you."

"I don't know. Damn, if somebody sees me, I'm dead meat."

"If we don't have insurance, you're dead meat anyway. Besides, I know he doesn't even think you could do anything like this. I know you're smart, Devon, but he doesn't see it. That shows how really smart you are. You've fooled him."

Devon hesitated, then asked in a wary tone, "The blanket is still in the Blazer?"

"Yeah."

"Gives me the creeps. Her stinking blood all over it. I didn't like the witch, but that was brutal."

"I know, Devon, but we need you to do this. You've got to."

I heard Devon sigh, then say, "Okay. I guess I better get going."

More movement. Footsteps near the door to the room.

"Raney?"

"Yeah?"

"Let me take her once before I go."

"Forget it. Goddamn, is that all you think about? We don't have time for you to jump some broad's bones."

"Hey, I might not come back alive. This might be my last chance."

"Christ, Devon, you're not gonna die. I'm asking for something simple. No one will even know you were in town. Just do what you need to do and come back. We can't afford to screw things up now. What if we don't have to use the insurance? What if everything works out fine, but he finds out you did it with her? You'd be passing up a million bucks. With a million bucks, you could buy yourself a whore every day for the rest of your life."

"Whores give you diseases. She's not a whore."

Raney laughed. "What, you falling in love or something? She's too old."

"That's not important. I want her."

"You want every piece of skirt you spend five minutes with. Go on, get going. Worry about her later."

He left.

I forced myself up to the window again, seeing and hearing the Blazer leave. I went back to the mattress, trying to sort out what they had said. The most I could make out of it was that there were at least four people involved in Sammy's murder: these two, the Goat, and someone they called the Pony Player. They seemed to trust the Goat ("our boy," Raney called him) more than the Pony Player. The Pony Player's blood, as well as Sammy's, could be found on a knife and blanket.

But nothing they had said told me much about who the other two were. I tried to silence the voices within me which said it didn't matter what I learned about them, since I was unlikely to be able to tell anyone else. I would survive. I fell asleep.

For some reason, Raney didn't bother me all day. He never came in and played the dice. I was able to sleep undisturbed by anything but the discomfort of my cuts and bruises. It was dark in the room when I was finally fully awake again, but the night was moonlit and I could see outlines of what little there was to see in my simple cell.

I heard Raney moving about, and could smell broth being warmed in the next room. When I heard the bolt to the door sliding back, I closed my eyes and feigned sleep. I didn't want to face his fists again, or even his knowing smile. I knew he stood and watched me, but he set the bowl down and left after a few minutes.

I drank it down as quietly as I could. I was hungry, and it didn't exactly fill me up, but it warmed me. I listened as Raney paced nervously. I lay there, becoming aware that Raney was still alone—Devon had not returned. I knew he was supposed to make a phone call to the Goat, but I didn't know the schedule. Apparently, he was late or nearly late.

I heard him move something against the door. The table. A silly precaution, given the bolt and my weakness. I began to think of that table as my ally. It would give an advantage to me.

The front door closed and I heard the truck drive off. I was going to have some time alone. It might not be more than about twenty minutes, could possibly be less, but I would make sure it was enough.

I picked up the bowl and made my way to the windows. Hopping on one foot with only one hand free was awkward, but I managed it. I pulled myself up on the overturned bucket so that I was near the middle window. I turned my face away and smashed the bowl into the thick pane. Glass flew and cold air came rushing into the room. I looked at the opening, and my hopes sank for a moment. I had hit it wrong somehow. There were no shards of the shape I wanted, and all the pieces were too small.

I had no time to waste. I hopped off the bucket, feeling small pieces of glass pierce the bottom of my bare foot here and there, but ignoring it. I moved the bucket to the right, closer to another window. I tried again. This time I didn't swing so hard and used only the rim of the bowl to strike the glass. Success. The glass fell more than flew this time, and the pieces were bigger. I worked a triangular piece free of the frame. It was about six inches long and three inches wide at the base.

Carefully holding my treasure, I made my way back to the mattress. Lying on my back, I felt along the edge of the mattress next to the wall, finding the spot where my right hand would lay. I pulled the edge toward me and slit the cover of the mattress with the glass. I hid the shard between the thin layers of batting.

I heard the truck return. I was running out of time. I felt quickly but carefully along the floor, searching for another large shard. He had come into the house by the time I found one. He was pulling the table away as I put it under the head of the mattress. I lay back down just as the door came open.

He hadn't noticed the windows when he drove up. But as he swung the lantern in, he began cursing me savagely. It was obviously the part of his vocabulary he had put the most time into. I wouldn't have minded listening to him refer in novel ways to various parts of my anatomy, sexual acts, kennel residents, and members of the oldest profession. But Raney, of course, didn't just shout.

He yanked me up off the mattress. I tried screaming at the top of my lungs, praying that with the windows broken, my voice might carry. He responded by cuffing me hard across the face.

Raney seemed to be operating on the assumption that I was as helpless as when he had Devon hold me, because the solid punch I threw into his nose caught him by surprise. I had about seven seconds of pure enjoyment out of that before he retaliated. I could only offer token resistance to him, kicking and hitting him, but mainly deflecting his fists. I held on to the vision of his bloody nose. It was worth it, I told myself, and that became my new inner litany.

I heard Devon before I saw him. He was shouting from the doorway of the room. "Stop it, Raney! Stop!" Devon raced across the room and held Raney's arms. I stumbled onto the mattress. For a moment, it appeared that they might come to blows with one another. But suddenly Raney dropped his fists and stormed out of the room. Devon looked around at the broken glass.

"What were you trying to do? You'll never get out of here through those windows. And now you'll just be cold. I heard you scream when I drove up, but no one lives anywhere near here. You could scream your head off and no one would know."

I tried to talk, but my mouth was such a mess, he had to bend close to hear me say, "Didn't know."

"You didn't know what?"

"No one near."

Raney had come back with a broom and dustpan. He threw them on the floor. "You do it, man. You pick up after her this time."

"Okay, Raney," Devon's voice was coaxing. Just like when he said my name. "Okay, I will. But don't hit her any more, okay?"

Raney shut the door and leaned against it, arms folded. Devon began sweeping up the glass. His eyes moved from Raney to me. I lay curled on my side on the mattress. Devon was right. It was damned cold in the room now. But, I kept repeating silently, it was worth it.

"What took you so long?" Raney said testily.

Devon kept his own voice calm and low. "It was out when I got there. I had to wait until they brought it back in."

"Damn. Didn't think he'd do that this time of year."

"I think he had a client with him, an investor or something."

"I had to leave this bitch here alone while I made the call. I'm gone fifteen minutes and look what happens."

Devon laughed, and after a moment, so did Raney. The two of them carried on like they were recording a laughtrack for "I Love Lucy" instead of standing over someone they had been beating the tar out of for two days.

"Man, when I came in here, I thought you were going to kill her."

"I wanted to. I wanted to. She'll freeze her ass off."

Devon looked down at me.

Suddenly Raney said sharply, "Pick her up."

"Why?"

"Just do it."

Devon shrugged and set the broom aside. I groaned as he started to lift me, and he looked at me with concern. "Damn, Raney."

"Just get the bitch off the mattress."

He held me close to him and stood.

As soon as he straightened up, Raney pulled the mattress back. He held up the shard I had placed underneath the mattress, the second one, for Devon's appraisal. I tried to hide my joy that the distraction was working. Now if they only would be satisfied that they had found my treasure, and not search further.

"She was going to cut our throats! That bitch was going to try to kill us!"

The look on Devon's face turned to one of cold fury. His hands tightened on me in anger. Raney stood up and laid the edge of the shard against my cheek. This was not something I had counted on. Being carved up was not on my agenda. I was afraid and I knew it was showing; I could see the pleasure of it on Raney's face.

"Let's cut her."

Devon's fury faded. "No man, he'll do worse to us. Like you said. He wants to work on her."

I tried to get myself back under control. I realized that this was getting harder for me to do. I ferreted out the anger I felt for them. Raney backed down, whether from Devon's warning or because he no longer saw fear, I don't know.

Devon sighed. Raney searched beneath the mattress, but finding nothing else there, walked out of the room with the glass. Devon sat down on the mattress, still holding me. I wanted him to let me go, leave me alone, and yet the warmth of his body took the edge off the cold.

He was stroking my oddly cut hair again, and he began rocking me. As bruised as I was, it made me groan again. He stopped and set me down as if I were a favorite rag doll. He left, taking the lantern and bolting the door shut. I was relieved, and closed my eyes. In a moment, I told myself, I would check on the shard in the mattress.

I reached over and felt the edge of it. I was about to draw it out when I heard footsteps. I quickly moved my hand. Devon came in. He didn't bring the lantern and I hadn't see him in the doorway, but I knew his step. His knelt beside me. I felt my throat tighten.

Something fanned out over me; he had brought a rough woolen blanket. He spread it over me, then tucked it in around me.

"See, Irene? I want to be nice to you. When you feel a little better, you'll see what I mean."

"Help me escape," I whispered.

"No, I can't do that. What would happen to my brother?"

"Brother?"

"Yeah. Raney's my brother. Half-brother, really, but I don't like that way of saying it."

He was silent. I wanted him to leave.

"If I helped you, my brother would be killed, and that would be like killing me. He's like my twin, even if we don't have the same dad."

This bit of genealogy was hard to absorb in my condition, but I remembered thinking they looked like brothers the first time I met them, in the shelter. As if remembering that same moment, he said, "Where's the journal, Irene? Tell me. I'm being really nice to you."

I didn't say anything.

"Tell me," he said softly, leaning close to my ear.

I turned my face from him. He laughed as softly as he had spoken, and left.

From beyond the door, I heard them talking.

"Man, you should have let her freeze. Teach her a lesson."

"She'll still be cold."

"Yeah. Pretty soon she'll be really cold." They laughed together.

Raney sobered first. "I gotta pick him up tomorrow. I don't want you trying to get into her pants while I'm gone."

"He's going to have her. Why should he get to have her and I don't?"

"Think about what he did to the old lady. Think about that witch."

Devon was silent for a moment, then asked, "Why are they following him?"

"He says they're following everybody who made out on the old lady's will."

"Even the cop?"

"I guess so." Raney laughed. "Can you believe it? We're beating the shit out of a cop's squeeze."

"She's gonna be a mess when he finds her. You can bet on that."

Their amusement over this lasted some time.

I could not make much out of what they had said at the time. I lay there trying to fold the throbbing of the latest blows into the back of my awareness. I felt along the mattress edge until I found the shard and pulled it out. I tore a piece of fabric off the bottom of the mattress, using some of the batting and the strip of worn cloth to wrap the wide end of the glass. I touched its sharp point, relieved it had not broken when Raney had moved the mattress about. Possession of a diamond necklace could not have pleased me more. Carefully, I returned it to its hiding place. I thought of Sammy and Mrs. Fremont. I thought of Frank. I admonished myself silently again and again, until I could hear the words beyond the border of my sleep: You will be able to do whatever you need to do to survive. You will live.

Twenty-six

I awoke when I heard Raney go outside the next day. Soon I heard the Blazer pulling out of the drive. I rubbed my skin wherever I could stand it, trying to warm up. I sat up and moved my arms. I was still sore here and there from my fistfight with Raney, but I wasn't really any worse off than I had been before. I checked the bottom of my left foot, and found it was not as tender as I was afraid it might be. I knew I would be able to put my weight on it when I had to. Would I be able to do whatever else I had to do? Yes, I told myself.

With Raney gone, I had no doubt that Devon would take his chances with me. I heard him pacing around nervously and felt my own tension rising. The sooner he came in, the better. I wanted it over with. Before long, either I would escape the cabin, or I would have cheated them of doing me further injury.

But his fear of the Goat was stronger than I thought. Devon paced and paced, as if he were as caged as I. Just as I was beginning to lose hope of a chance to try my plan, I heard the bolt slide.

Somehow, as he stood there, looking at me, my courage fled. He was much more physically powerful than I; even if I had not been beaten, even if I had more sleep and more to eat, he would still have been able to overpower me. A smile crossed his face.

"You're afraid of me, aren't you?"

I didn't answer, but drew deep breaths, trying to calm myself. This is your chance, I thought.

He closed the door behind him. I pulled the blanket up.

161

He grinned. "Yeah, I can see you are." He moved closer, and I felt myself tense. Survive.

He stood over me and stared at me. "Were you cold last night?"

I found some part of myself rebelling against my plan. My plan was to kill him, as surely as their plan was to do the same to me. But I was not practiced in it, and they were. Devon had kept me from Raney's excesses. Devon had held me and helped me rinse my mouth when I was sick. Devon had brought me a blanket so that I wouldn't be so cold.

Stop it! I told myself. Devon brought you here, kicked you, held you so that you could be beaten, whipped you with a hose, took part in the murders of two people and will make yours the third. Survive.

He was watching my emotions play on my face, though I had tried to hide them. He seemed wary for a moment, then grinned again.

Suddenly he reached down and pulled the blanket from me, tossing it aside. I shivered, not entirely from the cold. He dropped down on the mattress, straddling me. To my dismay, he grabbed both of my wrists, pinning them near my shoulders. Keep your head! I told myself.

He leaned down and kissed me. My lips hurt as it was, but my revulsion was stronger than my pain. I swallowed the bile that rose in my throat.

"I'm going to have you, Irene. I know you don't think you'll like it, but you will. It's going to be great. You'll see."

"Help me get away from here," I tried again.

He laughed. "I told you. I can't."

"You can. Please, Devon. Things will be better for you if you do. We can be together."

He laughed and let loose of my left wrist and hit me hard on the side of my head. I hadn't expected the blow, and it jarred me.

"You must think I'm a real moron. That's too bad. I know you're that cop's woman. You go ahead and think about that cop when I do it to you, Irene. I don't care. I just want to have you."

"He hasn't done much for me lately, has he? He's use-less." Forgive me, Frank, I thought. I needed Devon to be offguard. "But you've been kind to me. I've lain here thinking about you."

"Liar," he said. He reached down and grabbed my blouse, ripping it down the middle. He used the same hand to unfasten my bra.

I had to get control of my fear. I had to. I took deep breaths again. He mistook the meaning of those deep breaths, and I gained my first advantage.

"Goddamn, you are excited, aren't you?"

I reached up with my left hand and caressed his neck.

He smiled. He let loose of my right hand, and placed his hands on my breasts. It made my skin crawl, but I willed my face into a smile, or as much of one as I could manage through my puffy lips. I reached down and took hold of the shard, moaning to distract him as I pulled it loose. With his arms as they were, I would not be able to do it.

"Please, Devon," I said, and he had no idea what I was really begging for. I ran my left hand along his chest and up on to his shoulder, then to his neck.

"Get ready, baby," he said. I was.

He moved his hands down to my waist, and fumbled with the snap as he leaned over me. Now, I thought, now.

With all my strength, I drove the shard into his throat, thrusting it in with my right hand as I pulled his neck down with my left. I stabbed into the place my left thumb had found only moments before, the artery near his wind-pipe.

The shock on his face was complete. By the time he reached up to grab his neck, he had lost too much blood to remain conscious. He fell forward on to me, the life spilling out of him.

I had killed a man.

Twenty-seven

His lifeless body lay bleeding, pressing me beneath his weight. I managed to move him over enough so that I could breathe. I fought down the urge to be sick. I wanted nothing more than to get out of that room, to run out of the cabin, but I was too weak. I cursed that weakness, then calmed myself as much as I could, and moved my arms and legs beneath him. Gradually, I was able to position myself so that I could roll him off me.

The effort left me trembling. I drew deep breaths, trying not to think about the smell of his blood all over me, trying to concentrate on what must be done next.

Don't cry, don't waste any of your energy. Don't look at him. Get out.

I had no idea how long it would take Raney to return from Las Piernas. I got up from the mattress and hopped over to the door. I was shaking as I opened it, but felt a sweet release of emotion as I moved outside of that room for the first time.

I was in the kitchen. There were three other doorways off it. One led outside. The others led to a small living room that was obviously being used for Devon and Raney's sleeping quarters and a tiny bathroom. A quick look did not reveal the location of my coat and shoes. Devon's feet were larger than mine and I decided a big loose shoe would be more of a handicap than a help. It may have been my way of talking myself out of having to go back into that room, or having to touch him again.

I hopped over to the sink and washed my face with cool water, drinking it right out of the faucet. I was so thirsty, it was heaven. The desire to take a shower—to rinse Devon's blood off me—was strong, but I was too afraid to take the time. I grabbed a paring knife, the only one I could find in the poorly furnished kitchen, and the set of keys Devon had left on the table. I took his denim jacket off the back of a chair and put it on. I saw a broom in one corner, and turned it upside down to use as a makeshift crutch. I put the knife and keys in the jacket pocket, and made my way outside.

Using the broom was awkward, and being barefoot didn't help. I worked my way over to the truck. I took the keys out of my pocket and tried each one in the door.

Nothing.

I tried them all again.

Nothing. Devon didn't have a key to the truck.

I howled in frustration and pounded on the door of the tall vehicle, causing myself to lose my balance and fall hard to the ground. It hurt like a son of a bitch. I started to get up, when it occurred to me that I could at least make it harder for Raney and the Goat to catch up to me. I pulled out the knife, reached up under the truck, and cut the brake line.

I pulled myself up again, literally and figuratively. If I went down the drive to the road, it would be easier going and I would probably encounter other people sooner. The problem was that Raney and the Goat were very likely to be those other people.

I decided to follow the creek down instead. It would be less obvious. People liked to build their cabins along creeks, I told myself. There would be water to drink and sooner or later it would lead me to someone who could help me. I hoped.

When I got to the back of the cabin, I almost changed my mind. The cabin sat about twenty feet above the creek. The slope from the cabin to the creek was steep and covered with leaves and pine needles.

My decision was made for me when I heard the sound of the Blazer coming up the drive. I began my descent. I slipped and slid a couple of times, but made it down to the creek. I heard the doors of the Blazer slam shut. I crawled until I was under a bush that I hoped would hide me from their view, and waited, feeling myself break out in a cold sweat.

Within minutes, I heard an almost animal cry, a screaming wail of denial and grief that I knew was Raney's. He sobbed Devon's name again and again in loud cries. I felt it go all the way through me. I had killed Devon to survive, but I didn't rejoice in it.

Soon I heard his cries turn to rage. "I'm going to kill that fucking bitch! I'll kill her! I'll kill her!"

Another voice, the Goat. Lower, calmer. I couldn't make out what he was saying.

Raney began screaming again. "Fuck you! Fuck you! This is your fault! This is all your fault! Oh God, Devon!"

There was a gunshot.

Had one of them killed the other? No, after a moment I could hear their voices again. Raney's much quieter now. Then the sound of the truck starting and driving off. Had they left?

I heard someone moving around outside. The hair on my neck stood on end. I could taste my own fear. I listened. Nothing.

I waited a long time. Still nothing. Slowly, I pulled myself down to the creek, rinsing my face, calming myself. I felt for the knife, but realized I must have lost it in the fall down the slope. With small, careful movements, I made my way along the creek bed, trying to stay out of the view of the cabin. I would survive. There were trees up ahead that would hide me better.

"That's far enough," a voice said in front of me.

| Twenty-eight

He was pointing a gun at me. There was no need for a mask now. I would be dead soon, so why bother? Still, I was surprised. I had guessed wrong.

"Hello, Paul," I said, as if I were meeting him at a church social instead of after being his prisoner. And now his prisoner again.

He smiled, but there was no warmth in it, and said, "You're going to very much regret what you've done, Irene. Devon was my cousin. I loved him very much."

"As much as you loved your grandmother?"

I should have known what his response to that would be. Runs in the family. His blow to my face brought me to my knees. He put the gun up against my forehead and told me to stand up.

"Can't. You'll have to help me. Your beloved cousin did too much damage to my ankle."

His help wasn't gentle. As he reached to grab my shoulders, I saw a set of white ridges on his wrists. It was not a tattoo of a goat that Sammy had seen after all—she had recognized the scars of Paul Fremont's teenage suicide attempt.

He dragged me between the trees and up a slope that wasn't as steep as the one I had slid down. I was beyond being able to resist physically. I decided I wouldn't cry if I could help it. No tears, and no yelling or screaming. No telling him where the journal is. I had my rules in place by the time he let me fall into a heap in the clearing in front of the cabin.

I dreaded the possibility of being put back into the room with Devon's body, but Paul didn't take me inside. He stood over me a long while, as if deciding a course of action. I lay unmoving, as much from exhaustion as from fear.

He moved behind me, pressed the gun to my head, and flattened me to the ground by placing a knee into my back. My left arm was pinned beneath me. He grabbed my right wrist, pulling my arm up into my back.

"Uncle," I said, wincing.

He pulled it harder.

"What do you want?" I asked.

Without saying anything, he eased the pressure off it, moved it around so that my hand was to the side of my head. He held tightly to my wrist, pressing it to the ground. He kept the gun up against the back of my ear. I couldn't figure out what he wanted me to do.

My shoulder was on fire, having been stretched as far as it would go. Or so I thought. He proved me wrong by suddenly yanking my wrist up into the air with all his might. I felt a burning, tearing sensation. My shoulder, leaving its socket. Tears came to my eyes unbidden, but my teeth remained clenched, so I managed not to scream. He laughed and laughed.

"When Frank Harriman finds you, lady, you are going to be broken into so many pieces it will take all day to count them. Think about that."

What I thought of was a string of obscenities. I was drenched in sweat. I felt close to passing out. I longed to. I didn't.

He grabbed my right hand, never moving the gun from my head. He bent my right thumb part way back. My shoulder hurt so much, it was amazing to me that I could feel him pull at my thumb.

"You know what's coming, don't you?"

I did, but I didn't answer him.

When he broke the thumb, I broke my rule about crying out. The scream was something that seemed to happen on its own.

It was as that scream died that I heard the sound of a motor. Someone coming up the drive.

He heard it too. "Raney's back. Now I'll have to share

some of this fun with him. If I can keep him from killing you outright."

But I knew he was wrong. I had learned the sound of the truck, and this was not the truck. Hope rose up against my pain. The sound stopped before the vehicle had reached the crest of the drive, and we heard doors closing. Two doors. Now Paul knew as well as I did that this wasn't Raney.

"Come out where I can see you or she dies," Paul shouted.

No reply. He pulled on the arm. I didn't want to, but I screamed again.

"Let her go, Paul." Frank. Sweet God in heaven, Frank had found me. In the next instant, I wanted him not to be there, not to see me like this. That passed.

"I've got a gun pointed right at her head. If you and whoever you've got with you don't show yourselves, she gets a bullet."

"Let her go, son. It's too late. The sheriff will be here any minute." Jack Fremont was walking into the clearing. He came to a halt when he saw us.

"Don't call me your son, you asshole."

"Paul, please," Jack pleaded. "Please don't do this."

"Where's Harriman? Get the fuck out here or I'll do her right now. Take a good look at her if you think I give a damn!" There was a rising hysteria in his voice. Frank came into the clearing. He had his gun in his hand.

"Drop it, Frank, or I'll kill her right now."

He hesitated, but let it drop at his feet.

"Raney's dead, Paul," Jack said, moving closer. "The truck went over a cliff."

"Liar. Stay back. Don't come anywhere near me. I wish you were dead. I hope you go through hell."

"Is that why, Paul? You did all of this because I told you I was sick?"

"Not sick, dying. You told me you were dying. And I couldn't wait around for that old bitch to die. Not when I could make everybody think it was you. Killed her, then all I had to do was wait for you to die."

"She gave you so much," Jack said. "And you killed her?"

"She gave all right. Oh yeah. She gave me and Ma everything we could ask for. But she let us know it. Every damn dime, she wanted something back for it. We had to listen to her go on and on. We had to let her know where every penny had been spent. Made us live with her. Like she could buy us! Goddamn I got tired of always having to do things her way. But where were you all that time, Daddy dear? Running around on a motorcycle like some kid. Coming back just to break Ma's heart. I hate you."

"Let Irene go," Frank said. "She's never done anything to you."

"Oh no? Well, go on in and take a look at Devon. This bitch killed Devon and she'd going to die for it."

He grabbed me by the hair and cocked the gun.

"No!" There was so much anguish in Frank's voice, I could hardly bear it.

Paul laughed.

It infuriated me. "Fuck you. I hope he cuts *your* heart out."

"Just for that, bitch, I think I'll kill him first."

What happened next happened fast. Paul raised up off me a little to turn and point the gun at Frank. I rolled over against Paul's legs, trying to throw off his aim. Frank dove to the ground and Paul fired the gun. He missed, and as Frank picked his own gun up, Paul turned and aimed right at me. There was no doubt in my mind that he was about to kill me, but in the next second I heard a whistling noise and a strange *thunk*. There was a knife in Paul Fremont's chest.

"Dad?" he said in amazement.

"I couldn't, Paul." Jack said, his voice full of misery. "I couldn't just stand here and watch you do it."

Paul looked at me then, the gun still in his hand, a bright red stain spreading over his chest. For a moment I thought he was still going to pull the trigger, but suddenly he fell over.

Jack and Frank were running toward us. Jack was picking Paul up in his arms and weeping. Frank knelt next to me, reaching out as if he wanted to hold me, but then stopping, as if he was afraid of hurting me.

"Irene," he choked out. I lifted my left hand, the only part of my body that wasn't in an uproar of pain, and touched his face. He took it in his and kissed it. There were dark circles under his eyes and he looked haggard—as if he'd had less sleep than I. I've never been so glad to see anybody.

"You look awful," I said, managing a lopsided smile. It was good to hear him laugh.

The sheriff arrived not long after that. He seemed to know Frank. He didn't need to be convinced that I needed medical attention, and left a deputy behind at the cabins to ride with us to a nearby clinic. Jack drove while Frank gently held on to me in the backseat.

Frank and Jack explained what they could to the sheriff, while I repeated one thought over and over to myself: I'm alive.

The doctor at the clinic was on her way to another emergency when we arrived. By then I was thinking only of the process required to keep my molars together, knowing that if I opened my mouth, I was going to scream. Conversations being held by those around me were difficult to follow. I know explanations were made, and I recall the sense if not the exact words of Frank's protest and pleas. They brought me inside the clinic and Frank set me on an examination table. The doctor took time to quickly check over my injuries and give me an injection to make the ride down to the hospital bearable.

She watched me for a minute, and seemed to know when the injection started to do its work. She nodded to Frank, and he lifted me again. It still hurt, but there was a growing fog between me and the pain. The sheriff decided to stay and help her, and somewhere in the fog he told Frank he would be in touch and people said thank you.

Jack looked worried about me when he helped us into the car.

Frank held me again, softly stroking my hair away from my forehead.

I felt tears welling up. "Ruined my hair."

"Your hair is wonderful. Don't worry about anything. If you don't like it, you can let it grow back. Or I'll buy you a wig."

I felt myself grin at that, a silly numb-faced grin. My emotions were yo-yoing like crazy.

There was something important to tell Frank, I thought, as the pain slipped farther away. What was it? Something important, just sliding out of my mind's reach. Then I remembered it, but my speech was growing thick when I called out to him, and it seemed as if he were getting farther away as well.

"Right here, I'm right here. Shhh."

"One more of them."

"No, he's dead. His truck went over a cliff."

"No, one more."

"Shhh. Go to sleep. They're all dead. No one's going to hurt you. You're safe now."

"No," I said, but it didn't seem important after all, so I let myself float down into darkness.

When I came around again, I saw white lights rolling over my head. Frank was holding my left hand, moving alongside me. I gradually realized I was on a gurney, being wheeled around in a hospital. The painkiller was wearing off.

The doctors were happy I could talk to them as clearly as I could. They had already taken X-rays, and were anxious about not letting the shoulder remain dislocated. They loaded me up with morphine and yanked the shoulder back into place. I howled like a banshee. The embarrassment of that didn't last long; I passed out.

I came awake feeling panicked. It took me a moment to realize I was in a hospital room. Frank was watching me anxiously. I was very grateful to see him there, because being in another strange, small room was frightening the hell out of me.

"How do you feel?" he said.

"Scared," I answered, before I realized Jack was there too.

He came up beside the bed and said quietly, "Do you want me to leave?"

"No, Jack. *I* want to leave."

Frank took my left hand in his and I held on to it tightly while I looked myself over. I had an IV in my left arm. The bottom half of my right leg was in a cast. My right arm was in a sling, and I had a strange cast on it. The cast started below my elbow and covered my thumb. It covered my hand under my fingers, but the fingers were exposed. The hand was elevated.

"The shoulder and thumb were dislocated," Frank explained. "The thumb fractured as well."

The room didn't have a window. The panic wasn't subsiding. "Get me out of here," I said.

"They want to keep you overnight," Jack said.

"I want to go home," I said to Frank. "Please don't make me stay here. Take me to your house. I'll go to a doctor in Las Piernas."

That caused a fight with the doctor who was on duty that night. He gave me two choices: see a psychologist or be sedated. I refused both. He tried to talk Frank into keeping me there, but Frank stuck up for me.

Finally, we found a doctor who was sympathetic to my point of view, or at least understanding of my desire to avoid confined spaces. He even helped me to move out into the hallway, where I felt a little less anxious. Jack went to get a prescription for painkillers filled while Frank helped me into a robe he had bought for me while I was in surgery. I apologized to the nurses for being difficult. I wondered if I was going crazy.

Just before we left, the doctor who had helped us gave me a sedative, saying it would make the long ride home easier on me. I fell asleep before Frank had finished signing all of the paperwork for my release.

We were back in Jack's car. I looked up hazily and saw Frank's face, looking down.

"Are we going home?" I asked.

"Yes. We're going home."

I woke up a couple of times on the way, vaguely aware

of feeling troubled, but Frank would try to calm me and soon I would fall back to sleep. I heard Jack and Frank talking easily to one another, their voices like a lullaby to me.

We pulled up in front of Frank's house, and Jack helped him once again. The lights were on in the house, and I became aware of voices—Pete and Rachel, Cody yowling. I couldn't make out anything anyone was saying, except Cody.

Frank took me into the bedroom, and with Rachel's help took the robe off and got me into bed. Rachel left the room. Cody, somehow always sensing when he needs to be gentle, found a place near my left hand to lie down and purr at me, giving me little kisses on my knuckles. It roused me enough to look up at Frank as he kissed me softly on the top of my head. He stayed until I fell asleep.

He came in again not too much later. I became aware that he had turned on the light and was calling my name and holding me. I was busy screaming. The nightmares had begun.

| Twenty-nine

When I woke up enough to realize that Devon had not reached up and pulled out the shard and started stabbing me with it, that it was a dream, I felt like there wasn't enough air in the room. I was going to suffocate at any moment. I was sweating. Frank was looking worried. "I've got to go outside," I told him.

It must have seemed an odd request, but he gave into it without question, as he did many other odd requests that would follow over the next few weeks. He put on a light jacket and then gently lifted me up out of bed. He helped me to stand and to put on my robe. He picked me up

again, and carried me out to the backyard. He eased me
down into a chair on the deck, then sat next to me.

"Is this okay?"

I nodded. The night was cool, and I took in great gulps
of air, which smelled wonderfully of the ocean. I could
just make out the sound of the waves hitting the shore.

"Better?"

"Yes, much better. I guess after being locked up in that
room—" I couldn't finish.

He took my hand. We sat there like that for a while.

"I suppose I should tell you what happened," I said.

"When you're ready."

I shook my head. "I don't know if I'll ever be ready."
I looked over at him, trying to put myself in his place.
Would he ever be ready to hear it?

Tentatively, I began telling him the story of my three
days in the mountains. By the time I finished, he was sitting, head in hands. I knew he was upset, but still, when
he spoke, the anger in his voice took me aback.

"Why the hell did you go out to that field that night?"

"I've asked myself that question many times, Frank." I
swallowed hard, feeling the regret rise within me like a river.

He got up and paced again, shoving his hands in his
pockets, then restlessly taking them out again. "I just don't
understand it. You're smart. But I swear to God, Irene,
sometimes you do something so . . ." He faltered, having
finally looked over at my face.

"Stupid," I finished quietly.

"I'm sorry. I shouldn't have said that. It doesn't do any
good."

"You're right. O'Connor once said that some people
would hold faster to their stupidity than to their lives,
which was good, because it provided a way to get rid of
idiots."

"For Christsakes. That's not what I was trying to say."

I didn't reply.

"It's not your fault, Irene." He stared down at his feet.
"I should never have left you that night. I knew you were
in danger, and I left you. I'm the idiot, and you've had to
pay for it. If I had stayed with you—"

"That doesn't do any good, either. Maybe if you had come with me they would have killed you."

He was silent.

I thought of all the worry and self-recriminations my disappearance must have caused him, and at a time when he had plenty of other problems to contend with. I thought of how he had blamed himself for Mrs. Fremont's death, for his father's death. I had, quite obviously, put him through hell.

"Do you think," I asked, my throat tightening, "that you could possibly come to forgive me?"

"Oh God, Irene. That's crazy. Nothing to forgive. What happened is not your fault. None of it is your fault."

I couldn't speak. He came over to me then and said quietly, "Let me hold you."

I laid my head on his shoulder. We sat like that for a long time.

"Want to try to go back to sleep?" he asked, seeing me grow drowsy.

I nodded. "Let me try to walk."

It was slow going, and I was frustrated, but he simply said, "Be patient."

"Frank?" I said, as we reached the bedroom.

"Hmm."

"I haven't seen myself yet."

I saw his jaw tense, but he quietly walked over to the closet door. I knew there was a full-length mirror on the other side of that door.

"Wait," I said, just as he started to open it. Deep breaths.

"You don't have to do this now," he said.

I shook my head. "Go ahead, I'm okay."

He opened it and there I was. There *someone* was. I didn't recognize it as me. Not entirely. My face was a mass of dark purple bruises, my right eye still swollen. My lips were puffy. There were cuts here and there. My hair was cut in clumps, some an inch long, some three inches long. Lots of lengths in between.

Frank moved up behind me, and gently encircled my waist. He looked over my left shoulder. "This isn't how you look to me. And besides, this won't last long. We've just got to let you heal."

I'd like to report that I was a good little soldier, but the truth is, I burst into tears and started bawling like a baby. Frank rolled with it. He shut the closet door and took me back to bed, putting a pillow under my right hand to help keep it elevated.

"Sorry I'm such a pain in the ass," I said, as he started undressing.

He moved over to me and sat down on the bed and said, "Don't ever say that again. We'll do whatever we have to do until you're better."

"I'm scared, Frank. Really scared."

"I know you are. Anyone would be."

I didn't say anything.

"Do you want to sleep by yourself until—well, I'll sleep in the guest room if you need some time."

I realized that my despair was being misread. "No, Frank," I said, taking his hand. "I want you to sleep by me every night until the day I die."

"Is that a proposal?"

"A proposition, maybe. Lower those eyebrows. I'm not quite up to *that* yet—but soon. Come on, get in here."

He finished undressing, turned out the light, and carefully crawled in next to me. Cody jumped up and settled between us. I was weary, but I was also afraid that if I went to sleep, the nightmares would return. Frank felt my tension and gently rubbed the back of my neck, taking care with the shoulder.

"Frank? Could you turn the light back on?"

He reached over and turned it on, watching me for a moment.

"Are you in pain? Can I get you something?"

I shook my head. "I'm just scared."

"What would help?"

"I don't know. Hold me."

He did. Eventually, we fell asleep. I found out that even with the light on, the nightmares came back, so I let him turn it out.

* * *

Just as I finished awkwardly eating a huge breakfast the next morning, friends and family started coming by: Pete, Rachel, John, Mark, Barbara, Lydia, and Guy. At first I felt uneasy and embarrassed over my swollen, bruised face, but Frank apparently had not only warned them about my injuries but told them not to ask me about my ordeal.

I was grateful. Even knowing that most of my visitors were professionally curious, I didn't want to talk about it. I had had to go over all of it during a phone call from the sheriff, which was harrowing enough. While I managed to stay fairly calm and detached during that call, I found myself shaking afterward. I was unsure of my ability to keep my emotions in check; I would be fine one moment, irritable or on the verge of tears the next.

But my friends seemed to ignore both my bruises and my moods, providing both distraction and support. Frank never strayed far from my side. Normally, I would have rebelled against that kind of protectiveness on his part. But I was not inclined to make one of my typical declarations of independence: I only wanted to feel safe.

My sister even brought a little barbering kit with her and cut my hair, evening it out. She had to cut it quite short, but I felt much less freakish when she was finished.

I wore down easily. I sometimes fell asleep while people were talking to me. I inevitably woke up in a panic, struggling, sometimes screaming; the visitors would be long gone and Frank would be there, calming me down, trying to keep me from unhinging my shoulder. Sometime in the late afternoon, the doorbell stopped ringing, and he crawled in next to me for a much needed nap. Miraculously, I was able to sleep for a few hours without having a nightmare.

We were awakened when Jack called and offered to bring dinner over. We accepted, and when he arrived, I saw that he had apparently carefully thought out the menu: a savory stew with everything in bite-sized chunks. No one would have to cut up my food for me. "Here's to Irene's first full day back home," Jack said, lifting a glass.

Throughout dinner he told us stories of his life on the road, which had included more than one stint as a cook. At one point, he glanced over at me and caught me touching my hair, regretting its loss.

"Make the most of it," he said, rubbing his smooth pate.

"Of what?" I said bitterly. "At least you had a choice about shaving your head."

"Irene—" Frank began, his voice full of protest, but he stopped, then looked over at Jack.

Jack just smiled. "Relax, Frank. I was going to tell her sooner or later anyway. Just wanted to give her a little more time, is all."

"Tell me what?" I said, still irritated.

Frank looked uneasy, but Jack just grinned. "That I did have a choice," he said, "but I gave up trying to have an elaborate hairdo after chemotherapy."

| Thirty

"Chemotherapy?" Shock won out over chagrin, but chagrin was a very close second.

"Made life simpler. I don't even have to blow-dry this cut."

I stayed silent.

"Leukemia, currently in remission," he said with a bow, as if he had just finished singing a little song.

I stared for a moment, still not believing it. But as I looked at him, I gradually realized that I didn't *want* to believe it. I had lost both of my parents to cancer. I liked Jack, and I didn't want to hear that he had leukemia.

"I'd prefer," he added quietly, "that you don't let word of it get around. I told Frank and I've told you. But no one else."

I agreed to keep his confidence, but I was still shaken.

"I'm sorry," he said, watching me. "You don't need bad news right now, do you?"

"I had it coming," I said.

The subject was dropped for the moment. I stayed quiet, and allowed the two of them to distract me with their conversation as they cleared the table and washed the dishes. Frank built a fire and we adjourned to the living room. Cody, who had been staying close to me all day, opted for Jack's lap.

As the evening progressed, I began to notice that Frank and Jack talked and laughed together with the ease of longtime chums. They looked to be about as unlikely a pair as could be imagined, but they obviously shared a growing friendship. I wondered about it as I listened to them. It wasn't the only thing I was curious about.

"What's wrong? Is your shoulder bothering you?" Frank asked. I became aware that my face had set into a frown.

"Not really. And nothing wrong. I just wanted to ask you about a few things."

"Such as?"

"Such as, where was I when you found me? Where was that cabin?"

He shot Jack a look, but answered, "You were in the San Bernardino Mountains, near Pine Summit. They took you up to the rental cabins. Mrs. Fremont's rental cabins."

"Your cabins? Those bastards took me up to your cabins?"

He nodded.

"That makes me furious!"

"Me too," he said quietly.

I looked over at Jack. I suddenly felt bad about bringing the topic up at all.

As if reading my thoughts, he said, "Keep asking those questions, Irene. You must have more than one or two."

"How can you stand being around us, Jack? Don't we just remind you of it all?"

"Do I 'just remind you of it all'?"

"No," I admitted.

"Well," he said. "I guess you and Frank are just about the only people in Las Piernas I want to be around right now. You don't pity me. What happened, happened to all of us. Differently for each of us, but—I don't know—I guess I'm not making any sense."

"You're making perfect sense," I said. "Other people— well, it's easier to be with the two of you. You were there."

"That's it."

I turned to Frank. "What happened while I was gone? How did you find me?"

"I was home. I was worried about you and was just about ready to call the hotel and ask if you had left yet. If you were still there, I was going to have you paged and meet you there."

He didn't say anything more for a while. For long minutes, the only sounds were Cody's loud purrs and the crackling of the fire.

He sighed, then went on. "I got a call from the department, saying they had Brian Henderson's son on the line, and that he insisted on talking to me, that you were in trouble. They patched the call through; it was Jacob, and he was frantic. I guess he had found one of my cards in your car. When he told me what had happened, I told him I'd meet him back at the field. I made a quick call back to the department, than left. Drove like a maniac. I got there not long after Jacob. He was a mess.

"He told me that although he hadn't seen them drive up, as he was leaving he had seen a Blazer parked on the corner."

I smiled. "Thank heaven he saw it. I thought he would be too rattled by what was going on to notice it. I think that kid really is going to be a reporter someday."

He looked at me and shook his head. "God help him. Anyway, Jacob was a big help. And not just with the Blazer. But to go back to what was happening that night, we weren't there for very long when the black and white units were pulling up, and we had Jacob take us to where the body was. We made him take us along a different path, so that we wouldn't disturb footprints in the places where the weeds were matted down.

"To make a long story a little bit shorter, we found prints of three people walking toward where the Blazer had been parked. No sign of where you might have been taken from there. None of the neighbors had seen a thing.

"Somebody took Jacob home. He was really upset; blamed himself. To be truthful, I wasn't holding together too well by then myself. It was after dawn when we finished in the field.

"Jacob had told me about the message at the hotel. Pete tracked down the guy who had been on the switchboard at the Lafayette that night and woke him up to ask him about the call. Fortunately, they don't get many messages that late, and this one was unusual, so he remembered it. He said the caller seemed to be a young man. Of course, he didn't question a young man being named "Sammy." Found out the same message had been left at the Cliffside. There was no doubt that the girl was dead long before the calls were made. So you had obviously been set up."

"It was her heart on my doorstep, wasn't it?"

"Yes," he said.

I motioned for him to stop for a while. I felt tears welling up and tried to keep them from falling, but once again, my emotions refused to be reined in.

"I suppose there's nothing that can be done about her father?" I said.

Frank shook his head.

I wiped my tears away and asked him to go on.

"Whoever made the call had to know about your connection to Sammy," he said. "That pretty much had to be someone at the shelter or the newspaper. I tried the shelter first. The girl you had talked to at the funeral—Sarah—was missing. Paul said he was really worried about her and asked if we would let him know if we located her. I had gone back over the journal and made a list of initials from it. I was thinking of going over them with Paul, but then I remembered you telling me about Sarah's dramatics, sneaking the journal to you when he came into the room. For some reason she hadn't wanted Paul to know about the journal, and it made me decide to hold off."

Jack looked away from us when Paul's name came up. I felt damned awkward and I guess Frank did, too, because he hesitated.

"Maybe we could finish talking about this some other time," he said.

"No," Jack said tightly. "It doesn't matter. It's too late. He wasn't who I thought he was, that's all. Go on, Frank."

Frank waited, then hearing Jack sigh with impatience, continued with his story. "I went home and tried to sleep. I couldn't. Jacob called me, and asked if I wanted to get your car—in all the excitement, he had gone home with your car keys. I drove over to the Hendersons' and picked him up. We went back to your car and he followed me home. I invited him to come in, and Jack stopped by while he was there."

"I was being a nosy neighbor," Jack said. "I had just moved into my mom's place and saw somebody else pulling up in your car, Irene. I wondered what was up."

"Well, I for one am damn glad you were curious," Frank said. "I don't know how much longer it would have taken if both of you hadn't been there at the same time." He looked at me. "As far as I could tell, there were only four things that had gone on at the shelter that could have made you a target for someone: you had talked to Sammy, you had talked to Sarah, you had taken Sammy's journal, and you had asked around about members of the coven, particularly this 'Goat.'

"So I started asking Jacob if he knew the names of the people whose initials had been in the journal. I left out the ones for Romeo and Juliet."

Jack's eyebrows went up at this, but he didn't get anything for the effort.

"When I got to the initials DM and RA, Jacob said, 'Devon Morris and Raney Adams.' And suddenly Jack looked like someone had slapped him."

"I asked Jacob to repeat the names," Jack said. "They were Paul's cousins. Remember I told you he had lived with Cindy's sister for a while? Well, Devon and Raney were two of her five kids."

"Devon told me he and Raney were half-brothers," I said quietly.

"They're all half-brothers. I just didn't know Paul still had anything to do with them. I didn't know they were hanging out at the shelter. I doubt they were ever around at the same time my mother was there. She couldn't abide any of that bunch."

"You're right—at least, on the day I was there with your mother, Devon and Raney weren't around."

Frank went on. "Things started to look a little different once we knew they were related to Paul. You had seen Paul order them around; Sammy's journal mentions a connection between them and the Goat. Pete tracked Sarah down; she had gone to stay with an aunt in the San Diego area. She said she left because Paul had threatened her about the journal. She told Paul it wasn't in the shelter any longer and that he'd never find it. He grabbed on to her and she thought he was going to hit her, when Mrs. Riley walked in. He walked off and she packed up and left.

"We asked Mrs. Riley about it and she said Paul had kicked Devon and Raney out the day before the funeral. But she also said she was convinced that Paul had received a phone call from Raney very early Wednesday morning—she answered the phone, thought she recognized the voice—and Paul had taken off not long after he got the call. He hadn't returned until late that afternoon.

"So we put a tail on Paul, hoping he'd lead us to wherever Devon and Raney were. I figured he had to be the Goat. He was connected to the shelter, to Sammy, to Devon and Raney, and to Mrs. Fremont. And he knew about Jack's leukemia. So he stood to inherit. He probably picked the goat and Satanism because of Jack's tattoo. Paul was hoping Jack would be suspected of murdering Mrs. Fremont. I guess Sammy found out what they were up to. She probably threatened him by telling him she had a journal."

"She knew Paul was the Goat. She saw the scars on his arms," I said. "I saw them when—I saw them," I finished weakly, trying to not feel the memory in my shoulder and thumb.

Frank waited, probably wondering if I was going to burst into tears again, and went on when I didn't.

"I checked vehicle registrations for Devon and Raney. Devon had a registration for a Blazer. So now it was a matter of waiting and praying to God that Paul got back in touch with them before—well, before it was too late. Jack knew them by sight and I didn't; I only had a DMV photo. So he came with me to watch Paul and on Friday it paid off. We followed Paul to a place where he met Raney. Then we followed them up into the mountains. By then, we knew where they were headed.

"Sure enough, they took the Pine Summit turnoff. I didn't know what the situation would be, and Jack and I weren't really official—"

"You mean Carlson didn't want you working on this," I said.

"Well, actually, he let me work on it. I don't know if he felt sorry for me or what. He told me I seemed to be personally connected to every murder in Las Piernas, so I could work on a missing persons case. He knew I'd look for you anyway. But he didn't like the idea of Jack getting involved, and so we were sort of an unofficial back-up tail, you might say. Good thing, because Paul shook the official one.

"Anyway, like I said, I didn't know exactly what the situation would be, but I knew there were at least three of them, and Paul had other cousins. So I stopped off at the sheriff's station and told them what was going on. By the time we convinced the sheriff and his deputy to get up off their behinds and follow us up there, Raney had apparently started back down. We came across his truck—what was left of it. I was afraid . . . well, we stayed just long enough to determine there was only one body. The sheriff fooled around calling another unit but I couldn't wait. Jack and I took off for the cabins. You know the rest."

I know we all had our own mental pictures of what happened from there, and the silence that followed was an uneasy one.

"I don't know how I could have been so wrong about Paul," Jack said, just above a whisper. "I can understand why he hated me. I just never thought he was so bitter toward his grandmother."

No one said anything for a long time. I felt myself wearing down and told them I was going to call it a night.

Jack stood up, gently putting Cody on the floor. "I'll say good night, then. I'm glad we talked."

"Stay if you want to," I said. "I just don't have any stamina. I wish—" I didn't finish it.

"That you could go back to being your old self?" Jack asked.

"Yes."

"Give up on that one, Irene. Just about everything changes." And with that, he said good night again and left.

Over the next week or so, I tried to come to grips with the implications of just about everything changing. The first disappointment came with the unsettling realization that I was not going to heal overnight. I didn't like being so dependent on others, but that was the simple fact of the matter. There was very little that I could do for myself, even when I started to be able to hobble around a little.

There was also the fact that I was still feeling scared. Afraid that if I was alone I would be kidnapped. What were the odds? A million to one still made me break out in a cold sweat.

Looking back on it, that week I did more feeling than thinking. It was as if everything I had tried to repress during my captivity came boiling up and over me. The terror of it demanded to be acknowledged.

Frank's support was unwavering, but I doubt that we could have made it through that time alone. Fortunately, we didn't have to try. Lydia, Guy, Rachel, and Pete came by and spent hours with me, talked to me, watched me sleep, woke me from nightmares. Took care of and cared about me.

When I protested to Rachel that she should find something more enjoyable to do with her vacation, she said, "What, I don't look like I can make a decision? When I'm doing something I don't want to be doing, you can put the story in that newspaper of yours. *Basta.*"

Okay, enough. I didn't mention it again.

Two new friends were over fairly often: Jacob and Jack. Like my other friends, the first time Jacob came over, he was shaken by my appearance. But, like them, he recovered quickly. He was full of youthful energy and loaded with questions about working for newspapers. His father, I learned, had won the election. Julie's parents had put her on restriction, so he hadn't seen much of her. I imagined I would see less of him once she was paroled.

Jack seemed to need to be around us, and he came by several times each day. He brought groceries, helped Lydia and Rachel cook, talked hockey with Guy and Pete. He did errands that would have taken up Frank's time, allowing Frank to spend it with me instead.

Jack was solicitous to me, and kept me company if none of my other babysitters could be there, but usually he allowed the others to pamper me.

I woke up and limped out of the bedroom on Tuesday morning, and found him sitting on the couch with Cody, reading a book.

"Rachel had to leave for a few minutes," he said, looking up. "Need anything?"

I shook my head and slowly made my way over to a chair. "What are you reading?"

"Ovid," he said, and laughed at my undisguised look of surprise.

"I never know what to make of you, Jack," I said, then felt embarrassed at my own bluntness. As usual, he didn't seem to mind.

"No, I guess not. And I suppose that extends beyond catching me reading the *Metamorphoses*."

I nodded. Jack never ceased to puzzle me. Two days before, I had found him sitting on the couch, working with a notebook computer. When I asked why a biker needed a computer, he told me that the notebook had been his first indulgence after coming into his inheritance; he found he needed a computer to keep track of his mother's complex estate. I noticed that he had yet to go on a big spending spree; like his mother, he seemed to prefer to live simply.

"Okay," I said, "I give up. Why the *Metamorphoses?*"

"As for that, my mother read more Greek mythology than Mother Goose to me when I was a little sprout. So I guess I just wanted to remind myself of those days."

"Oh."

He closed the book and studied me. "What's wrong?"

"Nothing."

"Tell the truth."

"It's just a mood, Jack. Give me five minutes—or maybe less—and it will change."

"So talk to me before the five minutes are up. I'd hate to miss the full impact of this one."

"Just feeling frustrated."

"About your injuries?"

"Not this time—not any more than usual. It's just that I know there's a fourth person involved in all of this. The department won't let Frank work on the case. I'm in a funk because Frank can't seem to get anyone to even take the idea seriously."

"I guess they consider it a closed case."

"But it's not. This fourth man is still out there."

"How did you learn about him?"

I swallowed hard, pushing the suddenly sharp memory of the cabin away. "The second day I was up there. I heard Devon and Raney talking about him."

"You're sure? You were scared and in a lot of pain and—"

"I'm sure. There's another man involved in this."

"And you want him brought to justice."

"It's more selfish than that. I'm scared to death of him."

He idly fingered the pages of the closed book, then said, "Maybe you should tell me what happened."

Why I found it easier to tell that story to Jack Fremont, whom I had known only for a number of days, than to friends I had known for years, I can't say. He listened calmly, which somehow kept me calm as I sketched out the basics of what had happened.

When I finished, Jack was quiet for a while, then said, "There's no immediate help for feeling afraid, I suppose. You've obviously been through a lot, and it will take time before you feel safe again."

"That's why I was hoping that somehow we could find this 'Pony Player.' "

"You suspect someone in particular?"

I hesitated. I had suspicions, but they were based on

seeing a limo at a funeral and one brief conversation with Murray Plummer. I didn't even know how Malcolm Gannet might have earned the nickname "Pony Player." I hadn't had a chance to determine who else might be the Pony Player; as soon as I was able to go back to work, I intended to do some digging, but until then, I couldn't do much more than guess.

"It's not the kind of thing I'd like to say about anyone," I answered uneasily, "at least, not without more reason to do so. I'm just saying that I'll feel less afraid when the fourth person is caught."

"I think it would be a mistake to believe that would be enough," he said.

"You think there are *more* people involved in this?"

"No, no, that's not what I mean. It's a possibility, but not my point. I'm just saying that you need to start getting out and around a little, to work on overcoming your fears on your own. Don't let finding or not finding the Pony Player decide whether you do or don't get on with your life."

I was about to ask him what the hell he thought he knew about overcoming fear, when the word "leukemia" occurred to me.

"You're right," I admitted. "But I'd still feel better if I knew more about the Pony Player. I guess you don't think there's much hope of catching him."

"Irene, I'm living proof that you ought to expect the unexpected. I'd never tell you to give up."

I won't claim that I jumped right up, shouted hallelujah, and started dancing a jig, but I did slowly start taking Jack's advice. I began by seeing an orthopedist and a physical therapist, which forced me to get out for a while each day. I had to fight down panic every time I stepped out the front door, and clutched Frank's hand throughout each brief car ride to the doctor's office, but at least I wasn't cowering in the house.

That's how things were going until the day we went sailing. Like Jack said—expect the unexpected.

| Thirty-one

By the weekend before Thanksgiving, I thought Frank might sell me off to Sea World as the planet's largest living crab. I was restless and frustrated and tired of not being able to do things for myself. I felt like I wasn't getting any better.

In reality, I was making great progress, healing quickly and steadily, in perhaps everything but my nerves. Frank tried to be patient, but both the lack of sleep my nightmares caused him and my changeable moods took their toll, and after a while we started snapping at each other over little things.

We had a particularly nasty round about our Thanksgiving plans. He still wanted me to go with him to Bakersfield—while I worried that my casts and slings would be met with slings and arrows.

"Sure, Frank. I can see it now: 'Hello, Mrs. Harriman, I'm Frank's girlfriend. Live-in girlfriend. Yes, I know I look like I've gone a couple of rounds with Jack Dempsey.' "

"Irene—"

" 'Tutankhamen? The mummy? No, I don't think I am related to the Egyptian Pharaoh, but why do you ask?' "

"It won't be like that."

"You're right. It will be worse. 'No, no, Mrs. Harriman, even before this happened to me, Frank cut up my food for me. Do you have a bib I could borrow?' "

"You're going to be fine. Do you think I'd let anyone give you a bad time?"

"You go. I'll stay here."

"If you don't go, I don't go."

"Don't be childish."

"Look who's talking! You're been whining like a damned baby for the past two days."

"I didn't ask to be brought here. Send me home."

"That is a ridiculous suggestion and you know it." And at that, he stormed out of the house.

As with every encounter of this nature, once I had simmered down a little, I felt overcome with guilt. That in turn fed a kind of depression that I found difficult to fend off. And so it was that I went into a funk not long after he had slammed the front door.

Cody came over to me, leapt up into my lap, and made an irksome yowling sound, acting like he would like to bite me.

"Not you, too."

He turned around and gave me the cat version of a mooning and jumped down. Wonderful. Male bonding had gone a little too far in that household. I got up and started doing my Peg-leg Pete imitation, a lopsided pacing that only seemed to further irritate me.

Before long, Frank came back in and watched me thumping around. "Irene, that can't be good for your ankle."

I wanted to say, "Forgive me, Frank, I've been a jerk." What I did say was, "Leave me alone."

"I came in to apologize," he said, ignoring my snottiness. "Never mind about Thanksgiving. Maybe we can just spend it here together."

I stopped pacing and scowled. "You're being too reasonable."

He started laughing, and despite my efforts to the contrary, I found my scowl lifting into a grin.

"You're being impossible and you know it," he said.

"Yes, I am," I sighed, and eased myself down on to the couch. "I'm going crazy, Frank."

He sat next to me. "I know. What can we do about it?"

"I don't know." I was out and out glum.

Just then there was a familiar pattern of knocks on the front door. We both recognized it and Frank called out, "Come on in, Jack."

Jack took one look at us and said, "You've just had a fight, haven't you?"

Frank and I exchanged a look that was a mixture of surprise and shame.

"I knew it. Okay, that does it. I've been meaning to suggest this for a couple of days. Frank, have you got a pair of warm sweatpants that will fit over Irene's cast?"

I frowned, but Frank was answering, "Yes, I think so."

"Good. We're going sailing."

"What?" I yelped.

"We're going sailing. You know, a boat, the ocean, and a little breeze?"

"Forget it, Jack," I said. "I can't."

"Why not?"

I hesitated. "I just can't."

"You mean you won't do it," Jack said evenly.

"Okay, I won't."

"Not an acceptable answer. I'll be back in an hour. Be ready. I've got a big sweater that will fit over that harness you're in."

And with that set of directives, he left. Frank, damn him, was grinning.

"You aren't seriously thinking of doing this, are you?"

"Yes."

"Frank, he's crazy."

"No, he's making more sense than we have lately."

"I don't want to go."

"You love the ocean. Don't you miss seeing it?"

"Yes, but—"

"What would O'Connor tell you to do?" he asked.

"You fight dirty, you know that?" I said, then sighed. "I give in. I can't take on you and Jack and Cody all in the same afternoon."

"Cody?"

"Never mind. Let's get ready."

Frank went into motion. Seeing his enthusiasm, I felt a little twinge of guilt at the thought that this very active man had been cooped up in the house with me whenever he wasn't at work or accompanying me to the doctor's office. I decided that for Frank's sake, if not my own, I needed to go along with Jack's plan.

Jack returned with a sweater large enough to get on me without jarring my shoulder. Frank put a stocking cap on my head for warmth.

"Let's go!" Jack said.

Outside, we were waved to by a couple of neighbors and got a wide-eyed look from a cable-TV installer; otherwise no one was out on the street, so this venture out of the house wasn't too bad. We drove down to the marina; we were in our by-now standard arrangement of Jack driving while Frank sat in the backseat, next to me. Frank kept hold of my hand, but this time, I wasn't clenching it in fear. I traced my fingers over his, enjoying the feel of his hand, his closeness.

Above the rows of masts in the marina, the sky was a soft, cloudy gray. I was grateful for the sweater. There were people out and about, but the weather wasn't warm enough to draw a big crowd. We stopped at a sharp-looking Catalina 36. Jack told us the boat had been his mother's; he had lived aboard it when he first came back to Las Piernas. It was named the *Pandora*.

"More Greek mythology?" I asked.

Jack nodded. "Mom once told me that I shouldn't see it as a story which blamed the world's troubles on a woman; I should simply remember that the world would have been a very dull place if Pandora hadn't been inquisitive."

It was a calm day, just enough wind to move us along. The sea was smooth, Jack was an able skipper, and we made our way out onto the bay in an easy fashion. For all I cared, it might as well have been a sunny summer afternoon. Even though it was gray above and below, there was still something uplifting about being out on the water.

"It's good to see you smile, Irene," Jack said. I noticed we were all looking contented.

Frank made his way over and sat next to me.

"Any more news about the case?" Jack asked.

"Not much," Frank said. "Hernandez is working on identifying some hairs he found in Sammy's wounds."

Seeing Jack's look of puzzlement, he added, "Dr. Carlos Hernandez, the coroner."

"You mean he'll be able to tell who the hairs belonged to?" Jack asked.

"They don't belong to a human being. We thought at first that they might be from a goat. But they didn't match up with the goat hair samples he had. So now he's going through samples of other animals to try to match it up."

"Any other hair or fibers?" I asked.

"Some, but you have to remember that just finding a hair or a type of fiber doesn't prove much. Carlos is putting in whatever time he can on it. He verified that she wasn't killed in the field. And he did find wool fibers, so maybe those came from the blanket you heard them talking about."

Frank changed the subject after that, and I let myself be distracted from thoughts of Sammy's murder. I looked out over the water, felt the breeze, listened to the two men talking. We sailed out beyond the breakwater, and headed down the coast, away from the boats going to Santa Catalina Island. Although eventually I was feeling at ease again, I wore down fairly quickly. Frank noticed.

"You're tired, aren't you?"

I nodded to him.

"Take her below," Jack said. "Sleep for a while, Irene, and I'll take us back in."

Frank helped me down the companionway ladder and forward into a bunk. He lay down next to me, gently stroking my hair. He leaned over and gave me a long kiss. We hadn't kissed like that in a while.

"I have a good mind to untie those sweatpants," he said.

"Frank! Not with Jack right above us."

He laughed and left me. I fell asleep quickly.

When I woke up, we were back in the marina. Frank helped me up the ladder. Just as we cleared the hold, I saw a sleek yacht going by, looming above our much smaller craft.

"Whose is that?" I asked.

"Oh, that's Malcolm Gannet's," Jack said.

"Gannet?" I said, just as the name painted on the yacht's stern came into view.

The *Long Shot.*

"The Pony Player," I said, and suddenly felt the blood drain from my face.

| Thirty-two

"Irene? Irene? Are you okay?"

I looked blankly into Frank's worried face, my mind still flooding with images of being in a small, cold, dark room; of being beaten; of being afraid I would be killed. Dice rolling across a bare wooden floor.

"Sit down," I heard Frank saying, as if from a great distance. "Try to put your head down." I let him position me without resistance; I couldn't seem to will myself to do anything.

When I had recovered somewhat, I lifted my head and said, "Sorry," and took a few deep breaths. Frank and Jack were anxiously watching me. I was shaking. I started to talk to them, but it was no good. I wanted the fear to pass, but it was like waiting for a long freight train at a railroad crossing.

"He's the one," I finally managed, but my mouth was so dry it came out a whisper. "He really is the one," I said again. "Malcolm Gannet. The Pony Player."

"The fourth man?" Frank asked.

I nodded.

"How do you know it's Malcolm Gannet?" Jack asked.

"Devon and Raney kept talking about someone they called the Pony Player. They also said he was the big boy. They were afraid they might be set up to take a fall for Paul or the Pony Player. I got the impression that Devon and Raney didn't do the actual killing—they were there, but Paul or maybe this Pony Player were the ones that actually carried out the murders."

I thought over what I had heard Devon and Raney say, placing Paul Fremont in their cryptic references to Sammy's murder. I looked up at Frank.

"Paul had a knife. After they killed Sammy, he cut this Pony Player with the knife, so that it had both the Pony Player's and Sammy's blood on it. Devon and Raney had a blanket they were going to use in the same way—so that if they were caught, they had a way to protect themselves, to implicate this same Pony Player."

"That was when you broke the window," Frank said, remembering what I had told him. "Devon took the blanket and hid it somewhere in Las Piernas."

"'Right. Devon took a long time getting back to the cabin. When Raney asked Devon why it took so long, he said something like 'it was out' and talked about having to 'wait until they brought it back in.' I think he meant the yacht. Raney said he 'didn't think they would do that this time of year.' It puzzled the hell out of me at the time. Then Devon said something about a client or an investor being with the Pony Player. Maybe Gannet had the yacht out that night."

"So why do you think Gannet and the Pony Player are the same man?"

"His yacht is called the *Long Shot*—and a pony player is someone who gambles on horses. He wanted your mother's land. He was at her funeral even though he hated her."

"He didn't hate her," Jack said.

We both stared at him.

"He even dated her for a while. I was about twelve or thirteen. She figured he was after the beach property, but I'm not sure. They were rivals, but in some ways, that also made them respect each other. I think if they hadn't fought about developing the beach, they would have been friends, or maybe more. I used to watch the way he looked at her. I think he thought of her as someone unattainable."

"Maybe she was unattainable, Jack. But so was her beach property, as long as she was alive. I think she was killed because Gannet wanted it. You were ill. If she died, and you died or went to prison for killing her, then Paul would get the property, right? So maybe Gannet put ideas in your son's head. Maybe Gannet even planned the whole thing. I think the knife that killed Sammy can link him to her murder. And that blanket—that might do the same."

"Can you get a search warrant, Frank?" Jack asked.

Frank was quiet. The whole time, he was watching my face. "It'll be tough."

He saw my disappointment.

"Look, I'll try," he said. "I'll do my best. But he's powerful and all I've got is your word about something you overheard and guessed at the meaning of—" I started to open my mouth to complain but he motioned me to silence. "Settle down, I believe you. But we'll have to come up with some way to convince a judge to get a warrant."

I saw the hopelessness of it.

"I'll try," he said firmly. "But in the meantime, don't talk about this to anyone else, Irene. I mean it. If he is involved and he thinks you're on to him—please just don't say anything to anybody for now, okay?"

I nodded.

On the way back home, I resolved not to let seeing the *Long Shot* spoil a great day. When we got to the house, I gave a surprised Jack a one-armed hug and a kiss on the cheek.

"Thanks," I said.

"Why, Irene! If I had known I could get kissed, I would have taken you out on the *Pandora* long ago. At your service any time, my dear."

He left. Frank had a look on his face that bordered on jealousy, and it made me laugh.

"What's so funny?" he said testily.

I didn't answer, just hobbled over and gave him the kind of kiss that could make him forget his name and address. When I remembered mine, I said, "Do you think we could manage to work around my orthopedic supplies and take up where we left off this afternoon?"

He kissed me back, moaning softly. "I've missed you so damn much."

The guy had been tethered to me night and day for two weeks, during which I had been a regular pain in the butt. But I knew what he meant. I had missed him, too.

| Thirty-three

The phone woke us up when Frank's sister called just before six, saying she was in town and would like to stop by and see us. I had never met her before; she lives up in Bakersfield. Frank invited her to join us for dinner.

Like Frank, Cassie had light brown hair and gray-green eyes; there was a striking resemblance there. But she must have favored her mother otherwise. She was shorter than Frank and me, and slim, with delicate features. Those eyes, warm and friendly, were resting on me now.

"You must be Irene," she said, smiling and extending her right hand, but quickly changing to the left to accommodate my injuries.

"Good to meet you, Cassie."

As we made our way back to the living room, Cassie walked at a pace that allowed me to move alongside her without hurrying, and without making me feel like I was being babied.

"Well, is this the world-famous Cody?" she said, bending to pick up the final member of the greeting committee. Cody purred loudly and shut his eyes in contentment as she scratched him under the chin.

"That is indeed Wild Bill Cody, tramp and tomcat."

"The cat that scratched Frank's face!" she laughed.

"He's also an ankle-biter," Frank said.

Cody gave Cassie a look that tried to convey he was being slandered.

"He has sort of a combination cowboy name, doesn't he?" she asked. "Wild Bill Hickok and Buffalo Bill Cody?"

"When I acquired this wild cat, I remembered that as a kid, I used to mix those two names together, confusing things adults were saying. I also used to think that there was a song called 'My Darling Turpentine,' and that during Mass the choir was singing 'Cheerios, A Lady's Song.' "

She looked puzzled.

"Sorry. Catholic lore. The actual phrase was 'Lord have mercy,' or in Latin, *'Kyrie eleison.'* "

She laughed. " 'Cheerios, A Lady's Song'—definitely a happier-sounding tune."

We had made it to the living room by then. I eased myself into a chair and let them have the couch.

"So what are you going to feed me?" she said to Frank.

"Nice to see you, too, Cassie," he said sarcastically.

Soon they were talking about Cassie's husband, Mike, and her two sons, Michael and Brian. Turning to me, she asked, "Do you have any brothers or sisters?"

"A sister. Her name is Barbara. She lives here in Las Piernas."

"That must be great, being so close."

"It is," I said, thinking that Barbara and I might be close in terms of residences, but we couldn't match these two in affection for one another. I watched as they bantered with each other, teasing good-naturedly. Cassie in turn watched me, drawing me into the conversation whenever she could. Frank quickly picked up her cue, and did the same. We talked about my job at the paper, her job as a teacher, and Frank's nephews.

"So," she said, "where's the famous grandfather's chair?"

I was puzzled for a moment, but Frank jumped in with, "Was your grandfather famous, Irene?"

"You know what I meant, Frank," she protested. "I thought you told me you were going to move this woman, her cat, and her grandfather's chair into your place. I can only see two out of three."

Let's see you get yourself out of this one, Harriman, I thought with a grin.

He turned red and gave me a pleading look. Cassie laughed.

"Well, Cassie, after two weeks of my constant companionship, he's probably nailed that chair to the floor of my house. Your brother has had hell to pay since the day he brought me back from the mountains."

"She never used to lie," Frank said. "Must have been one of the blows to her head. But to keep you from sticking your nose in any farther—Irene never officially agreed to move in. Just this morning she wanted me to take her home."

That earned him the hairy eyeball from me, but he didn't flinch.

Cassie looked between us. "Uh-oh. Sorry, Irene."

I laughed. "Don't worry, Cassie, Frank is just gloating because he knows I'm not going anywhere, and wouldn't if I could."

Frank looked at me in surprise, then turned and said, "Cassie, I love you. Keep talking to her. God knows what she'll agree to next. I'll go to the store and pick up some steaks."

"Well, Irene, I have a confession to make," she said as soon as he was out the door.

I waited, not knowing what to expect.

"I didn't have any other reason to be in Las Piernas today—although I told Frank I went to a teacher's supply place down here—well, I did go to it, but only so that I wouldn't be a complete liar. Anyway, the confession is that I came down here because I just had to meet the woman who was able to get Frank to come back home for Thanksgiving."

"What?"

"I knew I would be meeting you next week, but Mom will be there and it's just not the same with the whole family scurrying all over the place. I guess I figured it would take something or someone special to get Frank to come to the house again, and I was right. I mean, I knew that you would be the one, because Frank has been so happy since this summer. There's been such a change in him since he started seeing you."

"Cassie, what are you talking about? What about Frank and the house? Which house—your mom's?"

She looked at me. "Uh-oh, I've done it again. He didn't tell you."

"Didn't tell me what?"

She cleared her throat. "Frank hasn't been inside my mother's house for three years."

"Since your dad died," I said slowly.

"Oh, so he did tell you."

"Not exactly. I know about your dad, but not about the house."

"Oh." She paused. "Oh." Sighed. "I guess you could say Frank didn't handle Dad's death very well. It was hard on everybody, but Dad and Frank were really close. I mean, we all were close, but Frank and my dad especially. Frank blames himself, I think. Maybe that's over, I don't know. We never talk about it. Anyway, Dad died at home, and Frank hasn't been inside the house since that day."

"But I know he's been back to Bakersfield since then."

"Yes, but he comes over to my place, meets my mother there, and drives back home. Once in a great while, he'll spend the night at our place. He usually refuses to come to Thanksgiving dinner. Sends my mom right over the edge every year. They start arguing about it in October, and don't stop until after Christmas, which he also spends at our house."

It was my turn to say, "Oh."

I guess the look on my face said even more, because she hastily added, "Don't worry about her. She's a bit over-bearing at times, but she means well. Frank can handle her, and I'll run defense for you. Oh God, I make her sound like a harridan. I hope I haven't talked you out of coming!"

"Not at all," I said, realizing that I might have a way to return some of the kindness Frank Harriman had showered on me since bringing me home.

I smiled, catching myself using that word. Home. Yes, I thought, this was home, even without my famous grandfather or his chair. I didn't want to go back to my house, but it wasn't just that. Frank's house was more than my refuge for the moment.

I looked back over to Cassie, to see her returning my smile.

Frank came back in with an armload of groceries. "Is it safe for me to be back in my own home?"

"Our home," I said.

"Good work, Cassie," he said. He began unloading the sacks, pulling out a bottle of red wine.

"In fact," I said, "I was just about to tell Cassie how nice it will be to know somebody besides you when we join the family for Thanksgiving dinner."

He stopped what he was doing and looked up at me, clearly amazed. He turned to his sister. "Cassie, I may have to have you over more often."

"What's with you, Frank?" she asked.

He didn't reply. He was looking back at me, and I liked being looked at that way. *Kyrie eleison.*

| Thirty-four

Frank was getting ready for work the next morning when the doorbell rang, so I answered it, and was surprised to see the coroner standing there.

"Good morning, Miss Kelly," he said, seeming uncomfortable.

"Hello, Dr. Hernandez," I said, gesturing for him to come inside. "Frank must have forgotten to cancel his order. He changed his mind about killing me yesterday."

He smiled. Frank had made his way down the hall by

then, and also seemed surprised to see Dr. Hernandez. "Carlos? What's up?"

"Good morning, Frank. Sorry to bother you at home. I, uh, wanted to talk to you away from the office."

Frank nodded. "Come on into the kitchen, I'll get you a cup of coffee. Okay if Irene hears this?"

He hesitated. "Only if it doesn't end up in the newspaper."

My curiosity was fairly raging. "I'm on medical leave," I said. "I know it's hard to see why."

"You look like you could still use a telephone."

"You're right. But I won't."

That seemed good enough for him, and he followed us into the kitchen. When we were all settled around the table, he said, "I don't suppose you or Pete were in contact with anyone from the county lab over the weekend, were you, Frank?'

"No. Pete should be by in a few minutes, but I'm fairly certain he wasn't, either. Why do you ask?"

"I dropped by on Sunday to review our caseload and to prepare work schedules for next week. I also wanted to do a little more work on the Sammy Garden case. I discovered that between the time I left Friday afternoon and yesterday morning, someone took a look through my computer files."

"And you thought it was me?" Frank asked, taken aback.

"No," Carlos said quickly. "I never thought it was you or Pete. That's why I came by. If you weren't the ones who asked for the information, I wanted you to be aware of what had happened. I know you have a . . ." He glanced over at me. "You have a personal interest in the files that were read."

Frank and I exchanged a look. "Which files?" I asked, the knot in my stomach already predicting the answer.

"Those having to do with the Fremont murder and the Garden case."

The knot tightened.

"How could you tell?" Frank asked.

"The computer notes the last date and time anyone

opens a case file. The display doesn't show up unless you ask for it, but I check it fairly often, as a way of managing our work—helps me to keep track of which cases aren't moving."

"Maybe one of your assistants was in on the weekend," Frank suggested.

Carlos was silent for a moment, then said, "Maybe. But other than the man who was on duty, no one is admitting it, and he normally wouldn't be in the part of the building where the computers are. These files are generally accessible on a 'read only' basis from either my offices or the D.A.'s office, but it's too early for any involvement from the D.A. As far as I can tell, the files weren't accessed randomly, the way a hacker might enter them, and no other files were opened. So who felt they needed to wait until the weekend to take a look? It disturbs me."

"Anyone you would suspect of doing this?"

"I'd rather not speculate, Frank, at least not yet. I just wanted to ask you and Pete to be careful about who you talk to. I have no idea what was being looked for; the files don't seem to have been disturbed, just read."

"You've got backups?"

"Yes, on disks which are kept in a completely separate area. I checked them. No one looked at the backups." He paused, glancing at me, then back to Frank. "I've never mentioned my conversations with you in my notes. I know you aren't supposed to be on either case, but no one has forbidden me to discuss them with you. I know you have reasons to be interested in both of them, and I haven't minded taking care of a friend."

"I've appreciated it," Frank said.

Carlos waved it off. "It's nothing. By the way, I think I've finally identified the hairs."

"The ones from the wounds?" I asked.

"So, Frank has kept you up on all of this. Yes, from the wounds. The hairs are from a deer."

"A deer?"

"Yes. Does that mean anything to you?" he asked hopefully.

"No," I said. "Not unless it means she was killed in the

mountains, where there might be deer hairs on the ground."

He shook his head. "I suppose it's possible, but why would she pick up deer hairs only in the wounds, and not on her clothing or other parts of her body?"

"The hairs are bound to figure in somehow, sooner or later," Frank said. "It's just too weird otherwise. We'll keep thinking it over."

"I'll do the same," Carlos said, standing up. "Thanks for the coffee. I'd better get going."

When Frank came back after seeing Carlos out, he leaned over and kissed me. "Maybe Pete and Rachel will be late this morning," he murmured into my ear. The doorbell rang. I was getting ready to disconnect it.

"See you after work, Frank."

"Count on it," he said, moving to answer the door.

The boys left for work, and I moved back into the kitchen with Rachel. I set the table while she cooked; I hadn't gotten around to one-handed breakfast-cooking yet. She was making a frittata, an Italian-style omelet.

"Sweatpants," she observed. "We should have thought of that sooner. Those look a little big on you."

"They're Frank's. I'm afraid this is the second pair that will have the elastic around one ankle stretched out."

"I don't think he'll mind." She smiled. "You seem full of energy today."

"I'm feeling better. I think a lot of it is mental."

She divided up the frittata and we dug in. I was chasing my first bite around the plate with my fork when she said, "How do you mean, mental?"

"Oh, I guess yesterday was a turning point for me." I managed to get the bite into my mouth. Rachel and Lydia were going to have me bursting my casts from weight gain. The frittata was great. *"Squisita!"* I told her.

She grinned. "Terrific! Not only do you like it, you like it in Italian. So tell me about yesterday."

I told her, leaving out details concerning the hours alone with Frank after sailing and after Cassie left. I told her about my decision to get out and about a little more.

"Sounds good to me. You want to go for a ride some-where today?"

"If you don't mind, I'd love it."

"I know—we'll go clothes shopping."

I looked at her doubtfully.

"For sweatpants and other things that would be easy for you to wear."

I thought of being in a store, around that many people, looking in mirrors at myself.

"On the other hand—" she began, seeing my brows fur-row, but I cut her off.

"No, Rachel, you're right. And I'll have you along for company, so I know I'll enjoy it."

We finished breakfast, and I did what I could to help clean up. The phone rang. It was Frank.

"Bad news, I'm afraid," he said.

"No search warrant."

"No warrant. I'm really sorry, Irene. I can't get anybody to touch it. I thought Sloane would see himself as a lame duck and go for broke."

Sloane had been appointed as acting D.A. when we lost our last one. His term would be over in January, but appar-ently it didn't make him any braver.

"Thanks for trying, Frank. I guess I was expecting things to go this way. Sounds like Gannet is safe."

"Try not to let it get you down, okay?"

"I won't. Rachel is taking me shopping today. I'm going to get some sweatpants of my own."

"I don't know, you looked pretty good in the pair you were wearing this morning. But have fun. Be careful. I'll see you tonight."

I hung up the phone and felt a surge of frustration and anger.

"You look like you need to punch somebody. What's going on?" Rachel asked.

"Apparently, Mr. Gannet is beyond reach. Frank says the D.A. won't go for a search warrant."

She studied me for a moment. "There's nothing worse than being fairly certain someone is guilty and not being able to nail them. Sorry, Irene."

"I guess I'll just have to put it out of my mind. Shall we go?"

But before we could leave, the phone rang again. It was Jacob.

"You remember Zoe—the lady at Rhiannon?" he asked.

"Yes."

"Well, I went in there the other day to give her some of Sammy's things. Mrs. Riley gave them to me to give to Sammy's parents, but I didn't think they would want the witch stuff. Anyway, I was talking to Zoe about Sammy and about you, and she said she'd like to talk to you. I've got her phone number if you want it."

"Thanks." I wrote the number down.

"She's kind of goofy, but she's nice."

"You probably tell people the same thing about me."

"No, I don't," he said, taking me far too seriously. "I mean, I don't tell them you're goofy."

"Well, thanks again, Jacob. Come by and visit sometime soon."

We hung up and I had a smile on my face.

"He's a good kid," Rachel said.

"That he is," I said, feeling my spirits rise a little. I dialed the number for Zoe.

"Rhiannon."

"Hi, Zoe. Irene. Jacob said you wanted to talk to me."

"Oh, Irene, yes! I have something for you."

"What?"

"Oh, let it be a surprise. A little gift from me to you."

That in itself surprised me, but I said, "I'll be coming that way a little later on. Maybe I can talk my ride into stopping by."

"Wonderful! And don't let that Leo's pride of yours keep you away."

Rachel was willing to stop by Rhiannon, but we decided to go shopping first. My orthopedist had given me a cane, and I took it along, not knowing how much walking I'd do. I seldom used it, since it tied up my only free hand.

We went to a store called Nobody Out. It's in a shopping district in downtown Las Piernas, where the sidewalks tend to be fairly crowded, so there were plenty of eyes on me. Rachel parked her rental car as close to the store as she could manage, about a block away. I found out that there was actually a certain amount of amusement to be had in watching people react to me. Wide-eyed and slack-jawed faces are fairly comical. I couldn't move very quickly, even using the cane, but I only got jostled once. After that, Rachel managed to block for me.

By the time we got to the store, I had worked off some of the disappointment I had been feeling about Gannet. I felt better. I felt a little wistful, too, since this was where I had bought my running shoes, and running was not going to be in the plan for some time yet. One more ability you will have greater appreciation for after it is returned to you, I told myself.

I had chosen to go to Nobody Out because I buy most of my sports clothes there, and that proved to be of help. Helen, a college student who works there part-time, knows me fairly well, and didn't fuss over the injuries.

"You ski into a tree, Irene?" she asked lightly.

"No, but that's a good story to have on hand."

When I didn't offer any further explanation, she said, "What can I do for you?"

I gave her an idea of what kinds of things were easiest to put on and take off. She went to work, and Rachel looked like a pack animal by the time we left.

As we were walking and hobbling back to the car, something made me turn around—a sensation of being watched.

A black limousine was pulling up alongside us.

I let the cane clatter to the sidewalk and grabbed on to Rachel so hard she dropped the packages. As she saw what had startled me, she said softly but firmly, "I'm here, Irene. I'll protect you. We're out on the street in broad daylight with people everywhere. He can't do anything to you."

I looked at her. She had left the packages on the ground and had taken a no-nonsense stance next to me. She looked so strong and determined that I relaxed a little.

I watched our mirrored reflections roll down as a rear

window was lowered. A tall, silver-haired man looked out at us and smiled. Under other circumstances, I would have said he was dignified and handsome, looking like a pillar of the community. But that same smile could have been seen on the face that led Little Red Riding Hood to say, "My, but what big teeth you have, Grandma."

"How nice to see you out and about, Miss Kelly," he said. "I'm Malcolm Gannet."

"I know," I managed. Please don't let him see how scared I am, I thought.

"No need to be frightened, Miss Kelly."

Well, shit. But I grew angry, so my prayer was answered. "What exactly do you want, Mr. Gannet?"

"I wondered the same about you, Miss Kelly. Remarkable reports have reached my ears. Your friend—well, really more than a friend, isn't he? Your lover? Your—"

"Say what you have to say," Rachel said in a low, commanding voice.

He looked over at her. "Miss Giocopazzi, isn't it? *Che piacere.*"

"So you've been to Berlitz. Glad one of us finds it a pleasure. Now, why don't you leave Miss Kelly alone?"

"I wonder why Miss Kelly won't leave *me* alone? Really, Miss Kelly. A search warrant? You wouldn't have found anything on the *Long Shot.* I guarantee it." That hungry wolf look again.

I said nothing.

"No use bothering by now, is there?" Rachel said. "I imagine you've made sure everything is just shipshape."

"Tell me, Miss Giocopazzi, how do you find time to act as nursemaid and chauffeur to Miss Kelly? Perhaps Detective Baird is less than fascinating company?"

Rachel's smile was cold enough to skate on. "You can find trouble without begging so hard for it."

"Miss Kelly—" he began, attempting to ignore Rachel.

"Leave Miss Kelly alone," she interrupted. "Go on home. I'll even give you something to look up in your Italian dictionary: *Va' a fare una bella cacata! Ti sentirai meglio.*"

She turned to pick up the packages, and not wanting to be left staring at him, I turned to help her.

I heard him mutter something to our backs, then the car drove off. I was trembling. I collected the cane from where I had dropped it. Straightening, I fought off the urge to cry.

"Irene. Don't let him get to you. He's just trying to scare you."

"I wasn't one-tenth as scared as I would have been if you weren't here. Thanks for sticking up for me." We slowly made our way to her car. "By the way, what was that last thing you said to him in Italian?"

She laughed. "I told him, 'Take a good shit, you'll feel better.' "

I gave her directions to Rhiannon. When we pulled up in front of the shop, Rachel looked at me with wide eyes.

"You're going in there?"

"Want to come along?"

"And have some old *strega* put the *malocchio* on me?" She held up her index and little finger on one hand like horns and spat three times between them.

I laughed and made my way into the store. The idea of Zoe putting an evil eye on someone amused me to no end.

"Zoe, do you do hexes?" I asked by way of greeting. I found I was beginning to enjoy the spicy smell of the shop.

"Hello, Irene! As a general rule, no. The main tenet of Wicca is 'Harm no one and do as thou wilt.' Hexes are not to be taken lightly." She had her back to me and was spreading some powder on the window sills of the shop. She turned and saw me, and took in my injuries with a quick glance. "You have a very strong spirit, Irene, which has served you well. I'm sorry you were hurt."

"I'm healing," I said. "What are you doing?"

"Oh," she said, smiling. "Putting out protection powder—an ancient herbal recipe for protection from thieves."

"Have you had problems with break-ins?"

"No, but I dreamed that someone broke in and stole an athalme."

I searched my memory. "A knife?"

"A ritual knife. Come into the back, I'll show you."

Setting the cane aside, I followed her through the narrow aisles, dodging boxes of herbs yet unpacked. She talked as we made our way. "There are four elements: air, earth, water, and fire. The athalme represents the air element. It is used to separate sacred ground from the rest."

"Separate it?"

"The athalme is used to draw a circle on the ground in an unbroken manner. It is never used to cut anything. Another knife is needed for cutting herbs and so on."

We came to a glass case filled with knives. Most had long, black handles. Zoe explained that most athalmes were black-handled. I glanced over some white-handled knives, and then my eyes came to rest on something that made me stand stock-still.

A knife with an animal foot on its handle.

"Oh, you've noticed the deer-foot knife," she said, seeming embarrassed. "I know, I should get it out of here. Maybe that's what the dream was about."

"Deer-foot?"

"Someone convinced me that some witches liked the representation of the Goddess in the hoof. I had four of them. This is the only one that's left, and I don't think I like it. In fact, I didn't like the auras of the men who purchased the other three."

"Were the others purchased all at the same time? By two brothers?"

She looked at me and said, "Yes, I suppose they could have been brothers, though I'm not sure. But they were here at the same time and bought the knives together."

I described Devon and Raney.

"Yes, that sounds like them. How did you know they were the ones who bought the knives?"

I hesitated. I knew she had been fond of Sammy. I didn't want Zoe to know that one of the knives might have been used to kill her. "I'm not sure. Just a feeling that it was something they might do. They're the ones who did this to me. Well, most of it."

She sensed my mood change and said, "Well, I told you

I had a little something for you." She pulled two stones out of her pocket. "I hope you will accept these with an open mind."

One was oblong and dark green, roughly the diameter of a pencil, a little less than two inches long. The other, nearly the diameter of a dime, was rounded and transparent, a light purple color. "Jade and amethyst," she said, as I took them from her. "Jacob tells me that you have trouble sleeping. The amethyst has long been regarded as able to cure insomnia, relieve pain and tension, even to give prophetic dreams. The ancients believed that jade gives health and long life, accurate judgment, and protection from nightmares. I want you to have these."

Doubt as I might that two little stones could do all that, the kindness of the gesture was not lost on me. "Thank you, Zoe. I'll give them a try."

"I'll miss Sammy," she said softly. "She was a bright and eager student of Wicca. She seemed happy just to come in here and ask questions about herbs and spells and charms. I enjoyed her company. May she sleep in bliss until she returns. Blessed be."

We both stood for a while, thinking our own thoughts. I rolled the stones over in my hand.

"Zoe," I said, "I'd like to buy that last knife."

She gave a start, and stared at me. But then she said, "Of course." She unlocked the case and gave me the knife. It was in a leather sheath and had a brass hilt on it. The fur on the handle was soft and the cloven black hoof on the end was hard and shiny. I couldn't unsheathe it with one hand, so she drew it out for me. The blade was about five inches long and had a blood groove in it. It looked mean enough, all right. I thought of a similar knife cutting out Sammy's heart, and felt sick.

Zoe sheathed the knife again and said, "Be very careful, Irene."

I forced a smile and reached into my pocket. I dropped the stones into it and pulled out the money to pay for the knife.

"No, take it," Zoe said.

I shook my head. "I'll pay for it. I don't want the protection powder working against me as a thief."

She smiled and took the cash. She gave me my change and put the knife in a bag. I gathered up my cane, then thanked her for the stones and told her I'd let her know if they worked for me.

Outside, Rachel was looking worried, and I felt bad about spending so much time inside the store. "What's in the bag?" she asked.

"Bambi's right foot," I said.

She made a face of pure disgust.

I reached into my pocket and held on to the stones.

| Thirty-five

As soon as we were back home, Rachel called Frank to let him know what had happened. He was furious with Gannet, but there wasn't much any of us could do about it.

As the afternoon wore on, I found myself fumbling with the stones in my pockets. It had an odd meditative effect, reminding me somewhat of how it used to feel to handle rosary beads, something I hadn't done in years. I was able to think things through a little more calmly.

I realized that Gannet would not be trying to intimidate me unless he thought I could in some way connect him to the murders. If he felt safe, he wouldn't have risked bullying me, especially not out on the streets of downtown Las Piernas. I couldn't figure out exactly what it was I was supposed to know, but it was clear that he was convinced I could cause him trouble. I mentally replayed the conversations I had overheard in the mountains, all to no avail.

Lydia relieved Rachel from Kelly-duty at about six o'clock that evening. She noticed I was feeling edgy, and so

I told her about the events of the afternoon. Since the day I told Jack what had happened in the mountains, I had found it easier to tell other friends about it, so Lydia knew why being caught out on the street with Gannet was upsetting to me. She had some novel ideas about fitting punishments for Mr. Gannet. Italians, I was reminded, had coined the term "vendetta." Still, as time passed without my being able to determine what Gannet was after, my nervousness increased.

We called out for a pizza, each drinking a glass of red wine while we waited for it. Jack stopped by and asked me if I wanted to go sailing with him late the next afternoon, to try to catch the sunset. I readily agreed. He left, we had a second glass of wine, and the pizza arrived. I was making slow progress through my first piece when Lydia suddenly said, "What if it isn't Gannet?"

"After the way he acted today?"

"There could be other reasons for that, Irene."

"Such as?"

"You're a reporter. It happens all the time—I know this isn't the first time someone has tried to intimidate you. Maybe he fears that you'll harm his reputation, write some story about him that will cause him to loose his standing in the community."

"I don't believe he's really worried about that."

"Sure he is. Or at least, he could be. He's a businessman. More than that—a developer. He depends on people in City Hall to cooperate with permits and zoning regulations and hand over all sorts of other approvals. If you wrote something implicating him in a murder investigation—especially this one, with Satanism being hinted at—you know no one on the City Council would go anywhere near him."

"He's probably got a certificate of ownership for every vote he needs on the council," I said.

"Cynic."

"Realist."

"Even if you're right, you've covered politics long enough to know that buying politicians never comes with a money-back guarantee. Gannet can't be that sure of their support. Abandoning him might mean some of them would have to scramble for funds from somewhere else, but that's

not as bad as being linked to a homicidal Satanist. Counter-
acting that kind of bad press is very expensive."

"Okay, suppose you're right. He doesn't want a story to
appear. That doesn't mean he isn't guilty."

"No, but it doesn't mean he is, either."

"I don't know, Lydia. I'm not in any shape to write anything up. Why would he be worried, when I'm not even
back at the newspaper?"

"You said he knew about the warrant?"

"Yes. He has highly placed friends, all right."

"Well, don't you see? You're already causing him to
call in his markers, just to keep any possible link with
these murder cases quiet. Even if he has nothing to hide,
he probably can't afford the notoriety an investigation
would cause."

I had lost interest in the pizza.

"Look, Irene, you could be right. But I'm just trying to
get you to keep an open mind about it."

"Maybe you're right. If it's not Gannet, I don't have any
idea of who else it might be. Maybe that's why I was so
anxious to have Frank pursue him—I don't have anyone
else in mind."

"You don't?"

Something about the way she said it caught my attention. "Am I missing something?"

She shrugged. "Ignoring someone, maybe."

"Who?"

"Jack."

"No way."

She didn't say anything, just went back to her pizza.

"Lydia, you can't say something like that and then just
go on eating. Jack *saved* my life, remember?"

"Did he? Or did he shut Paul up before he could tell
you who put him up to killing his grandmother?"

"Jesus Christ, Lydia! That is an incredibly cruel thing to
say."

"Forget it," she said, shoving her pizza away.

"Listen, I know he looks frightening, but he's really a
very gentle person. Every time I've felt down lately, Jack

has been able to cheer me up. He's smart and funny and—"

"Forget it!" she said again, much more sharply.

There was an awful silence. She started to stand up, but I reached over and took hold of her arm.

"No, wait—don't go. I'm sorry, Lydia." She sat back down. I shook my head. "Lately I seem to just steamroll over other people's feelings without thinking. If it's any comfort, you're not the only one I've done this to. Ask Frank. He's put up with a lot."

"I'm sorry too. I forget that you haven't really had time to deal with any of this yet. It's only been a couple of weeks. I never should have said anything about Jack, even introduced a worry about him. You're scared enough as it is. I'm certain Frank would never leave you here alone with someone who couldn't be trusted."

"Let's forget the whole thing. You're probably right about Gannet. And I'm sure that if you get to know Jack, you'll like him as much as Frank and I do. There could be any number of other people interested in Mrs. Fremont's land. I'm just not able to research that right now."

We settled into safer topics, primarily newsroom gossip. Sitting at the City Desk at the *Express,* Lydia had the best seat in the house for gathering it. We then went on to Catholic school memories, which have provided an unfailing distraction for both of us in times of trouble over the years. There was, for example, our running disagreement on how many days suspension I served for barricading Sister Mary Elizabeth in the school library in eighth grade.

Frank got home at about nine o'clock, and Lydia left. He looked tired. He took off his shoes, loosened his tie, and plopped down on the couch. I mixed a scotch and water for him; he appreciated the effort. As he drank it, I showed him the knife, and explained that Devon and Raney had bought the other three.

"So that's where the deer hair came from," he said, studying it. "I'll have to show it to Carlos. Of course, any number of these knives may be available at other places in town, but given what Zoe told you and what you heard

Devon and Raney say, I'd assume we now have some idea
of what the murder weapon looked like."

"If we found Paul's knife, could we prove anything
against Gannet?"

"I don't know. Carlos could run DNA tests on the blood
on the knife to see if it matched Gannet's. If it did, it
would be up to the D.A. to decide if that would help make
a case against him."

"The same D.A. who apparently decided to tell Gannet
you were seeking a search warrant?"

"We don't know that it was the D.A.'s office that gave
us away. To be perfectly honest, I doubt we could get
more than an accessory charge out of any of this, and a
good defense lawyer would be able to get him off without
a lot of effort." He paused, then said, "You're scared of
him, aren't you?"

"He knows who we are and where we live; he knows
our friends—he even knew Rachel spoke Italian. Just this
morning you asked about getting a search warrant, and he
must have learned about your request within minutes. He
found me out on the streets of downtown Las Piernas,
when only you and Rachel knew we were going shopping
at all, and when I was the only one who knew what store
we were going to, so someone must have been following
us. Yes, I'm afraid."

He was quiet.

"I'm afraid," I went on, "but I also realize that if he's
putting that much effort into trying to make us back off,
he's more afraid than I am."

"He's also unpredictable. And very possibly arranged
everything that happened to you." Hearing the anger in his
voice, I began to hope he never ran into Gannet on his
own; if he did, he was the one who was going to need a
good defense lawyer.

I had another nightmare that night, a real screamer. I woke
up to find Frank looking more concerned than usual.

"Jesus, Irene, are you all right?"

I nodded. "Just the strain of the day, I suppose."

"I swear I'm going to get a restraining order put on

Gannet. You haven't had a nightmare this bad since you first came home."

We settled back into bed, and he turned out the light.

"Frank?"

"Hmm."

"Who's coming over tomorrow, while you're at work?"

"Jack. The guy's been great. Don't know what we'd do without him." He felt me shiver. "Are you cold?"

"A little," I said snuggling closer. It wasn't the truth, but I couldn't bring myself to tell him who had been chasing me in my dreams.

Jack arrived just after Pete stopped by to ride into work with Frank the next day. By light of day, the dream fears receded and had no hold on me. Jack was no monster, he was a concerned friend. I went back to bed and caught up on my sleep, not waking up again until the early afternoon. But once I was awake, I felt restless.

Jack was sitting on the couch, reading more verses of Ovid's *Metamorphoses*. He looked up from it and assessed my mood in a moment. "Frank called to say he was working late again," he said. "I told him I might take you sailing if you were still up for it. Maybe Lydia and Guy would like to come along, too. What do you say?"

"Sure," I said, feeling certain that Lydia would refuse the last minute invitation; she probably wouldn't want to be out on the ocean with a man she thought to be a murderer. But when I called her, she readily accepted the offer, saying that she'd meet us at the marina coffeeshop.

A few minutes later, she called back to say Guy could make it as well. I detected a note of relief in her voice when she made that announcement. I supposed the company of a former professional hockey defenseman made her feel safer. I began to wonder if she had decided to go along because she thought I might be in danger from Jack.

Later that afternoon, as he helped me put on a sweater and shoe in preparation for our outing, Jack said, "Oh, I forgot to tell you—Frank said Bredloe had approved surveillance of Malcolm Gannet."

"What made Bredloe change his mind?"

"I asked Frank the same thing," Jack said. "He told me it was a combination of things. Bredloe was angry that there was some kind of leak of information between his office and the D.A. He was also unhappy to hear about what happened downtown yesterday. I guess that did it."

Cody made a pain of himself by streaking past us when we went out the door. "Get back here!" I yelled after him, an utterly useless command to give the willful little bugger. He stood in the middle of the street, staring back at me and twitching his tail, as if to say, "Come on, Gimpy, just try to catch me."

"Jack?" I pleaded.

Jack took one step toward him and he scurried beneath a cable TV van across the street. He crouched there, watching Jack. I could swear the cat was smirking.

"I can't wait for Frank to get around to installing that cat door," Jack said. "Are you sure you want Cody inside?"

"His dinner's in there."

Jack laughed. "He'll be all right, then. It wouldn't hurt Cody to miss a meal. But I'll put a water dish out for him."

The moment Jack opened the front door, of course, Cody hauled his gray buns back through it in a four-legged flash. No use starving if we weren't up for playing hide-and-seek with him. He had achieved one of his standing goals, to make me late whenever possible. Jack took it all in stride. He locked the front door and helped me out to the car.

We traveled at a snail's pace through late afternoon traffic until we made the turnoff down to the marina, which was virtually deserted. I looked for Lydia's car but didn't see it; Guy's Mercedes wasn't there either. "Don't worry about it," Jack said, reading my thoughts. "We'll just have a cup of coffee while we wait for them."

The moment we entered the small coffee shop, a large man I took to be the manager came out from behind the counter. "Hey, Jack! Long time no see! Got a message for you."

"What's up, Harry?" Jack asked.

Harry fumbled in the pocket of his shirt for a moment

and then put on a pair of bifocals. "Let's see. Lydia and Gee can't make it."

"Guy," I said. "He's French Canadian, so it rhymes with 'key'."

Harry scowled at me over the bifocals, then turned back to Jack. "I'll let you get back to your date with the professor here."

"Irene's a reporter," Jack said. Judging by Harry's deepening scowl, being a reporter put me on a par with attorneys.

"We miss you around here, Jack," Harry said, turning his back on us. "Drop by again sometime."

Jack grinned at me and said, "Ignore him. Harry was born grumpy."

"And never seen any reason to change my outlook," Harry called out, as Jack held the door open for me.

"We'd better get going if we want to catch the sunset," Jack said.

I tried not to make too much of "Gee" and Lydia's cancellation, and followed Jack outside.

On board the *Pandora,* Jack had to do almost all of the work, but he didn't seem to mind. He set the engine on idle, and I thought we would motor out, but we made our way out of the marina completely under sail. "Why did you start the engine if you weren't going to use it?" I asked when he turned it off again.

"Oh, just a precaution. The wind or the current might have shifted while we were leaving the dock."

A steady wind picked up off the starboard, and we managed to get out past the breakwater just as the sun was starting to set. The sunset was a glorious combination of colors and clouds and shafts of sunlight, making up what Lydia and I used to call "a religious sky"—a term I no doubt remembered as a result of our previous night's discussion.

Thinking of Lydia, I began to wonder if I had let my love of the ocean overcome my common sense. Maybe this was just as stupid as going into the field that night. Maybe the message Harry the Grump gave us was as phony as the one at the hotel. Maybe Jack didn't really have leukemia, and this was all a plan to—

"Irene? Is something troubing you?"

I looked up at him, startled right out of my maybes.

"What's wrong?" he asked. "Do you want me to head back in?"

Concerned. Not threatening, concerned. Everything in his manner and his voice said so. I exhaled. "I'm fine, Jack. Just letting my imagination run wild."

"You want to talk about it?"

I laughed. "Not this time, but thanks."

He didn't press me for more. He was looking out over the water, toward the horizon. With his scars, tattoos, and earring, he could have been a pirate. The pirate was suddenly grinning to himself.

"What's so funny?" I asked.

"Oh, I was just thinking about Cody's little stunt as we were leaving."

I shook my head, picturing the imp crouched under the van. Suddenly, something tugged at my memory. "Jack? Remember when we left the house on Sunday, the first time we went sailing?"

"Yes, why?"

"That van was there. On a Sunday. As far as I know, General Systems Cable won't come out on weekends, and they won't come by after five. Frank had them install cable at his house at the beginning of October, so that I could watch the Kings' games when we were there. It was a real hassle, because at the time, we were both working late. But this van was there after six o'clock yesterday, when Lydia arrived, and it was there again today."

"I don't remember seeing it there on Sunday. Are you sure you didn't see it when you went out with Rachel?"

I hesitated. "I don't know. Maybe I saw it both times."

"Maybe one of our neighbors works for the cable company now. Or maybe the van arrived before five, but they were still working when she got there."

"Maybe. But that must be one hellacious installation if they're back today."

"Mention it to Frank. He may remember about Sunday. In the meantime, he's got a tail on Gannet. You're out on the ocean, trying to enjoy a sunset. Relax."

I took a deep breath and tried to do just that. We had been sailing for a little less than an hour, and I was just starting to enjoy myself. The wind picked up as the sky darkened. Jack prepared to come about and head back into the marina, beginning a port tack. I decided that I was being paranoid about the van.

Two seconds later, there was a sickening screech of metal. We both watched the aluminum mast fold at the lower shrouds, and topple to the starboard side.

Thirty-six

The top of the mast, sails, and lines were swinging wildly around the deck. I barely managed to duck in time to keep my head from being hit by the boom. "Damn," I heard Jack mutter, but otherwise he remained remarkably calm. He hurriedly secured the boom.

"Can we still use the engine to go back in?" I asked.

"Not yet," he said. "I've got to secure all the lines first. Otherwise, we might wrap one in the propeller."

I was reassured by the way he moved about the deck: calm, certain of his actions. When the lines were secured, he came back and tried the engine, but he couldn't get it to start.

That earned another "damn," but he quickly moved toward the mast. "Can you get below on your own?" he asked, as he made his way forward.

I nodded, trying not to panic.

"Do you know how to use a radio? How to call the Coast Guard? Call PAN-PAN. There are instructions near the radio if you don't know how."

"I know how," I said, thinking through the sequence for

a distress call. Calling PAN-PAN would signal an urgent but not life-threatening problem. One step below a Mayday.

"Good. I've got to try to get the mast secured before it tears the boat apart." He attached a harness to himself, of the type that prevents a sailor from being lost overboard in a storm. Seeing my worried look, he added, "We'll be okay."

I clumsily made my way down the companionway steps, hearing Jack struggle with the mast. In the shadowy interior of the cabin, I found the radio and hit the power switch. It glowed to life. I switched to channel 16, the international distress and calling channel. I lifted the mike. Jack had printed the *Pandora*'s call sign on the instructions he kept near the radio. I pressed the mike button, saying "PAN-PAN," and turned to read off our identification. It was then that I realized that no other vessel would hear me. The mike cord had pulled away from radio.

Above me, Jack cried, "Got it!"

"Jack," I yelled up, "the radio's broken."

There was no immediate answer, but then I saw him making his way below. Even in the dimming light, I could see his face was set in a frown. "We dismasted because someone pulled the clevis pin on the upper shrouds on the port side and replaced it with a wooden dowel. It was only a matter of getting enough wind in the sails when we made the port tack."

I didn't really know enough about sailing to understand exactly what he was saying, but I managed to grasp the implication. "So it didn't happen accidentally?"

"No. It's part of the standing rigging. Someone intentionally changed it."

"What the hell does he want with me?" I said frantically. There was no need to explain who I meant.

"I don't know, Irene. To scare you, I suppose. So the only way we can beat this is to stay calm. We're not in as much danger as it looks. If I can't get the engine running, I'll try to jury rig the mast. Even if that doesn't work, we're not all that far off shore, and we'll be seen. I've got flares and other ways to signal another boat."

I nodded. "Let me know what I can do to help." I put

my good hand in my pocket and found my little stones. Anything to calm myself.

"You're safest down here for now. I only have the one harness on board, and it's getting dark. If we lurched and you went into the water with those casts, I'm not sure I could get you back on board without hurting you." As he spoke, he reached for a flashlight and turned it on. I felt an inordinate sense of relief when it worked. "They forgot to steal my flashlight battery," he said with a grin.

He tried to start the engine again. This time, it worked, but we didn't seem to be moving much.

He came back down and turned the cabin lights on.

"What's wrong?" I asked.

"I'll have to take a look. I can't get it to do much more than idle," he said, then made his way behind the ladder, near the engine. He moved the cover off the engine, flashing the beam of light over it. "They jammed the throttle linkage," he said after a moment. He moved out from behind the ladder and over to a low compartment, kneeling to open it, and then pulled out a padlocked foot locker. He took a set of keys out of his pocket and used one to open the lock. "I learned a few things before I got kicked out of the Boy Scouts. I've got spares for almost everything—no spare mast, I'm afraid—I do have the tools and spares we'll need to fix the engine."

As he opened the locker, his light-hearted manner was suddenly lost. His eyes widened, as if in shock. "Stole your tools?" I asked, looking over his shoulder.

But he just shook his head and rocked back on his heels, gingerly lifting a large, lumpy manilla envelope that sat on top of the other contents. In black felt pen, across the front of it, was scrawled, "Dad—Open only in the event of my death or disappearance."

"Oh God," he said hoarsely. He pinched the bridge of his nose and took a deep breath, as if trying to will himself not to lose his self-control. He shook his head again, then looked up at me and handed me the envelope. "Hold that for me, please." I took it from him, and hearing an object slide within it, was almost positive that we had just found the missing knife.

Jack, although obviously still shaken, went to work on the engine. After a few moments, he corrected the problem with the throttle linkage.

"That should do it," he said. "provided they haven't done some other damage."

"You think we'll be able to make it back in, then?"

Before he could answer, we heard the sound of an approaching powerboat. He gave me a tentative smile and hurried to the companionway. "They may have seen the mast and come over to help."

The powerboat drew closer. I felt the hair along my neck rise.

"Jack!" I called, but it was too late, he was already on deck.

I heard Malcolm Gannet's voice call, "Having a little trouble, Mr. Fremont?"

| Thirty-seven

"Stay where you are, Mr. Fremont," I heard Gannet say. "It would be inconvenient to shoot you now, but I'm not entirely opposed to the idea."

Looking desperately around me for a hiding place for the envelope, I moved beneath the ladder and wedged it between the engine cover and the hull.

Above me, I heard the sounds of two men boarding. Gannet had apparently brought help. Thinking over what Murray had told me of him, it made sense—he had said that Gannet couldn't swim and didn't know how to sail. I moved away from the engine and sat at the small table near the galley.

"Come on up from there, Miss Kelly," Gannet called.

"I can't," I called back. "I can't make it up the ladder

steps on my own." It was a lie, but I figured that if I could separate him from his assistant, we'd stand a better chance of evening the odds.

"Don't let him out of your sight, Stevens," Gannet said, apparently to the other man. "Mr. Fremont here is resourceful, as you can see by the fact that he has already managed to repair the engine. If he makes so much as a single move, kill him."

"Look Mr. Gannet," the other man said, "we were in a powerboat. We would have caught up to them no matter how fast he fixed his sailboat engine. His engine's not designed to—"

"—I don't need mariner's lessons at this point," Gannet said sharply. "That's why I pay you, Stevens—to mind the details for me. And right now, Mr. Fremont is the detail I'm paying you to mind."

I heard Gannet move toward the companionway. From the cabin lights, I could see his face as he loomed over the hatch. He wore an orange lifejacket over his dark blue sportshirt. His pants were white and neatly creased, and a jaunty white cap hid most of his gray hair. A picture of the gentleman yachtsman, offset only by the fact that he was pointing the barrel of a large gun at me. "Move to the bottom of the ladder, where I can see you better," he commanded.

I made a show of clumsily getting up and moving toward the ladder.

"Where is it?" he asked.

"Where is what?"

"Don't play games with me, Miss Kelly. I know exactly what you are up to. You plan to make that boyfriend of yours look like a hero in the police department. Oh, I understand that he needs all the help he can get—he's something of a burnout case, isn't he? An officer-involved shooting, assaulting another detective. Lord knows why they let him come back to work."

"Maybe because he knows how to track down people like you."

He laughed. "As I said, that's exactly the plan, isn't it? You hold on to the damning evidence—supposedly damning evidence—while Detective Harriman raises suspicions against me. Then, at the properly dramatic moment, you hand him Paul's confession and the knife. Detective Harriman is back to being the star of the Las Piernas Police Department."

I couldn't hide my reaction to the news that Paul had left more than the knife, but fortunately, Gannet mistook it.

"So I'm right. Save us all a great deal of trouble and tell me where it is."

"What makes you think I have it? Paul hated me."

"Don't waste my time! Paul made it quite clear to me that he desired you, to such an extreme that he saved you for himself. Wouldn't let Devon or Raney have a go at you. The mere mention of your name brought a knowing smile to his lips. And he wore that same smile when I asked him who had the knife and the confession. 'The woman who caused all the trouble in the first place,' he said. It doesn't take a genius to figure out that he was talking about you. Now, where is it?"

The woman who caused all the trouble. Pandora. The only thing we had in common was that our curiosity had been ill-rewarded. Gannet apparently hadn't made the connection to the boat's namesake. He was watching me with growing impatience.

"Don't you think Frank is going to wonder what has happened to us?" I said, trying to stall. "He has a tail on you, Gannet. You're the first person he'll suspect if anything happens to me."

Gannet laughed. "Thanks to a little electronic eavesdropping, I've known exactly what the two of you are up to. That's how we knew to prepare the *Pandora* for your little excursion this evening. Let Detective Harriman suspect whatever he wants to suspect. As you know, Miss Kelly, a suspicion is only as good as far as it goes. And the people who are following me believe I am still aboard the *Long Shot*. They'll actually provide an alibi for me. Meanwhile, the Pacific makes a magnificent rug, and you and Mr. Fremont are about to be swept under it."

"Did you get rid of that bloodstained blanket the same way?"

"Ah, Miss Kelly, you'll never know, will you?"

"We're not that far offshore. Don't you worry that some passing traffic from Catalina will see us? Or the Coast Guard?"

Gannet sighed. "You continue to waste my time. I can see you won't allow us to do this the easy way, Miss Kelly." He stepped partway down the ladder, so that his head was just below the hatch.

"Don't touch her!" Jack said angrily.

Gannet laughed. "You're hardly in any position to be giving orders, skipper. Besides, I don't plan to rush things. I'll give you a little something to think about, Miss Kelly, before I spell out any of my plans for you and Mr. Fremont." He reached into his pocket, never taking his eyes—or the gun—off me. His fist was closed over something. He stood watching me for a moment, and I didn't like the look of anticipation in his eyes. He moved farther down the ladder, held his fist forward, then shook it. I heard a familiar rattling sound.

Dice.

I felt the sound in my thumb, in my shoulder, in five places on my back. It sounded exactly like fear.

He stepped off the ladder and moved toward me menacingly. My knees weakened and I stepped away from him. He took another step toward me, and sheer panic seized me. Trying to step away, I stumbled and fell backward with a bone-jarring thud. It hurt, but for an awful moment, I was too afraid he would shoot me to worry about anything else.

"You son of a bitch!" Jack was shouting.

Gannet turned away from me, glancing up through the hatch, and yelled, "No, Stevens! Not yet. We need him for the moment."

From where I lay, I could see my cane, wedged on the side of one of the bunks. I looked back at Gannet, wondering if I could manage, left-handed, to free it and crack him over the head with it. A ridiculous notion, given the fact that I was flat on my back and he was armed and well out of striking range.

"Hold perfectly still," he said coldly, apparently reading

my intent if not my exact plans. He took some rope, and standing over me, laughed again. "I see your previous injuries are going to make this easier." Gun still in hand, he clumsily tied my good foot to my cast, then set the gun well out of my reach, laying it aside to put his hands beneath my arms. He pulled me to a sitting position. I couldn't help but yelp at the bolt of pain that sent through my right shoulder.

"Irene!" I heard Jack call, frantic.

"I'm okay, Jack," I called back shakily.

With an iron grip, Gannet stretched my left hand in back of me. He tied my left wrist to the support for the table, so that I was sitting halfway beneath the table itself.

"There, a nice, firm square knot," Gannet said in a low voice. His face was close to mine and he stank of cigarettes and whiskey. Apparently he had needed something to bolster his courage before playing at buccaneer.

He stood up. "Just in case you manage to free yourself from your bonds, I'm locking you in here. And should you try to crawl up those steps, you should understand that I'll kill Mr. Fremont the moment I hear you rattle the hatch."

True to his word, he closed and locked the hatch. The air around me quickly grew stuffy, and once again I had to force myself not to panic. Even though the lights were still on in the *Pandora*'s cabin, I pictured myself in a small, dark room in the mountains. I could not abide being shut up in a small space. I closed my eyes and forced myself to calm down.

I heard the sounds of the anchor being raised, of someone leaving the *Pandora,* and then the roar of the powerboat, heading away from us. Before long, the cabin lights dimmed briefly as the diesel engine of the *Pandora* started as well. We were under way.

I discovered the knot tied on my ankle was a granny knot, not a square knot, and gradually, by straining my cast and foot against it, it slipped and gave way. I twisted myself around, scooting myself farther under the table, so that I faced my left wrist. Using my teeth, I found this granny knot easier to loosen. Murray was right. Gannet was no sailor.

I worked my way to my feet. I opened a porthole, putting my face to it, taking in deep breaths to further calm myself. Only then was I able to notice the disturbing view before me: we were slowly moving farther out to sea. Sailor or no, Gannet was right about one thing. If he took us far enough away from shore, the *Pandora* could be destroyed with few traces left behind. Our bodies might never be found. I shook off visions of helping little lobsters grow into big ones.

Somehow, I had to stop the engines, to at least keep us within range of the traffic between Catalina and the harbors along the coast. Taking my cane as a weapon if needed, I turned to make my way aft. I hooked the cane on the ladder and moved nearer the engine, which still lay uncovered.

The working quarters were tight, and maneuvering within them was made all the more awkward by my casts. But I had learned to be more adept with my left hand by then, so I wasn't impossibly clumsy. I managed to remove the bilge plate. I found a pair of vise grips in the toolbox, located the fuel line, and pinched it closed. I quickly rummaged through the toolbox again, found the biggest wrench I could handle with one hand, and awkwardly stood up. I stayed behind the ladder, keeping the wrench in hand, the cane nearby.

Some minutes passed, during which I began to doubt my handiwork. Just at the moment I was sure I needed to start loosening every single bolt I could lay the wrench on, the engine choked to a standstill. The sudden silence didn't last long.

"What the hell did you do?" Gannet shouted. I felt a wave of relief. I hadn't been sure which one of them had stayed aboard, and I suspected Stevens would have been much more likely to be capable of getting the boat back under way.

"I didn't do a damned thing, and you know it," Jack answered angrily. "You've been watching me the whole time."

"Try starting it again," Gannet said.

Jack dutifully pressed the starter button, to no avail.

"What's wrong with it?" Gannet's voice.

"I'll have to go below to find out. Maybe your man did more damage than you suspected."

"It's a trick!" Gannet hissed. "She's done something to the motor."

"I thought you said she was tied to the table. She couldn't reach the engine from there."

"Never mind. Go on down the ladder and fix it. Hurry up. I've got the gun on you, remember."

The hatch opened and Jack slowly stepped down the ladder, Gannet hesitating to follow him too closely. Without so much as a glance in my direction, Jack walked toward the table and bent low, blocking it from view from the ladder. "Irene!" he said, as if talking to me under the table. "Irene! Wake up!"

"What's going on?" Gannet yelled.

"I don't know—something's wrong! I can't wake her up!" Jack shouted, his voice frantic. The man deserved an Academy Award.

Gannet's curiosity brought him to the ladder. He came down one, two steps.

"Irene!" Jack said again.

Gannet took another step down. His head just cleared the hatch. I held my breath. I couldn't knock him out unless he came down another step. But he stayed where he was.

"Step away from her!" he said nervously.

Jack shook his head. "She's hurt." If Jack moved, Gannet would know he had been tricked. I made a decision, tucking the wrench into my sling.

"Step back!" Gannet shouted, motioning with the gun. As the gun swung away from Jack, I reached through the ladder and pulled with all my might on Gannet's shin. Surprised, he twisted toward Jack and fired the gun as he fell off the ladder. Jack and I both fell on him, pinning him to the floor. Jack wrestled the gun away from him before he could fire again.

"Jack!" I cried. Blood was staining his left sleeve.

"Flesh wound," he said calmly, as if it were nothing more than a mosquito bite. "He's as lousy at shooting as he is at everything else. Are you all right?"

I nodded.

"Let me up!" Gannet said, apparently not enjoying having my cast in his kidneys.

"You've got to be kidding," Jack said, reaching for the ropes. "Irene, hold the gun on him."

I laid the end of the barrel against Gannet's temple. His face was beet red with anger. Jack started by pulling Gannet's lifejacket off, causing the beet red color to go to a clammy white. "He can't swim," I said.

"Even if he could, he'd never make it to shore. Especially not just kicking." He tied Gannet's hands behind him. Judging from Gannet's grimace, Jack made better knots.

"Stevens will kill the both of you!" he growled.

"I doubt it," Jack said evenly, dragging Gannet to his feet. "It will take him a while to understand that we haven't met him as planned, and then to turn around and find us. I'll be ready for him when he arrives." He went to a duffel bag and pulled out a pair of binoculars, a first-aid kit, and a flare gun. He went above with these, then came back down.

He opened another compartment and pulled out a knife. There was a visible tension in him now, and a look in his eyes that made me suddenly aware of a side of Jack that I had not really seen, or which I had ignored, until now. A very dangerous side.

He came up behind Gannet and grabbed his chin, pulling Gannet's head back hard, holding it against his shoulder. He laid the edge of the knife up against Gannet's exposed neck. When he spoke, his voice was deadly cold. "The last time I used one of these," he said into Gannet's ear, "it was to kill my own son. *My own son,* Gannet. Don't imagine for a minute that I would hesitate to kill the man who put a lot of crazy ideas into that boy's head. As you no doubt pointed out to Paul, I'm dying. What have I got to lose? In fact, it's a miracle that I haven't slit you from your fucking neck down to your balls already."

Gannet whimpered.

"We understand one another?"

"Yes," Gannet croaked.

"Then go on up that ladder." Jack moved back a step

and grabbed Gannet by the collar, then forced him ahead, up the ladder.

"Can you make it up here?" Jack called to me, his voice gentle and coaxing.

"Yes," I answered, finding my own voice shaky all the same. I took the wrench out of my sling, and putting the safety on the gun, tucked it where the wrench had been. I worked my way up the ladder.

"You said you couldn't make it up the steps!" Gannet whined when he saw me.

"Shut the fuck up," Jack said. The cold voice. He turned to me. "You've still got the gun?" The gentle voice.

I nodded, pulling it out. Jack reached for it, took the safety off, and handed it back to me.

"If he moves one inch," Jack said calmly, "shoot him."

I nodded again.

He took out the flare gun and fired it. The flare boomed, then glowed to life, lighting up sea and sky, a solitary firework arcing above us. Even as the light of it faded, Jack prepared a second flare.

We heard a motor approaching, all of us knowing it was probably Stevens. Jack set the flare gun aside, stood up, stretched, and picked up the knife again, smiling reassuringly at me. I wasn't especially comforted. He walked over to Gannet, yanked him hard to his feet, and held the knife to Gannet's throat, just as he had below. Gannet started whimpering again.

"When Stevens gets closer, point the gun at him, Irene," Jack said easily.

Unaware that his boss was now a hostage, Stevens pulled alongside and shouted, "What the hell is wrong? Everyone on the damned coast probably saw that flare." I tried to keep my aim steady and level.

"Cut your engines," Jack shouted.

Stevens finally took in the situation. Still, he hesitated.

"For godsakes, do it!" Gannet screeched.

The engines were cut.

"Good," Jack said, as if praising a small child. "Now slowly take your gun from its holster and throw it overboard. Do it very carefully."

He reluctantly did as Jack told him.

"Fine. I'll give you three choices, Mr. Stevens. Choice number one: watch me slice Gannet's gullet from stem to stern, immediately after which, Miss Kelly will shoot you. Choice number two: I push Gannet into the water, we allow you to watch him drown, and then Miss Kelly shoots you. Choice number three: you use your radio to make a distress call for the *Pandora,* and Miss Kelly doesn't shoot you."

Not surprisingly, Stevens chose number three. But even before he had finished raising the mike, we heard a Coast Guard cutter rapidly approaching. They turned on a highpowered beam, bathing the deck of the *Pandora* in bright light. I'm sure we made quite a sight. As they drew nearer, I saw a worried guy in a suit looking down over the rail at us.

Even worried, Frank Harriman was a welcome sight.

| Epilogue

The end table wouldn't do. Like almost every other surface in Beatrice Harriman's household, it was cluttered with knickknacks and mementos. Photographs. Doilies. Sea shells. Ceramic frogs. Nature abhors a vacuum; so does Frank's mother. I couldn't find a place with enough free space to hold the fine bone china cup and saucer in my left hand.

Frank was sitting next to me on his mother's white, very soft sofa, listening to her animated telling of news of his old Bakersfield friends. He was drinking his coffee. Bea Harriman was drinking hers. I was watching mine grow cold.

Unable to use my right hand, I couldn't lift the cup off the saucer. I thought about trying to set the saucer on my lap, but thanks to the softness of the sofa, my lap was at about a forty-five-degree angle. I couldn't even stand up.

I could have interrupted Bea Harriman to ask for help, I suppose. That would have been the smart thing to do. But I had the distinct feeling that Bea Harriman didn't like me much. Frank had warned me that his mother had been disappointed when he broke up with Cecila, a girlfriend from Bakersfield; he said it would take her some time to get used to the idea of someone new.

Someone new? Frank had broken up with Cecila five years ago. I couldn't credit all of Bea Harriman's coolness toward me to something that had happened that long ago.

All the same, there was no use in complaining over every little thing, I told myself. It was Thanksgiving, and the list of things to be thankful for was a long one. I concentrated on that list as I looked over the photographs.

I decided that I was being too sensitive about Frank's mom, probably in part because I was still worn out from Tuesday's rescue at sea. It had been a long night.

The Coast Guard had been very efficient. Within moments, they had boarded the *Pandora,* taken Gannet and Stevens into custody, and treated Jack's wound. Although we had a brief moment to reassure one another when Frank first came on board, things got hectic after that.

Jack shrugged off any attempt I made to express gratitude, saying that he knew he had scared me but that it wouldn't do to have Gannet think he wasn't serious. He asked me what had become of the envelope from Paul, and went to look for it soon after his wound was bandaged.

The Coast Guard went to work on getting the *Pandora* and the powerboat back to the marina, and soon took all of us aboard the cutter. I thought Frank and I would have a chance to talk then, but as soon as we sat down, Jack walked over and quietly handed Frank the envelope from Paul. It was still sealed. Frank opened it carefully and found not only a bloodstained knife, but a signed statement which described Gannet's role in detail. As Jack and I read over Frank's shoulders, it was clear that Gannet had initiated the entire plan to murder Mrs. Fremont.

As we read the confession, I glanced at Jack now and

then, anxious about his reaction. There was nothing personally addressed to Jack beyond the words on the outside of the envelope; the confession itself was both brutally explicit and absolutely unsentimental. No remorse, no excuses. Simply a means to protect Paul from a double-cross by Gannet.

As we finished reading, Jack walked away from us, to stand leaning against a rail. Frank watched him for a moment, then went over to him. For the remainder of our time on the cutter, they spoke to one another in low voices. Without hearing what they were saying, I could still tell that Jack seemed more at ease as a result of the conversation. All Frank would say about it later was, "Jack just needs some time."

Slow remedy, time.

When we finally got home that evening, we were both talked out. We had been met at the dock by members of the press (which included Mark Baker) and the police (which included Pete and Lieutenant Carlson); answering their questions had drained the last of our energy.

From listening to Frank, Pete, and Carlson, I learned that the police had already discovered the real function of the cable-TV van not long after Jack and I had left to go sailing. Frank had thought over the list of things I had said Gannet knew about us. While he was sure Gannet must have also had a connection to someone from the department or the D.A.'s office, Frank decided that even a friend in Robbery-Homicide couldn't have told Gannet so much.

Pete, who can make a badger look like a creature that gives up too easily, talked the department expert on bugging devices into dropping everything he was working on, and checking out Frank's house. The man suspected the cable-TV van the minute he laid eyes on it. Its occupant wasn't able to drive off before Pete showed him his detective's shield and asked to see cable company identification in exchange. No I.D. Lots of listening devices.

Most of the other members of the department weren't too happy with Mr. Gannet at that point, including Carlson and Bredloe. Frank realized that our plans to go sailing had probably been reported to Gannet. When we were late getting back, Bredloe didn't hesitate to ask the Coast Guard if they would initiate a search for us. The cutter had just cleared the breakwater when they saw the flare.

It was almost six in the morning before we got to sleep on Wednesday, which ended up being something of a lost day. Bright and early—very early—Thanksgiving morning, we got ready for the three-hour drive to Bakersfield.

Frank had helped me into the Volvo and put our overnight bag in the trunk. When he packed the overnight bag, I almost backed out of the whole deal.

"We're staying overnight?"

He looked at me and said, "Sure, why not?"

"I didn't know you wanted to stay there overnight."

"Look, you're going to have a hard time coping with the car ride out there and the day's activities. If we try to drive back tonight, you'll be tired and sore as hell."

It made sense, of course.

"We're staying at Cassie's?" I said hopefully.

He shook his head. "All they could offer us is a couch. We'll stay at my mom's."

"She's expecting this?"

"Yes, I told her we would be staying overnight."

"What about Cody?"

"Jack is going to feed him."

I couldn't think up any other objections right at that moment. I was trying to let the whole idea sink in. Somewhere on the 405 Freeway, it sank all right.

"What if I have a nightmare?"

"I'll be there."

"What? Your mom is going to put us up in the same room?"

"I don't see why not. I've told her we're living together."

"I'll bet that went over big."

"Irene, we're both in our late thirties. We're not a couple of college kids trying to sneak into each other's dorm rooms. If she hassles us, we'll get a hotel room."

I sighed. "I don't know, Frank. Age might not have anything to do with it. I don't want your mom to think I'm corrupting you."

That brought out a big enough laugh to make us ride along those little lane-dividing bumps for a minute.

I was enjoying the photos, and had stopped thinking about the coffee. There was the usual plethora of grandchildren's images one might find in any proud grandmother's home. There were a few of Frank and Cassie. And on the closest end of the mantel, there was a wedding photo of Frank's parents.

She was beautiful. She was fine looking now, but what a knockout she was at—how old? She looked to be in her twenties. And next to her was the spitting image of Frank Harriman. Or rather, the man Frank was the spitting image of. I studied it a little more. No, there were subtle differences. His father was a little broader in build. His eyebrows were different, and maybe, slightly, his chin. Hair color a little lighter than Frank's? Hard to tell from a black-and-white portrait.

"Irene! Oh, Jesus, I'm sorry." Frank was looking at me, awash with guilt and taking the cup and saucer from me.

His mother drew in a sharp breath. "No need to use the Lord's name in vain, Franklin."

"Franklin? Franklin ignored her and started to hand the cup back to me. "No, it's cold. I'll get you a fresh cup." He got up and strode off into the kitchen, leaving me with his mother before I could protest.

"I'm sorry, Irene. It was thoughtless of me."

I mouthed a gracious response while wondering if I was being overly sensitive again, this time about something I thought I heard in her tone. Lack of sincerity? Couldn't be. Could it?

Frank returned with the coffee, bringing a cup without the saucer.

They soon went back to Bakersfield prattle and I went back to studying photos while enjoying the coffee. I found my eyes drawn again and again to a handsome photo of Frank and his dad. Both men were in uniform, the father's arm around the son, his pride in Frank fairly bursting from the photo.

"About twelve years ago?" Frank was saying to me.

"Pardon?"

"We met here about twelve years ago?"

"Yes. About then. Just after college."

"How could you ever leave Bakersfield?" his mother asked me.

"Las Piernas is my hometown, and I guess I've grown attached to it."

"Frank used to feel that way about Bakersfield."

"Something smells great," he said, changing the subject. "When are Mike and Cassie due to arrive?"

"Are you hungry? I'll fix you something."

He was watching me polish off the last of my coffee, and took the cup from me so that my hand would be free. He made room for it on an end table by shoving half a dozen gewgaws aside with a nonchalance that said he'd had practice at it.

"No, Mom. I'm not hungry. I just wondered when they would be here."

"Oh, about noon. Listen, would you be a dear and pick up a few things at the store for me?"

"Sure. What do you need?"

"I made a list." She went into the kitchen, and we held hands again. We were getting to be like a couple of teenagers, sneaking affection when Mom wasn't looking. She was in there for a while, and I realized she was on the phone with someone.

"Are you okay?" Frank asked.

"You already asked me that."

"Are you still okay?"

"Fine."

"Sorry to be so boring with all the talk of people you don't know. I'll be sure to bring up other topics of conversation when we get back from the store."

"I'm enjoying the photographs, actually."

He looked over at them. It was apparent that he had seen them so many times that they were now just part of the furnishings. He smiled.

"That's one of my favorites." He pointed to the one of him and his dad.

"Mine too. You look a lot like your dad."

"I wish you could have met him."

His mom came back in with the list, and we forgot to let go of our hands.

"Ready to go?" he said to me.

His mother protested with surprising vehemence. "Oh, Frank, don't be ridiculous! Don't drag poor Irene all over town with you."

He must have felt me clench his hand.

"Why not? If Bakersfield is such a great place, I ought to show her around."

"She's lived here before, you said. And it can't be easy for her to get around in all of those contraptions. No, leave her here and let us get acquainted. Go on, shoo. I need you to get back here before Cassie comes over."

He looked at the list. "You sure you need all this stuff? With what you've got in the kitchen now—"

"Never you mind, Franklin. Now scoot."

He eyed her suspiciously. I knew that look. He thought she was up to something. He gives me that same look when I'm up to something. But she didn't waver in returning a look of her own that said there would be no further discussion on the issue.

He looked at me and shrugged. "Will you be all right?"

"Of course she'll be all right!"

Frank kept looking at me.

"I'll be okay," I said.

And so it was that I was left planted in a couch while Frank went off to run errands. As soon as he was gone, Mrs. Harriman excused herself, got up, and busied herself in the kitchen for a few minutes.

She came back out and seemed nervous. She kept looking at the clock. I decided to try to get a conversation going.

"How long have you lived there?" I asked.

"What? Oh, let's see. It will be forty-two years in December."

"It's a lovely home. You have quite a collection of—" What to mention first? "—of frogs."

She laughed, and started telling me about some of them, where they came from, who had given them to her. We were both smiling when the doorbell rang. She suddenly looked very flustered, then went to answer the door.

"Why, Evelyn! What a surprise!"

"It is?" I heard a woman's voice say. There was a murmur, then after a moment the voice said, "Oh. Oh. Yes." Then the voice was loud, almost as if the speaker wanted to reach the audience in the back of a theater. "Yes, I was just in the neighborhood and I thought I'd stop by."

More murmuring, and then Frank's mom escorted a truly exotic creature into the living room. She was heavyset and had blue hair. Her eye makeup was applied in such a way as to make her look constantly startled. Her cheeks were rouged in two bright spots. She appeared to be in her sixties. Her earrings were dangling papier-mâché bananas. She came in smiling nervously, clutching her bag as if I might rob her. But she took in my injuries and exclaimed, "Oh, you poor dear!" and shot Frank's mom a dirty look.

"This is Mrs. Parker," Bea Harriman said. "She's a good friend. She just happened to be in the neighborhood."

"You don't say," I replied warily. Something was up, all right, but Mrs. Parker looked like a poor choice for a conspirator. She seemed totally at sea. "Nice to meet you, Mrs. Parker. I'm Irene Kelly. I'm a friend of Frank's."

"You are? Oh, you might know my daughter then. Cecila?"

My turn to shoot the dirty look, but Mrs. Harriman wisely avoided my eyes. Mrs. Parker was really lost now, so I said, "I'm afraid I haven't had the pleasure."

"Oh, that's too bad. Frank and Cecila were so much in love. I tell you, he was crazy about that girl. Just doted on her. I'm sure Frank has talked about her to you. He was out and out silly over her."

I smiled, admittedly one of the phoniest smiles of my life, and said, "As a matter of fact, he has told me about Cecila."

"Really?" Mrs. Parker was delighted.

"Yes. He told me that they were together for a few years, that he followed her to Las Piernas, that she went back to Bakersfield, that he didn't follow. That he has no intention of following." This last I gave special emphasis as I looked over at Frank's mother.

"I wouldn't be too sure," Mrs. Harriman meowed.

Mrs. Parker looked extremely ill at ease. "Uh, are you from Las Piernas?"

"Yes," I said. I was trying to cool down. Mrs. Parker was clearly a pawn. I didn't like the game much.

"Oh, so is your family from Las Piernas?"

"I was born and raised there."

"Then why not have Thanksgiving dinner there, with your family?" Mrs. Parker asked innocently.

"Yes, why not?" Bea Harriman chimed in.

"I was invited here," I said.

"Won't your family miss you?" Mrs. Parker asked.

"My sister and her husband have plans of their own," I said. It might or might not be a lie. Barbara had never even asked me about Thanksgiving.

"What about your parents?"

"My parents are no longer living." I realized that I had said this same phrase to so many people over the last seven years that the sting had gone out of saying it. I usually said it as easily as "Please pass the peas and carrots." Somehow, this time, the sting was back. Maybe it was the holiday, maybe it was the strain I was under. Maybe it was because I felt like a goddamned orphan, even though that really wasn't the case. I took a deep breath.

Mrs. Parker was rather stricken, and even Frank's mom suddenly looked as if she realized she had overstepped a boundary.

It was at that moment that Frank returned. He walked in with a couple of grocery sacks and took everything—well, almost everything—in within ten seconds. He cursed with fluency and imagination and slammed the sacks of groceries down on the dining room table. I hoped he had bought eggs.

"Franklin!" his mother snapped.

He looked at Mrs. Parker. "Hello, Evelyn. Forgive my language. Would you please excuse us?"

"Hello, Frank," she said. "I was just leaving. I'll say hello to Cecila for you."

"Thank you," he said, but now he was glaring at his mother.

"I'll see you out," Mrs. Harriman said meekly.

As they left, he hurried over to me and sat down beside me. "Irene, I am so sorry. I didn't even get everything on her damned list because I had this bad feeling about leaving you here by yourself. But I never thought she'd stoop—I'm just so sorry. I never should have brought you here."

He scooped me up off the couch, and while I was glad to be out of the hole it put me in, I was startled.

"What are you doing?" It was going to be my question, but his mother asked it first.

"We are leaving," he said, his voice cold. As angry as I had seen Frank, this was a kind of rage that was scarier than any of the other forms I had seen his temper take.

"Frank, please." She was starting to cry.

"Crying won't work, Mom. You've gone too far this time. Don't ever even *hint* to me that I should come back here again. It's not home anymore."

As rotten as she had treated me, I felt sorry for her. She had tried something really dumb and it had backfired on her. By the time Frank reached the front porch, I asked him to set me down.

"Did I hurt you?" he asked, as if my voice had startled him into realizing that he was carrying me.

"No, and she didn't either. Not really, Frank." There was a big old-fashioned swing on the porch. I motioned toward it. "Let's sit out here on the swing for a minute before we climb back into the car. I need to talk to you."

"I'm not staying."

"Just sit here with me for a minute."

He gave in, some of the fight seeming to leave him now that we were outside. I let him get the swing in motion and we listened to its rhythmic creaking for a few minutes before I said anything more.

"I'm not crazy about your mom's methods, but I honestly think she just feels like she needs you. I think she's afraid she's lost you. She's lost her husband, and she doesn't want to lose her son."

He sighed, but didn't say anything.

"Your mom and I aren't off to a great start, but I'm not ready to give up. I don't want to become known as the reason you won't see her anymore. Besides, none of this is fair to Cassie. She's had to be the one your mom turns to all the time. You're down in Las Piernas."

"I just can't stand the idea of what she did today. It's embarrassing."

"Tell you what. You can have Kenny and Barbara, I'll take your mom."

He laughed. "No deal."

"See? Besides, you can't have Barbara. Kenny you can have at wholesale prices. But even though Barbara drives me nuts, she loves me, I love her. Go figure."

Another sigh.

"Go in and talk to her. I'll wait out here. If you decide we're leaving, I'll go with you and never bring it up again. If you want to stay, I'll survive. I think I've got my deer-foot knife here somewhere."

"Will you be okay out here?"

Good, he was going to do it. "My grandmother had a swing like this. I'm fine. Besides, Cassie will be here before too long, and those kids are dying to see the lady with all the casts on her."

He kissed me and went in.

They talked for a long time. Every now and then I would hear them shouting at each other. Frank is seldom a shouter; you have to really push his buttons to get a shout out of him. His mom must have been hitting them like a kid in an elevator. But I just sat in the swing and admired the garden, thinking that it was probably all for the best.

Cassie and Mike pulled up in front of the house before Frank came back out. The two boys got out of the backseat before their parents had a chance to open their own doors. "There she is!" one shouted, pointing at me. Brian, the four-year-old. Michael, at six, was slightly more restrained, but not by much. Both with light brown hair and freckles.

"Wait here, boys. Remember what I said." Mike

O'Brien was a tall blond with a dark tan. He gave me a wave and a grin.

"Be gentle, like when we pet Mutt," Michael Junior recited, as the four of them made their way over to me. Michael and Brian were each holding their hands behind their backs, as if for self-control.

Mike and Cassie probably hadn't expected to have the comparison to the dog be made public, but I laughed and they joined in on it, leaving the kids confounded. Cassie introduced me to her family.

"You're in Grandma's swing," Brian said by way of observation.

"Yes, I am. Would you boys like to sit on it with me?"

There was a moment's hesitation, but the casts were too intriguing. They hopped up next to me.

"Careful," Mike said.

"Where's Uncle Frank?" Michael asked.

"He's in having a nice long talk with your grandmother. That's why I asked you to sit with me on the swing."

"Where are your fingers?" Brian asked me, studying the sling.

"You can see most of them, can't you?"

"Yeah. And I can see your toes." This amused the two of them to no end.

"Where's your cat?" Michael asked, looking around.

"He's at home. Our friend is taking care of him."

"Where do you live?" Brian asked.

"She lives in a place called Sin," Michael said.

"Michael!" Mike said.

"That's what Grandmother said. She said Uncle Frank and his friend Irene are living in Sin."

"Grandma must have got it wrong, Michael," I said easily. "We live in Las Piernas."

"Oh. Where the beach is."

"Right."

Brian said, "When do we get turkey?"

"Soon," Cassie answered, but looked nervously toward the door.

Sitting was too much for the boys and soon they were

running around the front yard, playing tag, laughing and squealing whenever one tagged the other.

Cassie and Mike sat on the swing with me. Like Cassie, Mike was easy to talk to. He was telling me about his work with the Highway Patrol, when the door opened and Frank and his mom appeared, arm in arm. Before any adult could get a word in, the boys were rushing toward them, shouting, "Uncle Frank! Uncle Frank!"

"Hello, you little devils," he said and scooped them up, giving me a wink.

"You winked at her!" they both shouted.

"Yes. You caught me."

"Wrestle us!" Brian cried.

"Give Uncle Frank a break, boys," Mike said, but it was too late.

Frank was out on the lawn, the boys rolling and crawling all over him, amid more giggles and squeals. Mike grinned. "Well, Irene, I wish my kids would warm up to him a little." He stepped off the porch and joined the melee.

"Why don't you join us on the swing, Mom?" Cassie said.

Mrs. Harriman hesitated, avoiding eye contact with me. "I've got a dinner to get ready, Cassie." And she turned and went inside.

"We'll help!" Cassie shouted, undaunted. "Come on, Irene," she said.

Frank's mom looked between us as we arrived in her kitchen. "What can I do to help, Mrs. Harriman?"

"Please call me Bea." She paused then added, "I guess you've already been a great help to me."

I didn't hear any sarcasm in that, so I tried a smile. "I'm not very useful in this condition, but I'm improving in using my left hand. I'd feel better if there was something I could do."

"Why not let her stir the gravy, Mom?"

"Good idea, Cassie."

And so it was that the three of us got a chance to know one another better. Cassie was a masterful ambassador between us. Somehow she managed to get Bea and me to relax, to help with dinner, and get the boys cleaned up again when it was time to eat. I figured that as a working mother, she had learned to juggle this many activities long ago.

Frank sat next to me and helped to load up my plate with turkey and all the trimmings. When it came time to give thanks, there was plenty to give.

Brian was surprised to watch Frank cut up my food for me. "Look, Dad! Like you did for me when I was little."

This was topped a little later by Michael, who in all seriousness asked me, "Irene, what is it you want?"

We all looked at him.

"I'm fine, Michael. I've got all I want." I meant it.

"But Grandma said you were a wantin' woman."

Bea was mortified, but Frank started to howl with laughter and was soon joined by everyone but Michael and Brian, who exchanged that look that says adults are nuts.

"Did Grandma get it wrong again?" he asked when he could be heard.

"Not that time, Michael," Frank answered.

No one would let me help with the cleanup, so I sat outside watching the boys play. Brian had a toy clown that they were punching and flinging around, but the clown had the signs of being well-loved otherwise. Frank came out before long and sat next to me. Brian and Michael wore down and sat next to us. Brian wanted to sit on my lap, and Frank figured out a way for him to do it. "You have to sit very quietly," Frank said. "Irene has been hurt."

"How?" Brian asked, poking a hole in the clown's neck with his finger.

"We're not supposed to ask that, dummy," Michael chided.

"I'm not a dummy. Irene, can you take your casts off?"

"Not yet," I said.

"When you do, can I wear them?"

"They have to saw them off," Michael said with relish.

Brian's eyes grew wide. "How do you know?"

"A kid at school broke his arm and he had a cast and we all signed it and they cut it off with a saw."

"Can we sign your cast, Irene?"

"Sure," I said.

Frank laughed. "Boys, I wonder why we haven't thought of it up to now? That's a great idea. But I have dibs on the ankle cast. You guys can take the arm."

"I'm not sure I appreciate being divided up by you, Mr. Harriman."

But the boys were racing inside to ask Grandmother for marking pens. We went inside to a desk, so that my shoulder wouldn't bear the weight of my arm. The boys went to work eagerly and that is how the cast on my right arm was decorated with stick figures, unidentified swirls, airplanes dropping bombs, and the scrawled names of the artists.

They ran out of available arm cast and were eyeing the leg cast covetously when Cassie and Mike told them it was time to go home. They protested loudly to no avail, and I got a gentle kiss from each of them before they left. "Good-bye, Aunt Irene," Brian had said, and no one corrected him.

After they were gone, the house seemed a little empty. Or a little larger. Frank came over to me and asked me to sit on the swing with him for a while. He held me against him and rocked the swing back and forth.

"We have a decision to make," he said.

Uh-oh, I thought.

"We either stay here in separate bedrooms or go to a hotel."

I smiled. "Oh, is that all? Let's stay here."

He gave me a wry look. "I'm that easy to give up?"

"Not at all. I'll miss you terribly. But think of what it will be like when we get back home."

"You have a point. Aren't you worried about nightmares?"

"Lately I've been able to wake up from them a little more quietly."

"I've noticed. But I don't like the idea of not being there for you. I'll be in the room across from yours. Call me if you need me for anything—Mom or no Mom, okay?"

"Okay. Are you still going to undress me?"

"You really know how to torture a guy, you know that?"

* * *

But when it came time to get ready for bed, Bea shooed him out of my room and helped me instead. Even though she was another woman, it was embarrassing to me to have her do it. Frank knew all my tender spots and was able to avoid causing any additional discomfort when he helped. Bea tried, and I bore with it, but by the time I got into the bed I was sore in a couple of places; my blasted shoulder was already throbbing from when the boys had gotten overly enthusiastic about their artwork.

She tucked me in and sat on the edge of the bed. "I owe you an apology," she said after a while.

"I'd prefer we just forget about it and go on from here, if that's all right with you."

She nodded. "Frank's a man now. I guess I have to learn to let him make his own mistakes."

I laughed and she quickly said, "Oh, dear, I didn't mean that to sound quite like that."

"It's okay. Good night."

"Good night, Irene." She smiled, adding, "It's like the song."

She left humming it.

I heard her open Frank's door and say good night to him as well. "And you stay on your side of the hallway, you young goat, or I'll tan your hide."

I lay in the darkness, feeling restless without Frank beside me. Finally I fell asleep.

I suppose it was crazy to imagine that the pain and tension of the day, the new surroundings, and whatever else was playing at my mind would not lead to nightmares. What happened between the images of Devon and Raney stabbing me over and over with deer-foot knives and when I was fully awake is lost to me. All I know is that the light was on and I was sitting up in bed, sweating. Frank sat facing me, looking at me in a worried way. I was breathing hard and still feeling scared. I became aware that Bea was in the doorway, looking nearly as worried as Frank.

"I'll take care of her," she was saying.

"No. Go back to bed." No ifs, ands, or buts would have

worked against the tone. She must have realized that, since she left.

"Good morning, Irene. It's about three o'clock. You're at my mom's house." He saw me getting things in focus and gently lowered me back on to the pillows. Somehow, lying down again made me feel closer to the dream and I felt the terror of it again.

"Shhh," he was saying, and softly stroking my forehead and hair. The dream and the fear retreated. He leaned over and trailed kisses from my forehead to my lips, where he lingered a while. What dream?

He smiled a self-satisfied smile when he looked back into my eyes. He looked me over. "I don't think I'm going to be able to leave."

"What about your mother?"

"I haven't signed your cast yet," he said, ignoring me while he went over to the desk and brought back the marker. He pulled off the few covers that were still on me and turned his back to me, blocking my view of what he had started to do with the marker.

"What about your mother?" I repeated.

"Don't you like her?"

"Yes, I do, now that we're getting to know one another. What are you doing?"

Even without seeing his face, I knew he was grinning. "I think she likes you, too. In fact, I know she does."

"Are you glad we stayed?"

"Very glad. Are you?"

"Yes. What are you doing?"

"You'll see."

"Nothing too lewd, I hope. I don't want your mother to hate me again."

"I don't think she ever did. I certainly hope you won't think of this as lewd. Well, not too lewd," he laughed.

I groaned.

He was concentrating now. I could hear the squeaking of the marker.

"Almost finished," he said, obviously quite pleased with himself.

Bea chose this time to re-enter. Oh God, I thought. What is Frank drawing down there?

She was saying, "Listen, Frank, if you two were at least engaged—"

She broke off, staring at my right foot. Frank turned around and took my hand.

"Am I engaged, Irene?" he asked, grinning. He moved to one side.

There they were, in large black letters, each carefully colored in. Three words that would look up at me every day the cast was on:

Marry me, Irene.

| Acknowledgments

James Horner, former member of the U.S. Coast Guard, thirty-year veteran of sail racing and first winner of the Cabo San Lucas Race, graciously met another major challenge when I asked for his help with this book.

I am especially grateful to Dr. Ed Dohring, orthopedic surgeon, and Kelly Dohring, R.N., who answered all of my weird medical questions; to Sharon Weissman, Jenny Oropeza, and Tom Mullins for insights into political campaigns; to Detective Dennis Payne, Robbery-Homicide Division, Los Angeles Police Department; Debbie Arrington, *Long Beach Press Telegraph;* Bob Flynn, retired political reporter for the *Evansville Press;* to Danny Coburn and John G. Fischer for answering a host of inquiries; to Gaetano Di Lisio *(Tante grazie!)* for helping Rachel and Pete speak Italian.

Once again, I thank a long list of librarians, especially Eleanor Newhard of the Long Beach Public Library.

The individuals named above have helped with the research for this book, but I claim sole credit for errors.

My friends and family have given me unfailing support. Tim, I'm contacting the Pope about canonizing you.

Wendy Hornsby, Linda Grant, Beth Caswell, and Nancy Yost have kept me from going over the edge, and at times were too polite to point out the fact that I *was* over the edge. And like it or not, this time I thank She Who Will Not Be Thanked.